ICEHAVEN

Sum of all Tears – Book 1

Kim Cresswell and M.K. Chester

KC Publishing
Ontario, Canada

KC Publishing
London, Ontario Canada

Cover Art © 2019 - AKA Marketing & Cover Design

Cover Symbol Design Art © 2019 - Melissa Gamez

Edited by Excellence in Editing

Ordering Information:
Quantity sales. Special discounts are available on quantity purchases by corporations, associations, and others. For details, contact the publisher at kimcresswell@rocketmail.com.

ICEHAVEN/Kim Cresswell and M.K. Chester. – 1st edition.

ISBN 978-1-9995588-1-9

CHAPTER ONE

In the near future...

August Madison glanced at her watch, then back at her father, her shoulders tight with anxiety. "Minus seven minutes."

Anticipation flickered in his blue eyes as he smiled and watched the images of the dozens of military aircraft taking off from various airports throughout the United States and around the world on the mammoth digital screen inside the university's largest auditorium.

As chief climatologist of the International Climate Change Initiative, he believed he'd finally discovered the answer to the world's most pressing issue. With the oceans growing more acidic, dozens of animal and plant species becoming extinct, and the atmosphere ten degrees higher than a decade ago, widespread catastrophic weather events, each more violent and deadly than the one before had increased. Hurricanes, earthquakes, tornadoes, droughts, and horrific flooding due to rising sea levels had caused the destruction of some nations and continued to kill millions around the globe.

All of that was about to change.

"Can you check on Luke and Chloe?" her father asked under the increasing commotion surrounding them. "They should be here by now."

August frowned at the cause of her stress. She wasn't surprised by her brother's tardiness. He was always late, an eighteen-year-old who had an excuse for everything. All he had to do was pick up their younger sister from school and show up on time for their father's shining moment. Just be on time for once. Do what was expected. One time.

"I'll call him." August snatched her phone out of the back pocket of her jeans and hit speed dial. He finally answered on the fourth ring, right before voicemail kicked in. "Where are you? You're late."

"Chloe was poky leaving class."

August rolled her eyes, knowing her brother had been up all night playing video games with his friends. She'd bet her Yale tuition he'd been sleeping and hadn't gotten up in time. "Hurry up, Dad's asking for you."

"I'm pulling into the university parking lot. Wow, there's a ton of people here. I didn't know this was such a big deal."

She checked her watch again. *Five minutes.* "You've known your whole life how important this is to him."

"I'll be there in two minutes."

August ended the call and forced a smile for her father. "They'll be here soon."

He nodded and put his arm around her shoulder. "I don't want them to miss it. This will be a story you'll tell your own children one day."

She smiled, imagining a future where the climate wasn't the dominant issue of the day. Her father hadn't been this happy in a long time. Five years almost to the day her mother had passed away, he deserved some happiness.

While the auditorium filled to standing room only with faculty, students and media, excitement buzzed in the air. Her father really was about to make history, his experiment, his hard work, bringing them to this moment. She took a seat in the front row beside him and looked up at the screen. A low hum caught her attention. Unsure where the sound came from, she glanced over her shoulder, searching for her brother and sister, disappointed that Luke would probably be too late. The humming grew louder. August covered her ears, the high-pitched deafening sound too much.

An earth-shattering boom savagely rocked the auditorium.

The tile floor cracked and shifted under her feet. The seismic force catapulted her out of the seat, slamming her left shoulder and the side of her head into the floor with a hollow whump. Dazed, August staggered to her knees, then to her feet and reached for her father's hand, mere inches away through the smoke and dust. She couldn't get to him.

Phantom outlines of people bumped into her, scurrying by, searching for an exit. Screams, sobs, and moans filled her head. Blistering heat ripped through the room, as if the atmosphere was being sucked out by a high-powered vacuum. Her heart thrashed in her chest.

Where were Luke and Chloe?

She fought back tears as panic drove deep into her bones. Stretching out her arm, she reached for her father again and struggled against the growing clatters and groans.

A gale-force wind rumbled like a freight train, and the building blew apart.

"Daddy!"

Chunks of debris pelted down around her.

August tripped on something, maybe someone, and landed flat on her back. While she gasped for each painful, labored breath, electrical wires popped and sizzled around her and shot fiery particles everywhere.

Overhead, a metal beam swung wildly in her direction, like a giant pendulum. A pungent, suffocating odor, similar to lighting a million matches, filled her nostrils. An acidic taste touched the tip of her tongue and burned the back of her throat. Muffled quiet descended over her. The world blurred.

Then came the cold.

CHAPTER TWO

Arctic air sliced through August's lungs like a hundred tiny knives. She gulped her first breath and pried her eyes open one at a time. Adrenaline surged, and her heart took off like a rocket. Pushing her elbows against the frozen ground, she sat up and surprised a figure kneeling at her feet.

While the woman worked awkwardly with gloved hands to unlace August's boots, she stopped and looked up at her.

Her eyes widened. "You—you're dead!"

Fear rose in August's chest. And she remembered.

All around her, hard-pack snow and ice stretched for miles.

Everything was gone.

The university.

Everything.

Beneath the mounds of winter, remnants of scraps of metal, wooden planks, piles of bricks poked through, odd-shaped ghosts of what used to be. What happened? Where was her father? Her brother and sister?

While the woman rambled incoherently, August used all her strength and grabbed her by the shoulders and shook her. Her frozen joints shrieked with pain. "Where am I?"

The woman's watery eyes blinked between the black knit hat and red scarf draped around her head, shielding her face from the wind. "Icehaven."

The word meant nothing to August. No. There had been an accident at the auditorium at Yale University in New Haven, Connecticut, where she attended school. Her father's decade-long experiment to end climate change by stabilizing temperatures around the world had gone wrong.

Horribly wrong.

All she remembered was trying to grab her father's hand. By then, nothing could have saved them. A sound like high-pitched booming jet engines had overwhelmed her, and she raised her hands to cover her ears. "No. That's impossible."

Taking her opportunity, the woman shoved her backward with two hands and ran in the other direction, her frayed boots crunching with every rapid step. August bounced off the ice onto her butt, then slid backward until she slammed against the fender of a half-buried, charred car. Air exploded out of her lungs, and pain shot down her spine, her body. She doubled over, pulling her legs to her chest, and dragged in a stinging breath. Then, she released it.

Her piercing scream could probably be heard for miles, but August heard nothing. She only felt the extreme cold invade every fiber of her being. Within moments, the unrelenting chill blocked the searing pain and she straightened her stiff limbs, first her legs, then her arms. She glanced down at her blue fingertips and scrambled to her hands and knees with one thought: shelter. She needed to find refuge as soon as possible or she'd die. *Again?*

None of that mattered right now. August dragged herself to her feet and spotted bleary black dots against the white horizon. She blinked through tears and tried to focus. Were they moving?

She wiped her eyes with the back of her hand and tried again.

They were definitely moving.

They looked like fuzzy outlines of humans, other survivors, coming to help her or to kill her. Either way, she put one frozen foot in front of the other and resolved to meet them halfway.

The wind whipped around her, blasting ice crystals against every inch of exposed skin, sticking in her hair, soaking and freezing her jeans, sweater, and jean jacket within minutes. By the time she met the four strangers, carrying large backpacks and rifles, heavily clothed in winter coats and colorful blankets, all she heard was the monster howl of the wind. Maybe their lips moved, she couldn't be sure. She couldn't even tell if the people were men or women. August didn't care. Shivering uncontrollably, she fell forward, collapsing against them, hoping they meant her no harm.

"Get her something for her head, hands, and feet," a familiar female voice said.

After digging through their backpacks, a layer of comforting warmth encased her shoulders in the form of a pink shag carpet, secured by strong arms on either side. Another woman handed her white oven mitts with cows printed on them, men's gray wool socks and a fuzzy black headband.

Were they serious? August hesitated, then took the items, knowing they weren't anything she'd ever use as clothing on a normal basis, but grateful for anything to keep her warm. After putting on the headband, she sat on the carpet and took off her army-style black boots. While she finished putting on the extra pair of socks, someone handed her four plastic bags.

"Put them over your feet and hands. They'll keep them dry, keep the heat in. You don't want to end up with frostbite," a man said.

August took the bags and shoved her feet inside, tied them tightly closed, then put her boots back on. She slipped her hands into the bags and then stuffed her frozen fingers into the oven mitts. "Thank you."

"Where did you find her?" a man asked as he blocked the wind with his large frame and helped her to her feet.

The woman with white hair pointed then placed the carpet back over August's shoulders and head. "Over there by that beam. She was dead. I took her pulse and listened for her breath and a heartbeat. Nothing. I worked on her for thirty minutes. I was a nurse for a lot of years at Hartford Primary Care. I know when a person's dead. She *was* dead."

August tried and failed to laugh. The woman who'd tried to steal her boots had gone back, wherever back was, for help. At least she hadn't left her for an ice-filled grave.

A man's low, deep voice silenced the others. "Let's get her back to the bunker and see if we can get her warmed up enough to talk. If she came from that direction, she might know something."

August groaned as they trekked as a group, a clump of humanity buffeting the swirling air and ice that blanketed the endless frozen terrain. She couldn't tell them she didn't know anything, at least nothing that seemed logical or made any sense in this strange world. Even the sun didn't look the same, its fiery yellow-orange glow had changed to a dark shade of red, the light much dimmer, as if someone had shut off a gigantic light bulb.

She had plenty of questions for the strangers. Like where had the buildings and cars and civilization gone? Where were they, really? Who were they and how did they live in such harsh conditions? Why were they carrying weapons? First, she needed to make it to shelter before the sun dipped below the horizon and the temperature dropped beyond measure. August trudged forward, gritting her teeth. One thing she knew for sure. If any of this turned out to be her fault, her father's fault, she had to find a way to make things right.

• • •

Plodding across the slippery landscape for what seemed like forever, August's legs throbbed and blazed with fiery pain from the biting cold. The strangers hadn't said a word since they'd started their bone-chilling journey. All she knew was they were heading southeast on I-95. Ice packed shells of entangled and smashed vehicles with haunting statues of broken bodies in sculpted poses littered the once busy interstate she'd traveled so many times with her family. Carnage was everywhere, more visible in some areas than others.

With each cautious step, ice cracked and groaned under the heels of her boots. August held the carpet tightly around her body, her shoulders aching from the heavy weight. She stopped in mid-step and gasped.

Beneath her feet, a woman with black hair lay curled on her side, clutching a newborn baby in a powder blue bunting bag. The mother and child's eyes were wide open, staring back at her through the frosty glass-like tomb. Horrified, she looked away, sidestepping the buried family, wanting more than anything to erase the image from her mind. She'd be happy to get to their destination, out of the cold and away from the death and destruction.

"You can't think about the ones who are gone. It's too late for them. You have to keep moving," the female said.

August fought back tears and removed one of the bagged oven mitts to reach into the pocket of her jeans. She pulled her iPhone out and stared at the shattered screen, her hands shaking violently.

The man with the low voice, who appeared to be the leader, stopped and glanced at her. A thick layer of crystallized ice covered his eyelashes and mustache, making him look much older than he probably was. He had brown hair and kind blue eyes like her father. Her heart ached even more for her family.

"That thing won't help you. Nothing works anymore," he said through gray-blue lips.

August glanced down at the phone. She was hoping she could call her brother's phone and maybe find her family…if they were alive.

His hand touched her shoulder, and he gave her a little shove. "Keep moving or you'll freeze. We're almost there."

Wind blasted around them in gusts, cutting through the carpet tented over her head and wrapped around her body.

As they plodded past a gas station almost completely embedded in ice with its front door missing, August noticed the overturned and barren shelves inside. The cash register drawers sat open and empty. It wasn't as if money would help anyone now. On the floor inside the door, she spotted two large bare feet sticking out of a bump of ice. She glanced away, not wanting to see more.

"Where are we going?" The air stung her lungs and made her involuntarily gasp milky clouds of steam as she spoke.

"East Haven."

Thank God. They were still in Connecticut. August let out a breath of relief and started coughing when she inhaled a gulp of frigid air. "I thought we were in a place called Icehaven?"

"It's the name for the state of Connecticut. That's what they call it now."

August turned her face out of the wind and tried to process what he'd just said.

"I'm sure this is all confusing. We'll talk more once we get to the Army National Guard armory. We've been digging it out for two weeks."

Weeks? How could that be?

Panic bubbled up inside her chest and her head spun.

Impossible. She was at the university on Monday.

August shook her head, hoping the action would knock some sense into her, into the man.

He must be mistaken. He had to be...

Her feet were numb and frozen, and she wasn't sure she could walk much farther. She knew she had to. "Why don't we just stay at the gas station? We could light a fire to get warm."

"It's not safe here," the woman beside her said.

The man clutched the rifle tighter. "She's right. It isn't safe. The armory is secure, at least for now. We have some supplies: clothing, food, water, and whatever else we scavenge. But supplies are dwindling by the day."

Great. She'd either freeze to death or starve.

As they continued heading south, bleak crimson skies surrounded them. The sun lowered, and so did the temperature.

• • •

Darkness gathered around her. Barely visible from the outside, all August could make out was a massive four-story high bank of white with crumbled red bricks and wooden beams protruding in different directions. She headed through a number of narrow, chiseled ice tunnels and down a long set of stairs lit only by candles. She slowed her pace to allow her eyes to adjust and her vision to clear. With the wind blocked to a soothing wail, they hurried through a corridor of the building into an open area.

A small group of adults and one child, a toddler, clasped silver reflective blankets and huddled around two space heaters in the middle of the room, casting curious glances as she neared. They were dressed in mismatched winter clothing, some wearing military ponchos and wool hats. At her appearance, their whispered conversation stopped. Did she know any of them? Did they know her?

"This way," the nurse said and handed her a silver foil blanket.

August set the carpet down and took off the oven mitts and plastic bags and put them on a chair. She gratefully wrapped the blanket around her shoulders then followed the woman into another hallway on the opposite side of the room. "How many are here?"

"Unfortunately, too many."

Realization hit August in the heart. Too many people to feed, clothe and shelter. Had the world really come to that?

"What's your name?" she asked her host.

The woman unwound her scarf and grinned. "Snow Globe."

Was the woman serious? "That's your real name?"

"Actually, it's Sandy Globe. Everyone calls me Snow—especially now."

They continued, winding through a series of short halls until August couldn't remember how they'd gotten there. Probably on purpose, she thought. "Where are we going?"

"All newcomers need to meet with our leaders, no matter what time they come in. Even if we have to wake them up, which they hate." Snow came to an abrupt halt at a crossroads in the hallway, and August nearly ran her over. "You're in luck. They're waiting for you."

Facing these unknown people made the blood pound behind her eyes. What if they didn't let her stay? August shivered at the thought of going back outside, recognizing the armory provided the best protection. They had to let her stay. They couldn't just put her out, could they?

"Let's go."

August dragged her feet like she used to when going to a class she didn't like or a party where she didn't know anyone. Before she had time to arrange her thoughts into an argument about why she should be allowed to stay, they emerged from the deceptively short tunnel into a small room.

A decaying red and blue oriental rug lay beneath a long, bowed metal table. Behind the table sat three individuals, each passive face staring at her; two women, one man.

A woman with short red hair at the left end of the table greeted them. "Hello, Snow. Tell us about this one."

The nurse cleared her throat. "I was out scavenging with the others and wasn't having much luck. On my way back, I saw her in the snow."

The man in the middle raised his eyebrows. "Dressed like that?"

Snow shook her head and shot August a sideways glance. "She was dead. No pulse. I tried to revive her and couldn't."

"Apparently you could," the man said, combing his fingers through his bushy beard.

Everyone except for August laughed, and Snow's face turned red. "It wasn't by my effort. I was planning on taking what I could—her boots—then she sat up. Scared the hell out of me. I ran back to the group for help because the sun was going down and didn't know if I could get her in by myself."

At least the account of events was accurate. August stood still while they studied her like some kind of middle school science experiment. Did they still have schools? Probably not. Focusing on survival meant other things were impossible.

The other woman sitting at the table with almond-shaped eyes and long brown hair asked, "Is that all, Snow?"

"Yeah. If you don't mind, I need to get back to my kid."

"Of course," the man said as he stood and stretched his legs. "Thank you."

How civil everyone seemed to be. August's skin crawled for no real reason other than she was alone before the three-person panel without a clue if they would allow her to stay.

The woman sitting in the middle chair spoke up. "What is your name?"

"August—Madison."

"How old are you?"

"Twenty-two."

They glanced at one another, and the man sat back down.

"How did you end up out in the open, dressed like that? Did you run away from another group, settlement?"

What was he talking about? Settlement? "No. I don't know how I ended up there."

Even to her trained, logical mind, it sounded like a joke. But no one laughed.

The red-haired woman leaned forward. "Where were you from...before?"

"New Haven," she answered. "I lived there all my life."

Until I died...

The man's eyebrows drew together, making his face appear smaller. "What's the last thing you remember before you woke up today?"

August's eyes met his. He knew something, understood the strange thing that had happened to her. Or perhaps he knew who she was, who her father was. Was it safe to tell the truth? She had no proof they wouldn't use it against her. The longer she waited to answer, the more discomfort bloomed in the room.

"I was in the auditorium at Yale University, waiting for the climate change experiment to begin."

No one said a word. They traded glances again, then the man asked, "Are you saying *you* survived?"

Tears flowed, and August quickly brushed them away with the back of her hand. His question meant no one else had survived. Not her father, brother, sister or anyone else who had come out to support her father. With her throat too thick to speak, all she could do was nod.

"Amazing," the women said at the same time.

Then the redheaded woman stood and walked around to the other side of the table.

August felt a vague uneasiness and stepped back when she approached.

"It's late," the woman said, her accent something other than New England. "Let's get you something to eat and a place to rest. You can stay with me and my husband until we decide on the best course of action." Her green eyes gave nothing away except a sincere offer to help.

"Thank you."

The man also stood. A small smile flashed across his otherwise stern face. "Lydia will look after you. We'll talk again tomorrow."

Lydia rested a hand on August's shoulder and steered her toward another room with two sets of bunkbeds on either side of the space. "Don't worry, we'll get to the bottom of all this in due time. For now, you need food and rest. I'm guessing you may have more questions for us than we do for you."

CHAPTER THREE

Three miles from shore, on the deck of the *USCGC Eagle*, Brandon Church peered through night vision binoculars, his face stiff and cold from the biting wind weaving through the wool hat and two scarves wound tightly around his head and face. A few feet away, a fire roared. Spooky flames hissed and crackled in the metal barrel he'd found in the ship's kitchen.

He wasn't sure what he was looking for. They hadn't moved an inch in weeks, totally ice-blocked. There was nothing to see except for the same Boeing 747 that had crashed a mile from the cutter, its rear engines stabbing through a mountain of thick ice. After the event happened, he'd hoped to see some sign of life in addition to those who were on the cutter.

He hadn't seen any.

He blinked, trying not to go back to that day, unable to stop himself. They had just completed their mid-September six-week training at sea. The cold had blasted in phenomenally fast, on the heels of some type of peculiar scorching snow. Felt more like sand, or what he'd always imagined radioactive fallout would feel like: pelting, stinging, destroying and sealing everything in its path.

Fifteen minutes later, the nearest buoy registered a ten-degree drop in the ocean temperature and had plummeted since. They had experienced a day or so of radio silence, waiting for orders. They never came. Finally, the radio exploded with stories from survivors followed by hopeless, frightening quiet.

He'd heard people had frozen before they could find shelter and going south wasn't any help. The odd blast had flattened most structures, adding to the destruction and chaos. It was so cold now that the ship's figurehead, a golden eagle clutching a circular disk in its talons displaying the coast guard seal, was broken, severed by the unrelenting chill.

According to the ship's temperature gauge, it was minus 135 degrees Fahrenheit, colder than the Antarctic. Even standing outside for a few minutes, Brandon could barely believe the change. Being sheltered on the ship had saved him and the others, not that anything had been simple. The two-hundred and ninety-five-foot-long tall ship had its share of warm parkas, hats, gloves, boots, medical supplies, and food.

They were the lucky ones, for now.

His thoughts drifted to his parents. Had they survived? And what about August? Was she alive? He shook his head, convinced he already knew the answer. It would be difficult for anyone on land to outlive the cataclysmic climate change if he and the crew were barely surviving aboard the cutter.

Brandon had no idea what had gone wrong, but the ocean had morphed into a bumpy, dense field of ice as far as he could see. Everything turned white, frozen solid, including the ship's fuel lines and diesel fuel. The cutter's square and fore-and-aft sails, which once waved majestically in the wind, stood like statues weighted down in weird, twisted shapes, heavy with ice, bowing from the weight. He lowered the binoculars and looked up. Not one star in the strange red-tinted sky. Even the moon had disappeared.

"See anything?"

Brandon glanced over his shoulder and spotted Commander Dixon half-walking, half-sliding toward him with a flashlight in his hand. The bright white beam zigged and zagged with each unruly step and reflected off the icy teak deck. The man looked like a towering giant bear with all the layers of clothing he wore.

"Nothing, sir. The same as yesterday and the day before."

He frowned at Brandon's use of the respectful term. "You can drop the formalities, Church. Things have changed a lot in the past few days."

Brandon shrugged. He thought they might need to rely on some type of formal structure to help them survive. "Do you think we're the only ones alive out this way? I haven't seen any movement on shore. Have you heard anything on the radio?"

Dixon was quiet for a long moment, clearly contemplating the question, maybe thinking about his own family. "Absolutely nothing. What I do know is we have twelve officers, fifty crew members, sixty trainees on board and a day's worth of food left, maybe two if we're lucky."

Brandon did the math in his head. "That's not good."

"No, it's not." Dixon shifted from foot to foot and rubbed his gloved hands together. "I don't know what the hell happened, but this bad situation is about to get a lot worse if we don't do something."

"What do you want to do?"

"Ration what we have left the best we can and go from there. There isn't much more we can do except go all Donner Party," he joked about cannibalism, then sobered. "I think it's safe to say we've probably all lost our families."

Brandon heard the sadness in his commander's voice and wondered again about his own family. About August.

They'd grown up together, backyard neighbors as far back as he could remember. They'd even dated for a short time in high school but after her mother had died in a car accident, they became distant. He'd heard from friends she had enrolled at Yale while he was in his second year at the Coast Guard Academy in New London.

He glanced at Dixon. "Do you have a plan?"

"Not a bloody one. You?"

Brandon shook his head. "Water sure isn't a problem at this point. We can survive for about three weeks without food. It won't be easy."

"Glad you were listening in class." Dixon paused for a moment. "You're a fine cadet, Church. Your family would be proud."

"Thank you, sir."

"For God's sake, stop with that 'sir' crap. We'd better get back inside. I don't think we have to worry about pirate ships."

Brandon laughed. "Yeah, you're probably right."

"Sir! Sir!"

Both Dixon and Brandon squinted into the darkness on the other side of the fire. One of the crew members rushed to them the best he could on the slick deck. It looked like Morgan Hill, a cadet a year below Brandon.

Morgan slid to a shaky stop. "They're coming for us!"

Dixon's eyebrows rose. "Who's coming?"

"Five trucks. Driving across the ice toward the ship right now."

Driving? If the ship's fuel was frozen...how? Brandon looked at the man as if he had lost his mind. "Where?"

The cadet pointed past them. "Port side."

Dixon inched his way to the port side of the ship. Brandon and Morgan followed as quickly as they could manage.

"Give me the binoculars," Dixon ordered.

Brandon handed them over. Anticipation and excitement bore down on him at the thought that others were alive and coming for them.

His commanding officer stared through the lenses of the binoculars, his head pivoting back and forth. After a few seconds, he lowered the glasses. "What are you talking about? There's nothing out there."

Brandon squinted and also saw nothing. Morgan might be losing it.

"Over there. You should be able to see their headlights." The cadet pointed over the side of the ship. "Can't you see them yet?"

Yet? A shiver swept down Brandon's spine, and not from the cold.

A few more seconds went by and Dixon lowered the binoculars. "For Christ's sake. There is nothing out there. Get back inside. You're delusional."

The young man stared across the frozen ocean, then at Brandon, then at Dixon with confusion etched on his face. "But they're coming. I swear I saw them with my own eyes."

"You're tired." Dixon put his hand on the younger man's shoulder. "It's been a stressful few weeks. Go get some rest."

Shaking his head, Morgan walked away.

"This is exactly the type of thing we're going to have to deal with when the food runs out," Dixon mumbled.

Brandon wasn't looking forward to starving to death. There had to be another solution. They could walk across the ice, try to make it to land and hope against the odds that there were survivors somewhere and food. They'd have to try. He stared out at the flash-frozen water, fighting the hopelessness rising in his mind. He refused to sit here and wither away.

Then he saw them. Ten tiny headlights, growing larger by the second.

"Sir? Morgan was right. Look over there." He pointed toward the black boxy utility vehicles, their headlights illuminating their own shape against the polar-white barrenness, little more than moving shadows.

Morgan ran back and almost fell twice. "I told you!"

Brandon and Dixon glanced at each other, knowing nothing had been on the ice a few minutes before. Maybe they were the ones losing their minds.

Brandon turned to his subordinate. "How did you know they were coming? You couldn't possibly have seen them."

The man shrugged and didn't say anything for a moment. "I don't know. It's as if I could see things happen remotely before they actually occur. Not exactly like a dream, because it was too real. I could feel the wind and hear them talking. They're coming to take us to land."

• • •

Above the bunkbeds, a string of multicolored Christmas lights burst to life.

August smiled at Lydia. "You have electricity?"

"Solar. I normally don't use the lights when it's just me. My husband is out on an expedition. We spend most of our time searching for useful items to make life better here. Unfortunately, we aren't the only ones."

Her ominous tone underpinned a warning. August got the message loud and clear. She needed to find a way to make herself valuable if she expected to be fed. On cue, her stomach growled. She clutched her belly. "I'm so sorry."

Lydia chuckled. "Don't be. We hear it often around here. Let me share what's left of my food with you tonight."

What she had on hand included a can of sardines, a jar of dill pickles and bottles of water. "Water is the only thing we have in abundance. Purifying the water is a job here, so is scavenging."

August sat on the edge of the lower bunk covered with an army-green sleeping bag to eat the fish she'd never eaten before. She frowned at the sardines, even though she was starving. "Are you the leader here?"

The woman shook her head. "No. John Traxlor, myself, and Maggie McCallum. The three of us." She looked around the room. "John knew this place was here. Thank God. We lead and work together, each of us overseeing an area of need. If a newcomer joins us, they're given a task, required to pull their own weight. It's not really ideal. It's the way it has to be for all of us to survive. There are stiff penalties for not keeping your end of the bargain."

"Like what?" August asked.

"Let's just say that no one wants to go back out there."

Understood. "There are other communities—settlements?"

"Yes, so we've heard. Developing slowly all over the country wherever they can find refuge." Lydia sat next to her.

"Who were the people who found me? Do they live here?"

"That would be Davis, Rachel, and Henry. You already met Snow. Davis and Rachel arrived the morning after the event. Henry, that night. Davis owned a diner about a mile from here. Rachel worked for him—a waitress. I don't know what Henry used to do."

"He's the man with the deep voice?"

"That's him. He's the oldest here, in his sixties. I think he's still shell-shocked about what happened, as most of us are. Luckily, they found you." She took in a breath and let it out. "May I ask you something?"

August ate the pickle and washed it down with a gulp of cold water, holding off on the sardines for now. "Of course."

"Is your father Graham Madison?"

The water she just swallowed suddenly tasted like grimy sludge going down her throat. She didn't answer.

Lydia smiled, her hazel eyes sad. "I can see that he was. When you told us your name and where you'd been, I knew who you were. I'm sure everyone will know soon enough."

August's pulse sped up. "Is it a problem? Do people hate him? Hate me?"

"Hate is such a strong word when people are trying to survive. I think it's accurate to say there will be a lot of questions among the survivors about what happened that day and why. If word gets out, you're alive and here, it could put us in danger. I won't lie to you about anything because it's in our best interest to share what we know with you in hopes you will share what you know with us."

Her words seemed reasonable, but August's pulse didn't slow down. "I don't know what I could possibly share that would be of value."

"Did you study climate at Yale, like your father did?"

"Yes, environmental studies. I've been wracking my brain to figure out how something like this could have happened." She lowered her head. "All I know is I've lost my entire family. My entire world."

"Many of us have. There are a few theories about what sparked this new Ice Age. In due time, I expect you'll visit them all to see which might be the most valid. If this is something you want, then you must be honest with us."

August understood completely. "If there's a way to fix this, I have to try. No one expected this to happen. My father certainly didn't."

Lydia gave her a soft smile. "One other thing. You said you don't remember anything after that moment in the university auditorium?"

She honestly couldn't remember. "Maybe in time, something will come back to me."

The older woman tilted her head. "No, nothing will come back to you, August. No one who had experienced what had happened full-force could have survived. Very few people have endured the aftermath."

Her heart stuttered in her chest, and her stomach soured. "Then what happened?"

"You died," Lydia explained simply with a wave of her hand. "You know in your heart that's the truth. You also know…you came back to life."

• • •

Had Snow and Lydia been right? She had died and come back to life? August laughed under her breath then sobered. Something had happened. There had to be an explanation, a medical one.

After Lydia had given her a quick tour of what was left of the building, guilt plagued her thoughts. She didn't want to be here with people she didn't know without confirming if her family were alive or dead.

"Here, take this." Lydia handed her a red blanket with black stick people holding hands in a circle with white, swirling trim. It looked like something she had seen in a store in New Haven while shopping with her mother a year before she died. Mohegan Tribe women and children crafted them on the reservation in Uncasville about an hour from her home. She missed her family, missed the way life had been, so simple and easy.

"You'll need it even with the sleeping bag. The solar heaters always run out just before dawn. Not that the sun gives us much warmth anymore."

"Do you think the climate will ever go back to normal?"

"You're probably the only person who can answer that question. Have you thought more about what could have happened at the university?"

August lowered her head. She still couldn't figure out how she had died and come back to life—if that had truly happened. Was it an odd side effect of her father's experiment? Something else? "That's all I've been thinking about. It's a blank."

Lydia patted her shoulder then sat on the other bunkbed. Muffled voices drifted in from the main area of the armory, but August couldn't make out the conversations.

"I'm sure you'll start to unravel the mystery. In the meantime, think about how you can contribute here if you plan on staying."

"I have to find my family. They could be alive," August blurted out, then added, "I'll come back to help, I swear."

"You can't do that. You'll freeze or starve or worse. It's extremely unsafe with the Sproggs living on the summit at East Peak. They see everything we do. There are others you need to worry about, too."

Sproggs? The name sounded like a character out of one of her brother's video games. August stopped herself from laughing out loud. She had no clue what the woman was talking about. She felt as if she'd been transported to another planet, stuck in a horrifying alternate reality, like those old science fiction movies from the 1980s.

Lydia gave her a soft smile. "It must sound ridiculous. Sproggs are the survivors who have made their home at the peak. They're a nasty bunch of about fifty or so, living deep in the caves. They're always patrolling the area for anything they can use to stay alive: food and other supplies, including weapons. They will take what doesn't belong to them. They're not stupid. They're very strategic when they make a move. The others are more random."

A chill ran through her, and August began to second-guess her decision to leave to search for her family. "I'm not sure I want to know who the others are."

"They call themselves Bleeders. They show up out of the blue and force their way in and take what isn't theirs. They don't belong anywhere. They roam, unorganized, living in igloo-like structures they've built in various areas, fighting with each other and with anyone else when they get hungry enough. They're preppers. End of the world survivalists, knowledgeable about how to survive in this type of weather."

"They sound like mad renegades."

"Much more dangerous. We don't ever see them until they attack, even when we take precautions." Lydia's voice wavered, registering her fear. "Yesterday morning, we lost two men, friends. The Bleeders got away with nearly a full case of MREs."

August knew MREs were "meals ready to eat." She'd tasted them when the army recruiter came to speak at her high school. "I'm sorry they killed your friends."

Lydia looked away for a moment then back to her, her gaze intense. "We do the best we can to keep everyone safe. Sometimes it isn't enough. Anyone in the area who has survived knows we're here. It makes us a daily target. That's why my husband and others are out scavenging at night, to switch up the normal routine in case we're being watched. We're all trying to survive. It's a violent new world."

August wondered if there was any good news. Everything so far was doom and gloom. The woman was right. Life was tough enough living in a frozen wasteland without a bunch of crazy people killing each other for food and other necessities.

"After what happened yesterday, we have to ration what we have left until the delivery."

"Delivery from where? I thought your husband—"

"Don't worry about that right now. There's still so much you don't know." Lydia reclined on the bed. "You must be exhausted. Get some rest and John will explain more tomorrow when you'll have the opportunity to meet everyone and socialize. I'm begging you, August, please don't leave. If you do, you won't come back."

• • •

Brandon wasn't convinced the truck convoy had come to take them to land, and neither was his commanding officer. Dixon had gone to his stateroom to get his P229 DAK .40 pistol.

Whoever the people were inside the vehicles that looked like a cross between a Humvee and a box truck, there was too much at stake: the ship's food, medical supplies, and the extreme weather clothing. Not to mention the weapons and explosives used during their training exercises.

Brandon and a handful of trainees, including Morgan, watched as a dozen crew members and officers awkwardly lowered the heavy rope ladder over the side of the ship, preparing to welcome their guests.

Dixon checked his weapon and slid it into his coat pocket. "Are they coming up yet?"

"Any minute."

"I have a bad feeling about this."

"It's okay. They're here to help." Morgan stared wide-eyed at the commander. "Should I go and tell everyone to pack up, prepare to disembark?"

"Not yet. Let's see what they want first," Dixon said.

Brandon agreed with his commanding officer. For all they knew, their guests could be some sort of new world pirates only wanting to steal the ship's supplies. Or worse, kill everyone on board. Under the circumstances, anything was possible.

"Take this." Dixon reached into his other coat pocket and passed Brandon a handgun. "If all hell breaks loose, use it."

He knew how to use the weapon and was a good shot. Over three-quarters of the trainees on the ship had only received basic weapons training. He was sure the officers carried firearms. The thought eased his nerves a bit. Commander Dixon was a careful man, always two steps ahead of pretty much anything. He'd probably ordered the officers to arm themselves the second the vehicles had been spotted.

Morgan eyed the gun. "You won't need it."

His convincing tone didn't make Brandon feel better. He straightened his back and squared his shoulders. He looked at the weapon for a long minute then took the gun and put it into his coat pocket.

Dixon glanced at Morgan through runny eyes. "How do you know we won't need weapons?"

"I—don't know how I know. I just do."

Dixon's jaw tightened, and he shook his head. "Well, that's reassuring."

The cadet was beginning to creep Brandon out. How did he know the trucks were coming long before anyone could see them? Had the guy suddenly developed ESP or something?

"Come with me," Dixon said to Brandon. "Morgan, get some more wood on that fire and heat some water for coffee."

"Yes, sir."

On the ice below the bow of the ship, two people stood in the brilliant headlights of one of the trucks. Dixon pointed at them. "What do you make of that?"

Brandon raised the binoculars and peered over the side of the ship at the men standing in front of one of the running vehicles, wearing white Ghillie snow camo suits streaked with black or brown. They looked like feathered prehistoric beasts holding white camo rifles. They weren't Boy Scouts, although they seemed overly-prepared for the weather.

"Military? Maybe Special Forces?"

"My thoughts exactly, but you never know after what's happened. They could be anyone." Dixon leaned over the side of the ship. "Here they come. Five guests." His eyes shifted to Brandon and then to his coat. "Be ready in case shit hits the fan."

He gave the man a nod.

Moments later, the officers helped the first guest onto the deck. When all five were on board, Dixon went to meet them.

Brandon followed, uneasiness rattling his bones. He kept his hand securely wrapped around the grip of the gun. He gave the guests a once-over. They were all dressed basically the same in black parkas, black wool hats, and gloves, their faces covered with black scarves. Only the whites of their eyes were visible in the light coming from the fire. At least from what he could see, there weren't any weapons visible. That didn't mean much.

Tension filled the icy air.

"Welcome. I'm Briggs Dixon, commander of the *USCGC Eagle*."

The tallest of the group stepped forward. He held out a wool-gloved hand. "Graysen Marx. We're here to help you."

Dixon cautiously shook the man's hand.

"How do you plan on doing that?" Brandon asked, still apprehensive about the men's presence on the ship. "What if we don't need help?"

"And this is…?" Marx asked Dixon, tilting his head toward Brandon.

The man's eyes looked oddly distracted, moving from the commander, then passing over the crew on both sides of him and his men.

"That's—"

"Brandon Church, Junior Officer, Cadet, First Class, sir." He squared his shoulders and shoved his hands deeper into his pockets, his fingers curling around the weapon. He figured he'd add "sir" to show some respect, even though his gut was telling him something different.

Overhead, the mast housing the American flag creaked and swayed, unable to carry the weight of the ice any longer. A boom, louder than a crack of thunder, reverberated across the frozen water.

Heads raised at the same time.

"Clear the deck!" Dixon yelled.

Feet slipped and slid as the towering mast toppled like a giant oak tree. Brandon dove, submarining on his stomach, the deck shaking below him. He slammed into the back of Marx's knees, flipping him on his backside and sending him toward the other end of the ship, as if he rode a bobsled.

The pole crashed to the deck with a thunderous bang and shattered into splinters, narrowly missing the fire barrel. Shards and chunks of sharp ice propelled through the air like spearheads and rained down around them. Brandon covered his head with his arms, hoping he wouldn't be killed by the deadly frozen projectiles.

Seconds passed, feeling like an hour, followed by silence.

Brandon uncovered his head and looked around. He spotted Marx's men helping their shaken leader to his feet. Brandon sat up and squinted through the darkness, searching for his commanding officer. When he didn't see Dixon, he scrambled to his feet, his heart jackhammering against his ribs.

He spotted the commander's boots and shimmied across the deck to where the largest section of the mast had come down. His heart skipped a beat at the damage to the ship, and then to the men. Commander Dixon, Master-at-Arms Miles Johnson, and Petty Officer Percy Williams lay pinned under a large section of the pole that once held the American flag. Crushed to death by the emblem they'd sworn to protect and serve.

CHAPTER FOUR

August jerked upright at the sound of pops and bangs, her skin immediately sweaty and cold at the same time. She kicked her way out of the sleeping bag, both pushing and pulling at the warm fibers cocooning her body in a frenzy to get free.

Her gaze snapped to the bunk across the room.

Lydia wasn't there.

An unfamiliar male voice yelled from somewhere within the building, "They followed us in! Get on lockdown!"

Rat-a-tat-tat. Rat-a-tat-tat.

Screaming. So much screaming. Then she heard a child crying. Fear and adrenaline tunneled through her, driving her to do something, anything, as fast as she could, unsure how she could be of help or what she was about to walk into.

She thrust her arms into the winter coat Lydia had given her and fumbled to zip it up. After racing to lace up her boots, August ran to the open door. She stopped and peered into the hallway. Dim light came from the main area of the armory.

Shadows shifted.

August couldn't tell where they started and ended. She drew a deep, silent breath and held it. Letting it out, she crouched and stole a glance around the corner. She saw a tall figure wearing brown and white animal pelts and brown pants lined with buckles, trinkets, and fur. He had a long bird's beak covering his face except for his eyes and mouth, more frightening than any Halloween mask she'd ever seen.

Were these Sproggs? Bleeders? Or some other ungodly tribe?

"I'll ask you one last time. Where are your solar radios?" Birdman said, his voice vibrating down the hallway. "You know there are stiff penalties for lying. The proof is on the floor." He glanced at Lydia and tilted his head. "Your stupid husband should know better. The Bleeders don't play games."

He pointed his rifle at Lydia's head as she crouched next to the unmoving form of her husband. He lay sprawled on his back, his arms and legs at strange angles. She lifted her hands, stained red with blood, while tears streamed down her cheeks. Her mouth opened as if to scream, but no sound came out.

The air in August's lungs hitched, and she blew it out as quietly as possible while retreating into the shadows. Her heart thumped faster. What could she do to diffuse this situation? She knew there was more than one radio and she knew where they were kept, thanks to her tour of the armory. She peered around the corner again and spotted John trying to reason with the two men.

"You and the Sproggs have taken almost everything from us. We won't have enough. How do you expect us to survive? We have children here, for Christ's sake."

"Guess we'll raid the Sproggs when we're done. See what goodies they have," said the other man dressed in black pants and a woman's floor-length cream-colored fur coat.

Was he wearing pink lipstick? August squinted. He was.

Birdman raised the weapon and swung the barrel from Lydia to John.

Lydia looked up at him and wiped her eyes, smearing her husband's blood on her cheek. "No, we'll give you what we have. John, give them a radio and the sardines we have left."

"Marx isn't going to be happy about this," John grumbled.

August felt the fear crackling among the four involved in the conversation.

Birdman laughed. "Who gives a crap what he thinks? We don't get the luxury of having food and supplies delivered to us. You think we won't be getting into Liberty once we have enough manpower and weapons to take the place over?"

"That would be difficult to do," John argued, "And you know it."

Who was Marx and what was Liberty? August shook the questions away and crept down the hallway to the supply room. Once inside, she seized one of the radios half-hidden behind a case of water and tossed the canned sardines into a cardboard box to make them easier to carry.

No one else had to die.

She hurried back and stopped short, inhaling and exhaling before stepping into view, praying the crazy men wouldn't shoot her.

Birdman swung the gun around and aimed it at her.

She froze in her tracks.

His eyes drifted to the radio in her hand. "That's a good girl. She's new. Who is she?"

"Willow—my cousin—she arrived yesterday," John said calmly.

August didn't say a word and let him protect her with his swift response. If the Bleeders discovered who she really was, they might take her with them, do God knows what with her. Her mind sped through a million scenarios, none of which she wanted to happen.

The man stared at her, his beady eyes flickering as if he, too, had considered all his options. Finally, he blinked and barked orders to the other man, "Get the radio, Jett."

His sidekick sauntered toward her with a snide grin, waving his handgun in the air. He snatched the radio out of her hand, his eyes lowering to the box. "Those the sardines?"

"Yes," she replied calmly and sternly, even though she was trembling inside. August's gaze locked on Lydia, who gave a subtle shake of her head. She handed the box over slowly to the man, just to bug him.

He made clicking sounds and winked at her. "Pleasure doing business."

"Marx will make you pay for this," John said, his jaw tight with anger.

Birdman got in John's face, toe-to-toe with the man. "Only if he can find us, so if you know what's good for you, you won't tell him anything."

• • •

Brandon shut the door to the commander's private lounge, visibly shaking from shock at the death of Commander Dixon and the others. He shoved his hands into his pockets, then turned to Graysen Marx, the only other person in the room. With Dixon out of the equation, the crew displayed uncertainty, forcing him to step over others ranked above him to have a conversation with the civilian who'd come, apparently, to help.

Before he could find any words, Marx spoke, "I'm sorry about your crew members. It's one of many disasters in this new, unfortunate environment."

Unfortunate was an understatement. Brandon took in the man, his familiar name rolling around in his head like a loose marble.

The man removed his hat and gloves, unzipped his parka and took a seat in one of the two matching chairs. He seemed quite at ease in the cherry-paneled room, amid the stately furniture and patriotic emblems. His hair lay in waves, pushed back over an expansive forehead. His sharp gray eyes took in everything around him.

Brandon knew they should have cut the mast days ago. He knew the weight of the ice-laden sails would do something...terrible. Oddly, none of them could bring themselves to lay an axe on the thing and now, they had only regret for being prideful and patriotic. Taking a seat on the other chair, under the watchful eye of the ship's portrait, he let out a sigh, emotion catching in his throat. "How do we get off this ship?"

"We can talk about that. It might not be the best time." Marx sat back in his chair. "You can't be thinking straight after what happened."

Brandon hadn't meant to blurt out his end game, intending to negotiate, to learn his options, but the deaths up top changed everything. None of the crew would want to stay put, and none of them should. Except, from the reports they'd received, things weren't any better anywhere else. He drew back and asked instead, "What can you tell me about what's going on inland? We've heard reports of all kinds of things. What is the government doing about this crisis? We expected orders."

"Son." Marx leaned forward and rested his elbows on his knees, "There is no government. Not any longer."

He felt the blood drain from his face. "What does that mean?"

"From what I've been able to put together, the Yale scientist who set up the experiment to eliminate climate change did, obviously, more harm than good. It's difficult to say what happened first, but the weather churned so quickly that military airplanes, passenger planes, fell out of the sky. That started a destructive wave of fires in both rural and highly populated areas, D.C. included. The White House and Capitol were both heavily damaged. Then, the temperature plummeted, followed by that weird destructive snow. The United States you know is gone. The *world* you knew is gone."

Brandon closed his eyes, unable to imagine what the man had said. Communications had been destroyed—no cable or satellite television to get news 24/7. Cell towers down, electronic grids destroyed. So much worse than he wanted to believe. "Sounds like a horror movie."

"It looks a lot like one," Marx said. "I'm sure you've heard from various parties on your radio. There are communities taking shape, and that will continue. They'll keep finding survivors, merge together, pooling resources." He leaned forward in the chair, quiet for a moment. "Do you know who I am?"

Am or was? Because it seemed to Brandon who he was last week didn't naturally translate to who he might be now. Graysen and his men carried superior weapons, were dressed for the weather and used vehicles without frozen fuel lines. "I know the name, but you're going to have to forgive me."

"Fair enough. If the New York Stock Exchange still existed, I'd be the head of CT—CleanTech Group, Inc. We were one of the major financial backers for the International Climate Change Initiative. We pumped billions of private dollars into the research, readiness, and deployment of the project which, unfortunately, caused this disaster." He paused for a beat, then continued. "It wasn't our only project, and in hindsight, thankfully so. Nineteen years ago, we invested and helped build the prototype biodome settlement in Rhode Island designed for testing an off-earth colony on Mars, the first of its kind."

Brandon remembered reading about the settlement covering almost a thousand acres of farmland with interlocking biodomes. They called the place Liberty.

"The place survived the temperature drop, the ice?"

Marx nodded. "Although we took heavy structural loss to the north section, over three-quarters of the settlement survived, thanks to the space-aged steel frames and layers of thermoplastic."

Brandon tried to visualize the domed community. "Your weapons and transport make a statement about who you are."

"I suppose they do," Marx said. "The weapons are a necessary evil, as you'll soon find out. The biggest competition in the area is over food and ammunition, now that we've learned how useless traditional fuels are. We use a combination of solar, which is particularly weak right now, steam, and special biofuels made from sunflower and other nuts with a non-combustible antifreeze."

That made sense. It also made them a target. "Is that why you're here—for our weapons?"

"Yes," Marx admitted. "In part. We want to take you back to Liberty, with your food, weapons and anything else of value. We're not here to take what we want and leave you to die on the ice. On the contrary, we will find a place for you inside our community, give you work, a role. We don't turn anyone away, and I think you'll find the rules of society to be quite close to what you've experienced in the coast guard. Life there isn't easy, I don't want to give you the wrong idea. However, if you want to contribute to rebuilding a new society, Liberty intends to do just that."

"Rebuild it how?"

Marx's jaw tightened with a hint of frustration. Apparently, people lined up to go to Liberty without asking too many questions.

"You're a bright kid. The American bread basket is frozen solid. There will be worldwide famine, which is going to be the first obstacle to a content society. Our focus starts there and merges with technology, medicine, communications, and travel. You can pave your own way if you prove to have valuable skills, which most military members tend to have."

The cutter had been a hard target. Marx and his men simply arrived before anyone else could. Still, something about the offer seemed a little too good to be true. "What's the catch?"

Marx shook his head. "No catch. Come in out of the cold and help us navigate the new world. Yes, we need defense. Yes, we need military grade technology. We need a lot of things. Why not offer your crew—because unless I'm mistaken it's your crew now—the option to do what they choose?"

And what if some of the crew wanted to stay? What if some of them didn't want to give over the weapons or anything else? What then? Would Marx take what he wanted? "We can do that."

While Marx reached for his hat and gloves, he frowned. "You don't seem convinced."

Brandon didn't have any other offers as he reflected on the alternative of rationing food and starving to death. "My father taught me if something seems too good to be true, it probably is. Without any other options, I'm open to going with you and overseeing the transport of the items you feel necessary. All I ask is that I continue in that capacity until I learn more about what you're doing and what your larger needs are. The crew can decide for themselves."

"They'll go where you go," Marx said. "They obviously respect you."

Uncomfortable with the thought of taking over Dixon's leadership, he finally conceded. "Then I suspect they'll come with me."

"The sooner the better. It's not as if it's going to get any warmer."

Brandon stood, his body stiff. "We can start the off-load first thing in the morning after I see Liberty."

"Fair enough."

Minutes later, Brandon presented the option to the crew at the site where the mast had splintered from its base. They'd already removed the bodies of their fallen comrades, and he would make sure they were disposed of properly. His speech, short and sweet, sent a wave of palpable relief through the ranks. When he asked for a count of who was willing to leave for Liberty, every hand went up.

After dividing everyone into two groups under the watchful eyes of their guests, excitement filtered through the air. Brandon would leave with Warrant Officers Asher and Jacob Jotti, twins, men he trusted. He also chose Morgan in case the cadet had another weird premonition or whatever it was he had experienced earlier. It might come in handy if anything was off at Liberty. First Class Petty Officer Jackson Moss would remain behind with the rest of the men and women on the ship.

If Liberty truly was what Graysen Marx described, a utopia, then Graysen's men would return to gather the rest of the cadets, officers, engineers, and deck seamen along with the ship's food, clothing, medical supplies, and weapons.

No one argued. No one wanted to stay put or go out on their own.

Not even Brandon, not really. Not yet.

• • •

August's heart clenched. She sat quietly in the corner of the room and watched Snow and Maggie trying to comfort their friend with little success. Through red swollen eyes, Lydia brushed her fingers across her husband's cheek and kissed his forehead, then said goodbye.

Maggie's two daughters looked on from the hallway with frightened looks on their faces. The girls appeared to be somewhere between eight and twelve years old. They were two of three children August had seen so far. The youngest, Snow's little boy, was a toddler with golden, silky hair and bright blue eyes. August hadn't met the children officially, didn't even know their names. Instead, they had been thrown together after the Bleeders killed Dax.

While Snow and Maggie helped the grieving woman to her feet, the men carefully placed her husband's bloody body onto a shabby blue tarp and rolled it up. Afterward, John duct taped the tarp securely with the body inside.

"Be gentle with him," Lydia said, her eyes damp and puffy. "He deserves better than this."

"I know he does. He was a good man and friend," John said, his voice compassionate and caring. "We'll bury him close to the armory, so you know where he is."

Lydia nodded slowly.

The two men lifted the body, the heavy weight clear by their grunts and strained expressions, and headed to the door. As they passed August, she gulped down the hard lump in her throat.

There was a weird sense of finality to the scene, an unforgettable reality of what life was like now, that made her yearn for the life she once had. Even though she had only just met these people, she felt a strange sense of belonging which made her miss her family even more, pushing her again to find them. At the moment, the need to stay put was much stronger because Lydia was right. Danger lurked everywhere, and August had witnessed firsthand how things could change in the blink of an eye.

Lydia sniffled and wiped her eyes. "Come with me."

August looked up at her and stood. "Is there something I can do to help?"

"Not right now. I just want to talk."

Tired and hungry, she found it difficult to know what to say to Lydia about the loss of her husband. She followed her into their sleeping quarters, debating if she should say anything, not wanting to upset her more.

August found her voice after the woman sat on the bunk and stared blankly at the wall. "I'm sorry about your husband."

"He was a good man. You would have liked him."

"I'm sure I would have. I'm sorry I didn't get the chance to meet him." She paused for a long beat, feeling more uncomfortable by the minute, reminded how difficult it had been to say goodbye to her mother. At least she'd had the chance. Not like Lydia. "Can I make you a tea? I saw some on one of the shelves in the supply room."

"Not right now." Lydia glanced at the Christmas lights and smiled. "Dax loved Christmas and ironically loved the snow. He was like a big kid."

"You never had children?"

"We found out ten years ago I was unable to have any. My husband was fine with the news. So was I."

"Are there any other children here besides Maggie's girls and Snow's little boy?"

Lydia shook her head. "No. I forgot that you haven't met everyone yet. The man who's helping...bury...Dax is Maggie's husband, Ian. He was out with my husband, searching for supplies when the Bleeders followed them back. By that time, it was too late."

August counted only nine people, including the kids. The armory could hold a lot more survivors.

"The second expedition hasn't returned yet." Worry worked across her features. "They should have been back by now."

August hoped the others hadn't fallen prey to the crazed factions, especially the Bleeders. She shivered. Heavy footsteps in the hallway interrupted her thoughts and their conversation.

John poked his head inside the door. "He's in his final resting place next to the back door. I'm sorry, Lydia. I really am. It happened so fast. We didn't have time to secure the armory."

"We need to rethink our security plan immediately. Next time, we could all be killed by those barbarians."

There was anger in Lydia's voice, a hardness. It was understandable. She'd just lost the man she loved.

"I'll stand guard until the others return," John said.

"They're about an hour late."

"I know. I'm concerned as well." His gaze traveled to August. "We'll work on improving security tomorrow after the delivery arrives from Liberty."

Lydia looked down at her hands. "How?"

"We'll figure it out." He placed his hand on her shoulder and squeezed gently. "Try to get some rest."

After John left, silence and sadness occupied the room again. Lydia appeared completely broken, shoulders slumped, wringing her hands in her lap, fighting back tears.

"I'm going to make you a tea, whether you want one or not. It might help you sleep." August stood, prepared to leave the woman to grieve alone.

"Wait. You need to let me know the moment you remember anything about what happened at the university. It's important. There have been whispers among survivors that others have been experiencing strange abilities since your father's experiment. I doubt you're the only one who is special. But you have all the answers locked away, unable to remember. Think hard, August. You might be our only hope for survival."

• • •

After making Lydia a cup of tea, August noticed John sitting at a small table next to the front door of the armory with his rifle resting across his lap.

He leveled a stern gaze at her. "You shouldn't have done that. Now the Bleeders know your face."

She didn't feel like being chastised. She was tired, hungry, and watched a man die. "I don't care."

"You are too valuable an asset not to care." He slammed a fist down on the table. "We have trained to handle these kinds of meetings, August. Do you have weapons or combat training? It's bad enough they killed Dax. What would you have done if things had gone south again? If either of them had recognized you..."

She felt like she was having an argument with her father for staying out too late. "They didn't. I was only trying to help."

John bowed his head, as if having her here created too much stress for him, one more thing he had to manage.

"You didn't see Lydia's face." She'd never seen a person shot before. They all had a head start on her, and she needed to catch up quick, or she'd find herself on her own. "Teach me what I need to know. I want to help."

He looked up at her. "Lydia said you wanted to leave to find your family."

"I did. But after seeing what they did to Lydia's husband, I know I'm unprepared. I don't understand what's happened and what's happening now. I want to be an asset. I need to. Not just because I went to Yale. I want to know how to use a gun, stitch a wound. I'm young, strong and willing. Just teach me." Her plea seemed to hit the man where he lived and his expression softened.

"I'm glad to hear you've changed your mind. Look, we are sitting, literally, on a powder keg. There are munitions stored here. Nearly everyone is going to be angling to get their hands on what we have as soon as they find out. I can teach you how to use the weapons." He paused for a moment, then said, "I'll train you in the mornings to use some of the firearms and teach you some hand-to-hand combat, if you take inventory twice a week in the afternoons, recording what we have in food, weapons and other supplies."

"Deal." She didn't want to be defenseless and John didn't want them to be, either. Her family would have to wait. In all reality, they likely had died. Even though Luke had never made it to the auditorium, he'd been close enough to be affected. She needed to face reality. Seeking out her family made little sense at this point. Hell, she'd been in the auditorium and she'd died. Apparently.

"How do you know how to use the guns?" she asked, now that the tension in the room had receded.

"I trained here. That's how I met Dax. We were posted that weekend, the last to leave and lock up. We showed up with our families within hours of one another." He smiled. "We were definitely the lucky ones that day. Not so much today."

August realized the atmosphere of pain, grief, and loss was not temporary. Everyone had lost someone they loved. She wasn't special in any way. "Everything is gone, isn't it?"

Looking her in the eye for a long moment, John nodded.

August's heart sank. She lowered into a chair. She'd been so busy surviving, she didn't see anything else in front of her, even though the change had been obvious. No electricity. No cell phones. No internet. No public services. Nothing a first-world American was used to. Hashtag gone. In the blink of an eye.

"There is no government anymore, August. No centralized presence. There are some communities organizing, some stronger than others, like Liberty."

"Liberty?"

"The biodome settlement in Rhode Island. It's geofenced, well protected. They have some sort of energy there besides solar, maybe wind or even nuclear, for all we know. No one is sure yet. Thankfully, they agreed to deliver rations to us."

Some of what he was saying sounded vaguely familiar. "Graysen Marx? Is he involved?"

"Yes, it's his community. You know him?"

She nodded, putting a couple of pieces of the puzzle together. "He runs, used to run CleanTech, which funded my father's project. I've been in the room with him a few times, not that I'd say I know him. How did he know you were here? I mean from the outside, the armory pretty much looks like a big white camel hump in the middle of nowhere."

He was quiet for a moment and scratched his beard. "I have no idea."

Something stirred in her stomach. Had Graysen Marx known something horrible was going to happen with her father's experiment?

"Anyway," John said, disrupting her worries, "the biodomed settlement was designed by NASA using Graysen's company's money and technology. No snow or ice to deal with. They even control the climate inside and grow crops."

She'd kill for a bowl of fresh fruit right now. Something as simple as an apple would do.

"No one who goes there ever comes back to tell us anything more," he added.

"Do you lose many people who want a better environment?"

"Some. Although, getting past the Bleeders and Sproggs is almost impossible now. They're savages. They'll take what they want, including women, men if they choose. It's like the chaos of having no law to govern them loosened every horrible desire on Earth. They won't attack Liberty, though. It's too well defended."

"Why don't you just take everything you have here and go to Liberty? If Graysen Marx knows you're here, surely he's offered to take everyone in."

"The offer isn't the problem. It comes with every generous shipment of food."

She noted a shift in his demeanor, his eyebrows furrowing. "So, what's the problem?"

"You can't take anyone at their word," he warned. "Even us. Not everything is as it seems in this cold new world."

CHAPTER FIVE

Once Brandon, Morgan and Warrant Officers Asher and Jacob Jotti finished offloading the non-essential food items from the *Eagle* with the help of the rest of the crew, they found themselves separated into different vehicles for the ride to Liberty.

While there was no discussion of who would go in which truck, the men shared pointed looks as they ducked into their respective rides. Brandon cast one last lingering glance at the *Eagle*, his home away from home. He doubted he'd ever see her again, unless she remained moored in the ice for the rest of eternity.

As the truck engine idled, he ducked into the back seat of the all-terrain vehicle, overcome by the blast of the heaters pumping warm air. Jesus, he hadn't felt that kind of heat for days. He closed his eyes against the wave of gratitude that washed over him and wondered how long they would have to travel to reach Liberty.

"It'll take an hour, hour and a half, depending on conditions."

Brandon glanced at the driver who answered his question. Had he opened his mouth? He must have. With no further explanation, he tried to relax as the rest of Graysen Marx's men disembarked the ship and climbed into their vehicles. It was a tight squeeze, since they were carrying extra passengers and equipment.

The man to his right closed the door. "How long you guys been out here?"

"Since it happened." Since that weird, tumultuous day when things first stood still, then fell apart at the speed of light.

"You and your crew did great, compared to most. Lots of folks weren't that smart or lucky. I'm glad we found you when we did. You wouldn't have lasted much longer."

Brandon shrugged, stung by the realization they had been either sitting ducks or unable to sustain themselves of their own free will.

"It's not a knock, man. You'll see when we get there. You'll understand what I mean when you see what's happened to the country—to the world."

By his estimation, they wouldn't arrive until after midnight, if his watch could still be trusted. Brandon tried to ignore the apprehension stirring in his gut. He wanted to see what their new reality was going to be like and feared knowing at the same time. Feeling as if he might throw up at any moment wouldn't make them arrive any sooner. He took deep breaths and tried to imagine what the more desirable Liberty would be like.

In his imagination, he saw a warm and friendly environment where men like Graysen Marx stockpiled food and weapons to use to barter with outsiders. It couldn't be anything but.

The driver laughed. "You're going to be surprised."

"By what?"

"Nothing," the redhead said. "Just wait and see."

Silence descended, and Brandon watched Marx jump into his vehicle after waving his arm in a circle, signalling it was time to go. The trucks lurched forward and swung into a neat line, one after the other. Brandon's vehicle took the lead.

He watched through a small patch of the windshield as they retreated from the ship, feeling a twinge of guilt at being the first one out. He should have stayed until the last crew member had safely disembarked. Not that it mattered in any kind of formal sense, but those rules and regulations were what held teams together.

Would they be able to stay together inside Liberty? Only time would tell. No doubt some of the crew would adapt faster than others, and that might be the only difference. Was he the only one thinking ahead?

The driver shook his head.

Brandon stopped analyzing his thoughts so deliberately. Either he was losing it, or the redhead was reading his mind.

Come on, don't be crazy.

Taking a deep breath, he forced his body to relax, one inch at a time. Once his hands and feet were warm, his eyes grew heavy, even though each bump jerked him all over the seat. "Wake me when we get close."

Murmured agreement reassured him he wouldn't miss the lead-in to Liberty, and he let his guard down. He leaned his head back on the headrest, his restless mind finally releasing all the questions, all the problems he could never solve for himself or the crew. Within minutes, blissful nothingness took him swiftly, and he fell asleep.

•••

Brandon woke up to a hard elbow in his ribs. "Where are we?"

Headlights shone into the endless darkness and bounced off random, wind-formed boulders of ice. Blue, white and gray. The new landscape of America. The world.

"We're five minutes out, Newbie," the driver said.

Brandon grimaced at the nickname. He might have been the last to the table, but he had more skills than an adolescent with his first gaming console. "Thanks. How long was I out?"

"About ninety minutes."

It felt more like a couple days and still, he wanted to go back to sleep. Strange how no one really talked about Liberty, how the guys in the vehicle didn't share off-the-cuff stories about the place.

He didn't ask any questions. They wanted him to experience this for himself, and he had to admit, he felt a little nervous about going in. He'd never liked to experience new things without background information.

No, Brandon Church didn't like surprises.

The car slowed, and the vehicles lined up, single file, and idled. Try as he might, Brandon couldn't fight the darkness to see what was going on. The sound of muffled voices forced him forward in his seat. "What's happening?"

"Relax," the driver said. "We're at the checkpoint. We won't open the geofence until we're a hundred percent sure the area's clear."

"Clear of what?"

A long beat passed before he got the answer. "Problems."

What kind of problems did they have in the arctic badlands in the middle of the night? His skin crawled. People who wanted to stake claim to the things Marx's men brought into the settlement. He couldn't miss the underlying tension rising in the truck as they waited. If these guys operated the way most military units did, waiting didn't sit well. Made them sitting ducks.

"Here we go." The driver shifted the vehicle into gear, and they inched forward, not moving fast enough for anyone inside.

Brandon stared in amazement at the sparkling sapphire-blue lines as they drove down a ramp toward a large building. Behind the building, he noticed the hulking tall dome structures. "What the hell?" He twisted in his seat and watched the octagonal netting of laser-like light fall back into place behind them, then shimmered and faded to black.

"Geofencing," the driver volunteered. "The most advanced kind, of course."

Advanced for sure. He'd never seen anything like it on any military base or coast guard ship. "Is it weaponized?"

"No, it serves as a digital boundary and alert system. It allows us to respond quickly to intercept intruders before they get into the infrastructure. You can only see the light when you cross. Marx says it's fair warning to anyone who's not welcome."

Those thin lines were the only things holding the place together? Impossible. He wanted to see the looks on the faces of the others, of Morgan and the Jotti brothers, to know that they'd all seen the same thing. Marx had been smart to separate them. Brandon shouldn't have allowed it and tasted panic in the back of his throat now that they were inside. Would they be able to get out if they wanted to?

"This is it." The truck crept to a halt, ice crunching under the tires. "Marx wants you and your crew to get some rest. We'll bring everything inside."

Brandon said nothing, but knew damn well he'd be taking part in anything involving the ship's provisions. The group emerged from the trucks, and he decided to stay behind with his men to account for the items they'd brought with them. Marx oversaw the operation from a distance and only approached Brandon when they'd brought everything inside the concrete block building.

"Are we good?" Graysen Marx asked, slapping his shoulder.

Brandon nodded and peered out the open steel door. "There's no wind in here."

"No. Not anymore." He steered him toward a door with a handwritten sign that read *Survivor Processing*. "We'll have some bunks ready for you after you get checked out by medical. We can't risk anyone coming in sick. I want you and your men to be up for sunrise. You have to see it to believe it."

• • •

A chill touched August's face, panic washing away the remnants of sleep. She sat up in bed and rubbed her eyes, noticing the solar heater had died. The morning had come too quickly, and she felt as if she hadn't slept at all. Groggy, she glanced across the room at Lydia sleeping peacefully on her side, the sleeping bag enveloping her small frame.

Reddish-amber light filtered through a small area that wasn't covered with snow or ice in the window above her bed.

It was a new day, and with it would come new challenges. She had no idea what those challenges would be, but after Dax had been killed, anything was possible. She needed to be prepared.

Climbing out of bed, August tossed on her coat and boots then checked her hair and face in the small cracked mirror, hanging askew on the wall, next to a stack of unopened foil thermal blankets. As she straightened the mirror, the smell of fresh coffee surrounded her.

John's hushed voice came from the doorway. "Ready to get started?"

"I know it sounds silly under the circumstances, but is there a comb or brush, something for my hair?"

"Check the supply room. There should be some, as well as a toothbrush, toothpaste, and whatever else you might need, including clothing and warmer boots. Might not be the type of clothing you're used to, though. There's a clipboard on the wall to mark off what you've taken. We need to track every single item this close to the supply delivery."

At least she could brush her teeth and hair. A shower—not so much. "Thanks."

"Coffee's on." He grabbed the heater from the floor. "Looks like it's going to be scrambled eggs for breakfast this morning."

She raised an eyebrow, wondering where they had gotten eggs.

As if reading her mind, John said, "What's left of the MREs. Today's your lucky day."

August smiled, thankful for a meal and a cup of coffee, even though she wasn't much of a coffee drinker. She preferred hot chocolate or green tea. At this point, she couldn't be picky. She'd accept anything hot to warm her.

After brushing her teeth and fixing her hair to look somewhat human, she changed into a pair of military-brown cargo pants that were a size too big and an oversized heavy sweatshirt with a hood, then tossed on her coat and the men's black extreme weather boots she'd found in the supply room. She quickly stuffed wool gloves, an extra pair of socks, and a hat into her coat pocket.

In the main room, a fire raged deep within the crude-looking barrel stove constructed from a dented and scratched steel drum that was vented up to the ceiling and through the wall to the outside of the building.

No one else was awake. August wasn't even sure what time it was. Her watch was useless, broken in the university auditorium. She was happy the braided leather bracelet she'd made years ago was still in one piece. She stared at the worn brown leather and smiled, remembering a much happier time. Not that it really mattered now. There were more important things to worry about. Like staying alive—surviving. She stood in front of the fire's warmth and rubbed her hands together.

"Ian and I built the stove. He's kind of like MacGyver. Can put together almost anything we need," John said. "The stove serves its purpose, at least until we run out of things to burn. Coffee's in the pot on the table."

August poured herself a cup and stared at John's rifle leaning against one of the wooden chairs.

"How did you sleep?"

"Not well. It's going to take some time to adjust to this new life, especially after what happened last night."

"It's unfortunate—losing Dax. He'll be missed. There aren't many men left here. Seems like we've been losing too many people lately." He pointed to the battered chair. "Sit."

She took a seat and sipped her coffee, her thoughts turning to Lydia. August hoped the woman could get through her loss.

"Ian's outside standing guard. He said these tasted pretty good, directly from the army barracks in Newington, delivered by Graysen's men when they first found us. The barracks is one of the few places the Bleeders and Sproggs haven't raided yet. Too far of a walk in the cold, about twelve hours. I'm sure they'll try to hit the place once they figure out how to get there."

"Why hasn't the military helped with food and keeping the peace?"

"As far as we can tell, most were killed in the event. The ones who survived were taken to Liberty to supply security to the settlement." He passed her an MRE and a pouch.

"What's this thing?"

"A flameless ration heater."

August picked up the pouch and inspected it. "Cool. How does it work?"

"It's pretty simple."

August watched him tear open the top of the pouch and slide the MRE inside. He opened a bottle of water and poured in a small amount.

"Only fill it to between those two lines on the back of the pouch."

She picked up her meal and followed his lead.

He pushed the MRE down in the pouch, folded the flap, and slipped the pouch into a cardboard holder. "Lay it flat for a minute for the water to activate the heating. After that, lean the package on an angle against something for about ten or fifteen minutes."

A hot meal. Her stomach rumbled, reminding her how hungry she was. Anything would taste good, well, except for sardines.

"Can I ask you something?"

John clutched his cup with both hands and nodded.

"Lydia said there's been some talk about others being different after the experiment, changed, able to do things they couldn't before. Is that true? Are there others?"

"There has been some chatter from a few in the group. Harper McGee is a couple years younger than you, I think. A tough kid."

Excitement stirred when she learned there was someone else around her own age. "Where is she?"

"Out with the others gathering supplies. They still haven't returned."

The worry in his voice and on his face was obvious in the lines across his forehead and at the corners of his eyes. "I'm sure they'll be back soon."

"I hope you're right. Harper claims she can see glowing colored outlines on people's skin. An aura of some sort. She never experienced it before the event. Has no clue what it means. No one does. Except, she noticed the Bleeders and Sproggs have a cloudy dark red glow around them."

Because they're killers?

He paused as if contemplating what to say next, his gaze traveling to his coffee then back to her. "Lydia and Snow are convinced you were resurrected from the dead. Maggie, too. I believe them."

Not that dying and coming back to life made any logical sense. A shiver snaked through her body at the thought.

"Have you remembered anything else?"

"Nothing. It's as if something important is locked away in my mind and can't come out." August glanced at flames inside the stove. "Do you think it's possible maybe I wasn't dead, to begin with? You know, like people who wake up in a morgue? Apparently, it happens all the time."

"Anything is possible, I suppose. But I believe Snow. She's a good nurse, worked in the ER for many years."

She had a feeling John knew more than what he was willing to tell her.

"I'm sure you'll remember what happened. Don't force it. It'll come to you." He took a sip of his coffee and passed her a plastic spoon. "Eat up. We have a busy morning planned, and it begins with hand-to-hand combat and ends with weapons training. You're going to need your strength. You're going to wish you never begged me to train you."

• • •

Brandon tilted his head right, then left, and stared through the transparent hexagonal cladding of the dome. Outside, the sky had been a dingy, muted shade of red but in here, definitely more orange. Sort of looked normal, the way it used to be.

He'd woken an hour before dawn, eager to see what Graysen Marx had been talking about. He felt the tepid air, pleasant and comfortable, compared to the blasting winds he experienced on the deck of the *Eagle.* A person could live in this environment without changing everything about life. It almost made him forget what it was like on the outside.

He closed his eyes, inhaled deeply, and caught the faint scent of musty soil coming from the tall potted tropical plants clumped together at the far end of the room. He would never smell the salty tang of the sea, never witness the changing colors of the season again. God, he'd loved to go hiking in the mountains in the fall. All that had ended. As he marveled in the sky's color growing brighter, he wondered what he might find joy in now.

Behind him, a door opened and closed. Heavy footsteps sounded, and two very expensive Gucci loafers landed beside him. "You beat me to it."

Brandon looked up at Marx, who wore dark gray pants and a black long-sleeved shirt with an unusual emerald green emblem: a sun with spiked hooks that looked like tentacles and anchors inside the design. He wondered if the unique symbol had a meaning. The man's hair was perfectly slicked back and glistened in waves at the nape of his neck.

"I wanted to see what it would be like to sit for a few minutes and not freeze to death."

"Amazing, isn't it?" Marx crouched beside him and followed Brandon's line of sight to the horizon. "We'll get used to it one day."

"I don't think I ever will."

"Believe it or not, one day people won't remember the previous environment. Sooner than you think since modern medicine has also taken such an enormous hit. Lifespan is bound to decline, not just from the change in environment."

"Except for now all the bacteria and viruses are frozen, too."

"That's true in the majority of cases, although nature always finds a way to adapt. Our first obstacle must be the climate. Only then will human beings be able to combat other opponents, like disease."

Brandon noticed something else. Birds singing and a dog barking in the distance. With the joyful sounds, his eyes misted over. He blinked, unwilling to let Marx see him affected this way.

He hadn't missed the sounds of nature until he heard them again, and they were beautiful. Still, he housed all his questions for a time when he wasn't so nervous for the answers he wanted to hear. He needed to be able to discern between truth and lies.

"Your crew is still asleep. Do you want to wake them?"

Brandon shook his head. "They deserve some rest."

"They aren't as curious as you."

"Maybe not," Brandon said with a shrug. "What time are you heading back to the ship to pull in the rest of the crew?"

"In about a couple of hours. My men just got up and are having a meal. Do you want to go back with them?"

He wanted to return to the hard-packed snowscape less than anything he could remember, even when he got the crazy vaccinations the military had put them through prior to training exercises. "I should."

"We'll make room," Marx reassured him, then stood and offered his hand. "Come on, walk with me to the chow hall and get some breakfast, then I'll link you up with the convoy."

Brandon allowed Marx to haul him to his feet, then fell into step beside him. He saw little outside the parameters of the settlement other than the sky, scrapheaps of snow and ice and rows of gigantic blue solar panels. Miles away, to the east, he spotted what was left of a crumbled skyscraper in downtown Providence. Had anyone who worked there survived? He also couldn't piece together how Liberty worked, how extensive it was, or how the current climate inside was sustained over miles.

"How is air distributed throughout the settlement?"

"We have numerous electric motors run by solar and steam that supply clean air throughout the different ventilation systems. We use a geothermal heating system to maintain the dome's various ecosystems. Some areas require additional heating, others less."

It sounded complicated to Brandon, but he understood most of what the man was talking about.

Marx directed him down a long corridor that gave off the illusion of having glass walls and ushered him through another metal door on the left that opened into the chow hall. The first thing he noticed was the space was warmer than the processing area.

"This is where the Liberty Guard take their meals, three times a day," Marx said.

So, there was a military presence. Brandon didn't know enough about the men yet to call them a *force*. He wanted to watch and listen, glean every detail that could make a difference in the big picture. "Definitely better than where we were."

Brandon glanced around. From what he could tell by the intricate steel framing and roof of the dome, the processing area and the chow hall were located in a giant sphere. The room was set up like most military mess halls he'd seen, crowded and loud with rows of tables and benches featuring cafeteria-style food service. His nose instantly picked up the scent of eggs and, if he wasn't mistaken, bacon. His mouth watered at the strange normalcy, considering how much life had changed. For a second, he felt like he was at home, having Sunday breakfast with his parents.

Brandon followed the man to the line. Voices hushed, and eyes followed them the second they were spotted. He estimated there had to be at least a hundred and fifty men in uniforms, remnants of US military uniforms, either desert brown camo or digital green with requisite boots and caps, having breakfast.

Did Marx's men respect him, or fear him? Brandon couldn't tell. So far, he didn't fear him—not exactly. The man didn't give off any aggressive vibes. Assertive, yes, since he was the one in charge. He also observed four cameras anchored against the intersecting tubular steel frame of the dome. He didn't know if the cameras were functional. If they were, it was clear everyone was under constant surveillance. That didn't sit well with Brandon.

"You're a man of few words." Marx motioned to him to get ahead of him in line. "I'm sure you have questions. Everybody does when they arrive."

"Does everyone come in the back door?" Brandon picked up a metal tray from the stack.

"No. We have three other entrances at different locations in the settlement. One where we process survivors, another for those coming in who are ill, and one that we use as a second major security area. All are well-marked and guarded. The Liberty entrance is only for the guard."

Only four entrances made the settlement sound small, considering the size of the place.

"What would you like?" a male server asked.

Brandon's attention moved to the row of hot food in metal warmers. "A little bit of everything. And one of those apples."

The server frowned. "You're restricted to—"

Marx's hand landed on Brandon's shoulder, and he addressed the man. "He can have whatever he likes, today only."

"Yes, sir." The young man begrudgingly loaded Brandon's tray with a hefty scoop of scrambled eggs, three slices of bacon and two pieces of toast.

"Thank you."

After getting a coffee, they sat at the end of the only nearly-abandoned table: Brandon on one side, Marx on the other. He didn't like the way the man studied him, his blue eyes squinting. Brandon returned the favor and stared back at him.

"What's on your mind?"

"The men on the *Eagle*."

"That's very noble of you. We'll get to them quicker today since we know the way. They must be anxious to disembark."

"I'm sure they are," Brandon said between delicious bites of bacon and real—not powdered—eggs. "We've all been trained to rely on each other. I'd consider it a tough sell for at least half of them to be a part of something they don't know or understand."

Marx nodded. "This has been a rough transition for everyone."

"I don't know about that." Brandon raised his eyebrows. "You're still wearing Gucci shoes."

Humor disappeared from the man's chiseled features, although he still smiled. He leaned over his tray of food. "I take good care of them."

Brandon swallowed the lump of food threatening to stick in his throat. He didn't need to underestimate his host or the current situation. What he needed to do was inhale the rest of his food because he'd be rationed later, then leave here to get the rest of his crew. Keep his mouth shut and get along until something happened that he couldn't go along with.

For now, this unusual place with its warm air was the best shot for his crew to regroup and make decisions on an individual basis of what they wanted to do next. Including him.

CHAPTER SIX

In the cold basement of the armory, August peered at the stacks of menacing-looking crates filled with weapons. Nervousness worked through her and elevated her heart rate. The number of weapons stored below her sleeping quarters was scary, and she wondered if she really wanted to know how to use them. *I have to do this.*

"As you can see, there's a lot to protect here," John said.

"Do the Bleeders and Sproggs know about the weapons?"

"Not yet. We need to make sure they don't. Graysen Marx does. He just doesn't know how many." Turning to one of the guns, he quickly changed the subject. "That one is an AR-15. Powerful and deadly. Real easy to squeeze off a few dozen rounds before anyone knows what hit them. Exactly what you'll need to fend off a major assault."

"What's your weapon?"

His lips curled into a faint smile. "You ask too many questions."

Missing her family, sadness filled her. "My father always said the same thing."

"An M16. It's what I'm used to. We'll start small, work our way up to something bigger. I want you fully trained by the end of the week, so you can go out on supply runs with the others. What we get bi-weekly from Liberty is never enough. They don't always have everything we need."

She eagerly eyed the crossbow atop a box of ammunition. She'd never seen a one up close before and didn't realize how big the weapon was.

"I can teach you how to use the bow after we do some basic training. Get your coat off. You won't need it."

She took off her coat and placed it on one of the wooden boxes. John did the same.

He stood in front of her, his knees bent with one foot in front of him. "The first move is called the long knee."

As he showed her move after move, including elbow strikes to the back of the neck and chin, an up knee, throat punch, ax stomp, and something called a nutcracker choke, his voice grew louder. "Stop hitting like a girl. Hit hard. You're fighting for your life."

They continued to practice, and instinct told her she needed to step up her game. August put more of herself physically into each maneuverer.

"Harder! It's you or your attacker!"

Huffing and puffing until sweat built up along her hairline, she bucked back and forth with each hard blow, but held her ground, ready for the next hit.

John twisted and got behind her, catching her off-guard. His elbow smacked into the soft spot at the base of her skull.

Stars flashed in the back of her eyes. She blinked and choked down a groan. Pain extended down her spine, and the room spun. Her father's voice weaved through the dizziness.

"Don't worry. Nothing is going to go wrong with the experiment. The chemically-treated particles will do exactly what they're supposed to do..."

August staggered then dropped to one knee, afraid she'd lose her balance completely. She closed her eyes to get her bearings and felt John's hand on her arm.

"You okay? You took a hard one."

She inhaled and blew out small bursts of air until the vertigo subsided then gave John a brave nod. "I'm...fine."

"Let's get you up." He grasped her arm and helped her to her feet. "Now you know why it's better to practice with a sparring pad rather than a human."

Legs shaking, August leaned against the wall. The smack to the back of the head made her remember a glimpse of a conversation with her father, but she still didn't know how it fit into the big picture.

August rubbed the back of her head and gave in. "I remembered something. My father said something about the chemically-treated particles doing exactly what they're supposed to do."

John's brow furrowed in thought, and he didn't say anything for a few minutes. "What do particles have to do with anything?"

She shook her head and shrugged. "I wish I could remember."

• • •

After the final members from the *Eagle* had arrived, Brandon directed them to the chow hall, just in time for lunch. Watching for telltale signs of shock and awe, he secretly felt proud. None of them wandered and stared as if they'd arrived at Santa's Workshop. Instead, through the occasional wide-eyed moments, they kept to themselves.

Filtering through the food line, they naturally segregated in the corner of the room, where they could sit together and talk in whispers. Brandon took a seat at the end of one of the tables.

One of the cadets held up a chicken leg. "Where are they getting this food?"

"Why wasn't this place destroyed?" another asked. "Everything else was."

Brandon ducked his head. He didn't have all the answers, only more questions.

"Who is this guy, Graysen Marx?"

"He was a rich philanthropist who made billions in scientific research, energy and other things. He was a major financial backer of the climate change experiment that put us all here."

Gasps ensued at the realization. Then, more questions.

"Is he trying to fix it?"

"Did he know this was going to happen?"

Raising his hand to deflect the questions, Brandon mulled over his biggest one: *Did he know this was going to happen?* One would think, having inside access to the project only money or knowledge could buy, the capacity to see this coming could have possibly presented itself.

What kind of man lets the planet freeze while he saves only a few?

He shuddered at the answer. The kind of man who wanted assets, leadership, something out of the situation only his kind of money could buy. Did they want to be associated with someone like that? They might be better off in the new tundra than inside, if that was the case.

The redhaired driver, Roman Shipley, appeared beside him. "We've got some free time. Why don't you pick three of your crew to come with you to take a quick tour of the area? We'll start getting the rest processed, cleared by medical, and assigned to their living quarters."

It was an offer Brandon couldn't refuse. Making eye contact with Morgan and the Jotti boys, he pulled them out of the group with a nod. Asher and Jacob nearly ran to be part of the tour, while Morgan hung back, his brows creased.

"What's up?" Brandon asked. "You don't look too thrilled."

Morgan looked at him. "I keep getting a bad vibe here. Not sure why."

"We've been through a lot." Brandon patted him on the back, his instincts on high-alert in case his friend was right. "I'm sure it's nothing."

Morgan's eyes traveled to the guards finishing their lunch. "Yeah. I guess you're right."

The cadets fell in with Shipley and struggled to keep up with the man's long, ambling strides. They followed him out of the chow hall, down two dozen stairs and through another door that opened into a mammoth concrete sewer-pipe-looking corridor, wide enough to fit two lanes of traffic.

"These tunnels connect the biodomes together. Some stretch for twenty, fifty miles. The tunnels also run all along the perimeter. Makes it easier to get around. The design isn't perfect, but it works. All the electrical cables run underground, fully insulated, constructed to withstand the harsh elements of Mars—"

"And here, apparently," Brandon said.

Asher, Jacob, and Morgan gawked in awe with round eyes. Brandon was also wonderstruck by the sheer circumference of the tunnel. The men continued walking a few hundred yards then stopped at an intersection. Shipley pointed to a huge area on the left neatly lined with golf-cart like vehicles, mini-buses, pickup trucks, and box trucks painted dark metallic gray, almost black, with the same green emblem on the doors that Graysen Marx had on his shirt.

Asher grinned at his brother, then at the others. "Cool!"

"How can you drive down here?" Morgan asked, scratching his head. "I don't see any ventilation for exhaust fumes."

"All the vehicles inside the settlement run on water. Not like we have a shortage of the stuff now. The water treatment facility is found on the west side of the settlement. We have two biofuel processing and storage areas located at the north and southeast end."

Whoever designed the place had thought of everything by making it eco-friendly long before the world changed. Brandon wondered again if Marx had known the ruinous climate shift was going to happen, since the encampment appeared to be a much needed, convenient safe haven. He pushed the thought from his mind and watched Shipley open the door to one of the buses and wave his hand. "Hop in, boys."

When everyone was loaded up, their tour guide jumped into the driver's seat and started the engine.

"How many people are living here?" Morgan asked.

Shipley put the bus into gear and pressed his foot on the gas pedal. "About four thousand souls."

"That's all? I can't believe it. That can't be. Does that include people who were already here running the place?"

"Unfortunately, that includes the seven hundred who were here before we were ice bombed."

"Do you think Mom and Dad made it?" Asher asked his brother quietly.

"They're probably gone."

Shipley's answer wasn't what Brandon had expected to hear either. He shut his eyes and wished they could go back in time. That wasn't many survivors for the size of Rhode Island. Most of the world's population had more then likely been wiped out. Mass extinction. His parents...his friends...August.

All they could do now was make the best of what they had and try to think about the future. It was much different from the future he'd imagined growing up. Reality kicked in, and the atmosphere shifted to solemn silence.

Ten minutes later, the bus came to a stop, and Shipley shut off the engine. Brandon and the others exited the vehicle and followed the man up a flight of stairs.

"Exactly how large is the settlement?" Jacob asked.

"It was about an eighth of the size of Rhode Island before things went to hell."

Brandon absorbed the news as if he'd expected it, but Morgan's head exploded. "Come on, man. That's huge. How's that even possible?"

"The prototype idea began a long time ago and was shelved. Then the project was finally completed last year. Took nineteen years to build. The geofence makes all the difference. I'm no scientist, so don't ask me how, but Marx saved this portion of the state from the most devastating part of the fallout."

Jacob jumped in next. "You expect us to believe some damn electric fence helped save Liberty from destruction?"

"Not at all. Marx can and will tell you the story. He doesn't hold back. He deployed the geofence immediately after the event began, which means this place didn't suffer as much damage, compared to the rest of the state."

Brandon struggled to comprehend. Between the domes and the geofence, life was basically saved from the destructive climate change. "Loss of life?"

"We lost many. There are areas near the coast where the fence didn't hold well because of the shifting boundary. Those areas are a complete wasteland. At least the devastation wasn't total here, thank God."

"What were the losses then?" Brandon asked, knowing full well what they were on the outside.

"Estimates are somewhere between thirty, forty percent. Our domes on the north and northeast side took the hardest hit: infrastructure, crops, animals, and humans."

"I don't believe you about the geofence. Seems far-fetched," Morgan said.

The Jotti brothers nodded.

"Believe what you like. I expect you'll see enough here to convince you over the next few days." Shipley flung open the door. "Take a look."

• • •

Humid warm air hit Brandon first, and a butterfly landed on his shoulder. His jaw dropped open. Morgan and the Jotti brothers' mouths gaped, too.

"Holy crap," Morgan said, shaking his head in disbelief.

Brandon's eyes widened at the bumblebees buzzing. He looked at Jacob and Asher, who stared in amazement at what stood before them.

Inside the vast arched dome, a mountainous vertical garden, at least two hundred feet tall, took center stage. Orange, yellow and red vegetables blazing in various shades and sizes peeked through lush deep green leaves. Drastic beauty contrasted with the dismal world outside.

About thirty men and women in black coveralls picked vegetables and put them into plastic bins then hauled them down along the railed walkways that wrapped around the vegetation to the bottom.

"We have three vertical gardens, enough fresh vegetables to feed everyone here, and then some. Nothing goes to waste. Marx makes sure of it. We take some rations out to an Army National Guard Armory in Icehaven."

Brandon looked at him, confused. So did Morgan and the brothers.

"It's what Marx calls the state of Connecticut. Just like Rhode Island is Liberty now, as a centralization of the new government. We're getting ready to send a food convoy out today, if any of you want to join us. No one looks forward to going outside. When you're helping people, you do what you have to do."

Although Brandon still had a million questions, a quick glance at his friends told him they were down to help civilians on the outside. Wasn't it their duty? "We're in."

"Good. Because every able-bodied person pitches in at Liberty, has a purpose, whether it's this kind of work, farming, running the water treatment system, you name it. Like I said, most of the infrastructure made it through the storm, but eventually...well, you know how it goes. Things like that don't age well, so Marx has the Council putting together a training program to pass on vital information to survivors coming in."

Brandon's eyebrows rose. "The Council?"

"You'll be meeting with them. They'll help you decide on what your jobs will be here, if you and your crew choose to stay."

"I thought Marx ran everything," Jacob said.

Brandon thought so, too. Maybe he was wrong about the man.

Shipley turned them around, and they walked back toward the stairs. "After the event, the state government took on a different form because of our new circumstance. They call themselves the Infinity Council."

•••

Outside, a harsh wind howled and nipped at the small amount of exposed skin on August's face. Cold air filled her nostrils, and she adjusted the scarf around her face. After officially meeting Maggie's girls, Olivia and Emma, and Snow's little boy, Noah, John officially introduced her to Henry, a small man with broad shoulders and a booming voice.

While Henry made his rounds around the perimeter of the armory with his rifle ready to shoot if necessary, August clutched the Sig Sauer P320 with both hands. She aimed at the makeshift shooting range John had constructed between a cluster of trees, using stacks of empty sardine cans and piles of wood. With teeth clattering and her cheeks going numb, she fired. The shot missed and bored into one of the tree trunks. Ice rained down from the deformed branches and glittered in the pale scarlet light. The cloudless sky looked like some sort of strange russet twilight she'd see in one of those end of the world movies.

This *was* the end of the world, she reminded herself.

There were no birds or wildlife, vanquished into wintry graves after her father's experiment. The thought made her sad. She loved animals and had volunteered at one of their local rescues during high school as part of a community project. The reality of this life was surreal, mind-boggling, terrifying. What would happen if Graysen Marx stopped delivering food to them? What would they eat? There was nothing to hunt or trap. They'd starve...

Henry's voice came over John's walkie-talkie. "You're trying too hard. You need to relax."

August shoved the depressing thoughts aside and tried to stay focused, knowing she needed to learn to protect herself and help protect the others. She had been at it for almost fifteen minutes and she still hadn't hit anything. Not much of a great protector.

She lowered the gun and pressed her lips together, frustrated by the cumbersome thick gloves she was wearing, making it difficult to grip the weapon properly. About to throw in the towel, she glanced at John. "Maybe I'm not built for this."

John raised her arms before she had the chance to lower them completely, directing her not to give up. "You have to be. Try again. Bend your knees more. Loosen your grip slightly, and don't think so damn hard about the shot." He paused and took a breath, his voice strained. "You came back to life for a reason. Don't forget that."

She looked at him with confusion. There was no reason for anything that had happened. She wasn't any type of reigning queen prepared to rule the new world. August laughed to herself. Her only purpose at the moment was to hit the targets before she turned into an ice sculpture. Determined, she lined up the sight and inhaled and exhaled heavily. She squeezed the trigger. *Pop.*

Cans scattered and skyrocketed in every direction.

She grinned like she'd won Olympic gold. "Woohoo!"

"Do it again," John said.

August raised the gun and aimed at a piece of decaying wood. Another gunshot cracked. The bullet punched a hole into the top of the wood, splintering it into pieces. After making a dozen more shots and hitting the targets dead on, she lowered the weapon, pleased by her accomplishment. It wasn't as difficult after all.

"Tomorrow, I'll have you try a semi-automatic rifle. A lot easier to make a hit when you're spraying bullets."

"And the crossbow?"

He laughed. "Yes, the crossbow."

She sucked air between her teeth, excited to learn how to use the different weapons. Cold air burned her lungs and felt like stabbing sharp ice crystals. Something as simple as breathing was painful. Even her teeth hurt. Ready to pack it in, she handed John the gun.

"Keep it. At some point, you'll need it. You have to be prepared to kill. Don't think for one second the Bleeders or Sproggs won't kill you. A split-second hesitation means life or death."

Her stomach flip-flopped. The thought of killing another human being made her beyond uncomfortable, but she understood she might not have a choice.

Henry's voice bellowed over the walkie-talkie again. "John! We've got injured!"

August twisted her head and peered over her shoulder at the armory. An arm waved frantically a few hundred yards away. John took off running.

Then she saw them. Three nomads with two sleds. Again, she had no idea what gender they were because of the heavy outerwear covering them from head-to-toe. August shoved the gun into her coat pocket and headed across the ice.

When she made it to the armory's entrance, John and Ian were on their knees in front of one of the sleds with a woman who appeared to be unconscious. All she could do was stare at the expanding ugly bloodstain on the left thigh of the woman's pants. The others huddled around the sled, and August immediately saw the concern in their eyes.

"Is Harper going to be okay?" a woman asked, unwrapping the scarf around her face.

John frowned. "It doesn't look good, Rachel."

August's gaze traveled to the other sled, carrying a pig inside a block of ice and a tall wastepaper basket full of frozen chocolate bars, potato chips, and other goodies. They must have raided a vending machine somewhere.

"Davis, what happened?" John asked.

"We were ambushed by Bleeders outside East Shore Park," the man said, holding his arm at the elbow. "We had to wait it out, circle around and come back through Tweed Airport."

"Are you hit, too?" John asked.

The man rubbed his forearm and grimaced. "It's minor, just a graze."

"Ian, you okay? Rachel?"

"We're fine," Ian said for the both of them.

"Help me get her inside," John nodded to Henry then glanced at August. "Tell Snow and Maggie to get the medical supplies ready."

August looked on in horror then rushed inside.

• • •

After being ordered to elevate Harper's legs with two rolled up blankets, August's hand shook as she cut open the young woman's pants with a pair of dull scissors.

When she was done, Snow glanced at Maggie then pressed wads of cloth on the wound. "Pass me the scalpel, tweezers and the suture kit."

Maggie rushed and opened a battered brown suitcase and handed the nurse everything she asked for.

Snow held out the tweezers to August. "You wanted to be useful, learn everything you could. Here's your chance."

She stared at the nurse, regretting opening her mouth to John about wanting to learn what she could, including medical stuff.

"Hurry up. We don't have all day."

August blew a strand of blond hair out of her face and reluctantly took the tweezers, her hand still visibly trembling. "I don't know what to do. I might hurt her."

"I'll guide you through it."

"The bullet's in the tissue. You'll do fine," Maggie said in a calm voice.

Snow prepared the suturing kit. "Don't worry. It missed the main artery. There's isn't much more damage you can do. I'll make an incision, then you remove the bullet."

August's heart pounded. Obviously, the women had done this before. Probably numerous times. She wasn't a nurse. Far from it. She hated the sight of blood. She glanced at Maggie, hoping the woman would step in to help or take over. When she didn't, August gulped hard and waited for Snow to clean the wound. Then she made a two-inch incision.

Snow nodded when she was ready. "It's open enough now. She can't feel anything. She's out cold."

Shaking, August bent and inserted the tip of the tweezers into the oozing wound, searching for something to grab onto. When she felt metal-on-metal, she thought she had the bullet, but didn't. She kept searching, digging deeper.

Harper's eyes popped open, and she abruptly sat up. "Like hell, I can't feel it." She tore off the wool hat she was wearing, revealing black hair styled in a pixie cut with pale blue highlights.

Maggie put her hand on the woman's shoulder and gently pushed her back down. "Please stay still. We're almost done."

The young woman let out a heavy sigh and laid back down. "Who is she?"

"This is August. She's new," Snow said.

"Great. I have a newcomer performing surgery on me." Harper's eyes widened. "Wait. Can you see the golden aura around her? It's really bright. I've never seen a golden one before."

Maggie and Snow looked at each other and shook their heads, obviously not seeing anything. Neither did August. She stopped and looked at Harper, trying to figure out exactly what the woman was seeing that no one else could. Maybe she was mentally ill or something.

"Is gold significant?" August asked.

"No idea. Of course, if we had internet, I'd be able to go online and find out."

August cringed and continued working to locate the bullet, poking and prodding the flesh.

Harper gave her a measured look. Her brown eyes flickered and narrowed. "Jesus. Can you try to be gentle?"

"I think this is probably going to hurt more." August finally got a good grip on the end of the shell and extracted it, probably not as gently as she could have. She held the bullet up in the air like she'd won a prize. "Got it."

"Good thing. Because I was just about ready to punch you in the face."

Snow shook her head. "Relax, Harper. That type of behavior isn't allowed. You know that. I'll get you stitched up, get you some pain medication."

The young woman rolled her eyes. "Fine."

August wasn't sure she wanted to get to know the woman. Even though she had a thin, willowy frame, she had an attitude like a whip and sounded like she had a tough life before the world fell apart. She'd probably been a mean girl. August had witnessed that type in action all through high school.

After Snow finished stitching the wound, she stripped off the latex gloves and tossed them on the table. "You're lucky. A few more inches—"

"Yeah. Yeah. Lucky as hell to have survived a gunshot wound while living it up in an icy apocalypse. I couldn't get any luckier."

CHAPTER SEVEN

Brandon waited outside the closed metal double doors, listening to the muffled voices inside, unable to hear what was being said. Kind of like when his parents used to disagree. Growing up, he'd known they were talking about important things, never once letting him see them divided.

These weren't his parents. This was the Infinity Council, the leadership of Liberty. It was a far-fetched name for a group of survivors who happened to get lucky inside the settlement. He shouldn't be nervous, but somehow this felt more important than facing his parents after he'd made a poor decision. He took in a deep breath and exhaled.

The doors cracked open, and a slender woman in black plants and a black shirt motioned him inside an expansive room with a vaulted ceiling, to face a long conference table.

Brandon was still wearing his USCG uniform, his movements crisp in the face of scrutiny. Or lack thereof.

He counted five council members who looked at him, glanced away, peered at anything except for him. Just how did one get a seat on the Infinity Council? Money? Power? Prestige? He sensed none of that, only boredom and something else he couldn't quite put his finger on.

Graysen Marx stepped up beside him, laid a hand on his shoulder, and addressed the council. "This is Brandon Church—"

"Junior Officer, Cadet, First Class."

"He was aboard the coast guard cutter we came upon. He and his crew have joined us for the time being."

"Welcome, Mr. Church." A small voice came from a man at the center of the table. "Are you happy with your accommodations here? Do you have everything you need?"

"Yes, sir. Everything is great." Brandon squinted at the nameplate in front of the man. *Mr. Wallen.* "We're relieved to be in out of the cold."

"What arrangement has Mr. Marx made with you?" an older black woman with a friendly smile asked.

"Ma'am?"

"I assume he's made an offer to you and your crew to remain inside Liberty?"

"Yes, ma'am. It's very generous. We're to meet at the end of a week to determine who wants to stay."

Marx cut in. "Some may want to venture out to see about their families."

The woman frowned. "I see. How nice for them."

Brandon didn't miss the friction between the two. "Ma'am, it was my request. I don't expect too many will want to return to the outside."

She leaned over the table. "Well, what do you expect them to do here?"

Marx cleared his throat, and she sank back in her chair.

"I expect most will opt for the Liberty Guard or other security work detail. They're already trained and can have an immediate impact."

She pushed her chair back from the table. "What kind of impact?"

Marx tilted his head and raised his fingers to his temple.

Mr. Wallen cleared his throat. "Motion to approve the addition of the crew who decide to stay, pending work assignments."

Brandon shook his head. "Wait—what's happening?"

"Seconded," the man to Mr. Wallen's left said.

"All in favor?" came from the woman in the center.

Four hands went up. Only one remained opposed.

"Miss Petty, what is your objection?" Marx asked. "Approval needs to be unanimous."

"The young man seems to be confused. Why rush him and his crew through before they've reached their individual decisions? Could it have anything to do with the additional equipment you pulled from the ship?"

Marx stepped forward, his expression unreadable. "Miss Petty, you are out of order."

Brandon's hands turned to ice. He'd assumed the Infinity Council ran Liberty. Clearly, Graysen Marx ran the council and Liberty through them.

He spoke up, hoping to diffuse the situation. "No, no I understand. I'm not confused. We voluntarily brought the equipment from our ship. Mr. Marx expressed we would further negotiate those particular items."

Brandon lied. Marx had never said any such thing but now seemed like a good time to grab any bonuses he could. Judging by the rising red flush in Marx's face, he hadn't expected anything of the sort coming from him.

An amused smile bloomed on Miss Petty's face. "Is that right, Mr. Marx?"

"Yes, that's correct."

"In that case..." She laid her hands flat against the tabletop. "You have your unanimous approval. Mr. Church?"

"Yes, ma'am?"

"I do hope you'll stay. You'll do well here."

Mr. Wallen pounded a gavel once against the table. "Dismissed."

Brandon walked out behind Marx with a tickle of amusement he kept hidden. He didn't dare express the sentiment to his host, who turned to him the moment the doors closed.

"Do you think you were being clever?"

Brandon felt the color drain from his face. He understood he'd taken a step, but a step he needed to take when the opportunity presented itself. "It's my job to take care of the crew and those systems. We did agree to that."

Marx took a deep breath and stepped back. He raised a finger as if admonishing a child. "You understand there is no United States of America any longer, don't you?"

Being talked down to had never gone over well with him. "Of course, I do. It's hard to miss. I want assurances from you that my crew will not be bribed or bullied into staying if that's not what they want to do."

"You already have my assurance. This, of course, implies you will be staying."

Brandon locked eyes with him. He hadn't truly considered leaving. Being manipulated didn't exactly roll out the red carpet. He shook his head and wondered how much longer Ms. Petty's services would be needed on the Infinity Council. He kept his tone friendly. "You said the end of a week. We'll start there and see where we end up."

Anger glinted in the back of his eyes, and he gritted his teeth. "I'll stand by my word. Each crew member makes their own decision."

"Agreed."

Once they reached the doors, they parted company. Marx turned right, Brandon headed in the direction of the crew's quarters. As he walked the corridor, he thought about what he was going to tell the crew about the conversation inside the room. He could poison them against Marx, then what? Where could they go? So, what if Marx liked control. Who didn't? That didn't automatically make him a monster. It could simply mean he ran a tight ship.

But that's not what his gut told him. And his gut had never been wrong.

•••

Later that afternoon, Brandon tried not to be surprised by how heavily armed the food convoy went out. They'd been isolated on the ship, the only threat coming if food supplies ran low. From what he'd seen inside Liberty so far, life appeared stable if not downright great, compared to the outside. Other than the weird meeting with Marx and the Infinity Council.

It was different out here.

He watched the LED headlights skip off the ice and slice through the red haze, a persistent shine bright enough to give everybody a migraine in the hour they'd been driving.

Shipley downshifted and slowed the vehicle. "Look alive, boys."

The attitude in the truck changed to alert in a split-second. Hair rose on the back of Brandon's neck. He wasn't sure why.

The four trucks stopped at the end of an ice-caked hump in the washed-out silver landscape. He pulled the hood of the Ghillie suit over his head, his heartbeat thudding in his chest behind the plate of armor meant to keep him alive. He saw no opening, no door and yet they'd stopped.

"Hustle time," Shipley said.

Doors opened, and the men climbed out.

Brandon saw a man pop up from behind a tall block of ice, then another farther down, like a twisted game of whack-a-mole.

Asher shouldered him. "Tunnels, maybe?"

He could be right. Brandon slung his M16 over his shoulder and picked up one of the crates from the back of the vehicle and fell into a fast-moving line behind Morgan. Ten boxes of supplies snaked down the tunnels and to a set of stairs, around a tight corner, and into a wider room layered with shelves and boxes. They took turns dropping the weight, one on top of the last until they were done.

Only then did Brandon have a moment to take a good look around. He recognized the military outpost by the cinderblocks and types of shelving.

"It's an Army National Guard armory. One of many in Icehaven," Shipley said.

He was almost used to the man answering all his questions before he could say a word out loud.

"They're all assembling in the drill hall."

With a nod, Brandon ducked out of the room and down another winding tunnel, emerging into what once was the drill hall.

An estimated dozen people lined the walls, three children among them. He was surprised and concerned there were so few. As his eyes adapted to the bleak solar-powered light, he tried to make out the personal specifics of the individuals, an impossibility with the winter gear they were wearing. One of them, a woman perhaps, wore a fresh bandage across her thigh, a faint red stain seeping through the white. Beside her, a taller figure with wavy long blond hair stared at him with vivid ocean blue eyes. Eyes he'd recognize anywhere. His heart sped up. *August. She was alive!*

His body broke out into a cold sweat, and his pulse raced. He walked across the room to speak to her.

At the same time, Shipley stepped to the center, beside who Brandon could only assume to be the head of the armory. "John tells us you've had some losses. As always, Liberty's doors are open to anyone who wants to come back with us."

"Screw you," the injured woman growled. "You promised us protection."

Brandon's gaze flicked to August, who shrugged at the open hostility of her friend.

It didn't faze Shipley. "We can't protect you out here. You know that. You have your weapons. We bring food and supplies. That's the deal we made."

"We understand the deal," John said. "But you only brought half of what we agreed to. What's going on?"

"Unfortunately, we need to cut back some—on a lot of things. Not just goods and food. Personal things. Moving forward, Liberty is mandating one-child households for all communities we end up forging ties with. The statistics make the mandate necessary. There isn't enough food for a growing population, at least not yet."

Gasps flew from the survivors. While Brandon believed the scenario existed, he couldn't believe Liberty's reach—Marx's reach.

Tension electrified the room. A woman stepped into the void with one child on either side of her.

"We'd like to go back with you."

"Maggie. No," a bundled figure chastised her.

"I have my girls to consider. I want them to have a better life than living out here."

John raised his hands. "No argument. No judgment. We all have the freedom to come and go as we please. Do you have room for them?"

Shipley nodded.

"Don't go. It's dangerous. They're glowing red like the Bleeders and Sproggs—except those four." The injured woman pointed to Brandon, Morgan and the Jotti brothers.

Brandon exchanged glances with his unit leader. There was a strange acknowledgment in the back of the man's eyes like he understood what the woman was talking about. Brandon sure didn't. No one in the room was glowing red.

Maggie remained silent for a few minutes, contemplating. Apprehension shone on her face. "We'll wait until the next delivery before deciding."

"You are welcome anytime."

"How will the mandate be enforced?" John asked, glaring at Shipley.

"Voluntarily. Everyone likes to eat."

Goosebumps pimpled Brandon's arms. Would they really withhold food if people didn't adhere to the mandate? His mind charted all the possible scenarios that could end badly. A mistake, multiples, what happened then? Dread spiraled through his gut.

"We'll be back in two weeks. We should have some better communications set up. There's new equipment coming from military outposts. Being in contact more regularly will help us all."

Brandon's gaze caught August's. Her eyes didn't look round or scared, like everyone around her. Instead, they were narrow slits. She didn't look happy about Liberty's one child mandate...or maybe she wasn't happy to see him.

As most of the group disbanded, he hung back, hoping to have a moment with her.

She rushed to him, her cold hand folding over his. "I—I can't believe it's you."

He wanted to hug her and never let go, but all he could do was return the gentle squeeze of her hand. "I thought you'd died."

"I did," she whispered. "How did you get here? Can you stay? Can we talk? Why are you dressed like that?"

He looked down at the pallid Ghillie suit and shook his head, understanding implicitly what he'd signed up for, at least for now, part of his contribution to the new society. "I haven't been with the Liberty Guard long. The rest of my crew is at the settlement in Rhode Island."

"Oh, of course, no, I understand."

Brandon leaned closer and kept his voice low. "August, what do you mean, you died?"

She glanced away, and he realized Shipley had his eye on them.

August pressed something into his hand. A quick downward glance made his heart jump at the token from their past. The leather bracelet she'd made at summer camp. The same summer he'd first held her hand and dared to give her a quick kiss.

He put the meaningful trinket into his coat pocket and glanced up at her. Their eyes met. "Come back with—"

"We need to go—right now," Morgan said in a frantic uneven tone. "Just beyond the trees—there's a bunch of them."

Brandon stared at him, convinced the cadet had suffered some level of brain damage from the cold. But he also knew Morgan had seen Marx and his men long before anyone else. Maybe he wasn't crazy.

"What's he talking about?" August looked at Brandon confused. Her gaze roamed over his shoulder.

He turned to see his unit leader behind him, listening in on the conversation. "Move it, Church."

Seconds later, gunfire thundered.

• • •

"Sproggs—coming in from the west!" Ian shouted from deep within the tunnels.

Fear screamed inside August's head.

Brandon and the other guards ran out of the room. She hastily put on her hat and gloves then yanked out the gun John had given her, the weapon suddenly feeling almost at home in her hand.

John snatched up his rifle leaning against the wall. He pointed to Henry. "Take the women and children to the supply room. Lock the door. Snow. Get the medical kit in case we have injured."

Everyone scattered.

Hurried foot steps thudded behind and ahead of August. She stayed close to John and raced through the ice catacombs. Davis and Rachel followed, their feet pounding.

Outside, a wall of stabbing cold air took her breath away. August inhaled sharply then exhaled, her own breath clouding her vision.

Blinking through the puffy steam, she poked her head out around the side of the ice mound.

On the other side of the trees, flickers of movement danced.

She counted twenty people in bulky black and metal armor over winter clothing. Some wore gas masks and scarves, others sported vintage brown leather goggles, like they were heading to a Halloween party. Except they carried real weapons.

One hulking form stood out from the rest, dressed in a yellow snowsuit, black fedora, and a red and white molded mask with a bloody skeleton emerging from the man's mouth. He hoisted a frozen head stuck on the end of a pole proudly. In his other hand he held, a sword, a very long shiny sword.

John slid up next to her between Davis and Rachel and aimed his rifle toward the trees. "The one in the mask is the ringleader."

"Goes by the name of Witness. He's a mean bastard," Davis said.

They all looked mean—insane.

Not only had the environment changed, so had what was left of civilization. August steadied her hands and tightened her grip on the gun. "What do they want?"

John kept his gaze glued ahead. "Everything they can't have."

Her body tingled in panic, and her hands shook.

Brandon and the rest of the guard crouched, their hooded white camouflage suits blending in with the bleached landscape. They cautiously relocated to various positions around their trucks.

She couldn't fathom how they had vehicles that ran in the polar chill. Maybe she could use one of their trucks and go search for her family. Intermittent gunshots echoed and crushed her thoughts.

John grabbed her by the coat and dragged her back behind the ice.

Seconds later, silence.

August peeked her head around the corner again. Frantic wind whipped at her eyelids. Sproggs appeared, then disappeared behind the tree trunks and ice-loaded branches in a hideous game of hide and seek.

"We'll take the west side, see if we can get a good shot—take out a couple of them," Ian said, glancing at Rachel and Davis.

John gave them a nod. "Be careful."

Brandon pulled down his hood and glanced over his shoulder at August, his light brown wavy hair fluttering in the wind. He took a few steps and set up next to one of the vehicles, closing in the area between them and the renegades.

As Ian, Davis, and Rachel sprinted along the ice in front of the armory, automatic gunfire rattled and sparked the air.

One of the guard members collapsed against the truck door. Another slumped at the edge of the back fender then toppled sideways onto the ground. Blood spilled across the packed ice from the man's head.

Her heart thumped. She was worried about Brandon, scared something would happen to him. She couldn't believe he'd survived, was grateful he had. He was a familiar face, a piece of home and what life was like before—

"Ambush!"

August and John spun at the same time.

Four Sproggs barreled toward them with chains and sticks.

August aimed and fired. The shot hit one of the men. He dropped to his knees, clutching his chest.

John smacked the butt of his rifle hard into the side of another man's head. The man twirled and slammed to the ground.

In the flurry of motion, she heard gunshots coming from Brandon's direction and his voice. "August, watch out!"

A man in a dark-colored coat wearing a long white wig underneath a wool hat had a dog collar around his neck that had 'BEAST' engraved on it. He grunted and bowled into her, spinning a rusted chain high in the air, and lassoed her wrist. August flinched from the pain when the chain hit. The gun flew out of her hand. Every ounce of John's training kicked in, a violent dance for survival. She stepped back out of range of the man, her eyes glued to his, trying to decipher his next move.

He bent, scrunched his face, showing his yellow teeth, and drove his head into her side like a bull.

August twisted and jerked up her knee and drove it upwards with all her strength. She heard his jaw crack. He fell backwards groaning, almost pulling her off her feet with the chain. She rapidly unwrapped the rigid metal and tossed it aside.

Nearby, Ian wrestled a man on the ground while John chased after another one, stopped, and fired his rifle. A bright red bullseye spread across the back of the man's navy coat, and he fell forward.

After Ian knocked the last hoodlum out with a chunk of ice, he climbed to his feet, huffing and puffing. His eyes traveled to one of the men she'd taken down, clutching his jaw, mumbling through clenched teeth.

Ian looked at her and pulled his hat down over his ears. "You did good."

Her body shook to the same tempo as her voice. "I can't believe I did that."

"What are we going to do with him?" Ian asked.

"Let him suffer," John said. "He'll either die out here or go back to the peak. He doesn't deserve our help."

"What about the other one, the one I shot."

"He's dead, August. Good riddance."

Bile rose in her throat. Horrified by what she'd done, she choked it down.

The growl of an engine roared against the wind.

"They got one of our vehicles. Go after them!"

Ian, August, and John glanced at each other and hightailed back to the ice hump in time to see a truck speed off east past the trees. The rest of the Sproggs had disappeared.

Brandon and two other men jumped into a truck. Plumes of exhaust bloated out of the back of the vehicle. The other guards stayed behind and attended to their downed men.

August stood in silence, rubbing her wrist. Days ago, she'd gone from being a happy-go-lucky student at Yale with a family, working on her bachelor's degree, to killing someone—on purpose.

Their new world was venomous, unforgiving. She was fighting for her life and the lives of others. As taillights disappeared, August wondered if she would see Brandon again.

CHAPTER EIGHT

Inside the stark enclave of his private quarters at Liberty, Graysen Marx paced a straight line from one end to the other and ground his teeth together. What he wouldn't give for just one goddamn day where things would go as planned. As *needed.* Couldn't everyone—anyone—see what he was trying to do?

He balled his hands into fists and longed to rail against those who opposed him, a list growing by the day. In this frozen, broken world, why couldn't one thing happen the way it needed to for him to move forward?

He corrected himself. For *Liberty* to move forward.

A moment of clarity helped clear his mind. He couldn't allow his anger to get the best of him. He took a deep breath and slowed his frantic movement. He needed to be on top of his game.

He was amazed to learn how organized the Sproggs were during his men's first run-in with them. Getting away with one of their vehicles could put them in danger. He was positive the group planned on heading to the army barracks in Newington. Half of the weapons had already been taken by his men and brought to the settlement. The fifty percent still sitting there worried him. If the gang got their hands on the weapons cache, they would be in a good position to attack the settlement. His settlement.

They had also lost one of their most loyal guard members, and that tragedy would not go unavenged.

He would make sure the second injured man was well cared for, beyond what a typical citizen of Liberty would have. He knew the encounters with the outsiders were dangerous. To ask his men to risk their lives on a near-daily basis meant giving them rewards for their allegiance, Brandon Church among them.

Time and experience would be the young man's best teachers, show him that being in the guard provided the best opportunities, top protection, the best of everything in this changed world. By and large, the guard obeyed out of loyalty and because going hungry was not an option anyone would choose. They knew what life was like beyond the geofence.

He'd have to keep an eye on the new recruits who decided to stay and work either in the guard, as part of the internal security teams, or in other areas throughout the settlement, depending on their skills. Roman had divided them, as instructed, to quickly integrate them with the rest of the population, to keep them from forming any type of opposition. He made a mental note to check weekly on their progress. Bringing in so many young, able, and smart men and women had been a risk. But the rewards outweighed the risk. Liberty now had extra power to keep the settlement secure.

A loud knock forced him to turn. "Enter."

The door opened, and Roman stuck his head inside. "You wanted to know when Darren Kelly was awake, sir?"

The young man who'd been wounded. "Yes. Come in. How is he?"

He entered and closed the door behind him. "He'll be fine. The doc's not sure about saving his eye, but he's lucky to be alive. No brain damage from what they can tell. He can move all his limbs. They'll know more in the next couple of days."

"How were things otherwise at the armory? Still squatting on the munitions?"

"You know it, sir. Cutting rations in half was brilliant. I bet they're thinking hard about giving up and coming here."

"We'll squeeze them as long as necessary. If they don't change their minds and come join us, then we'll have to take them. Like we did in Newington."

"They've lost another member to a different bunch of lunatics. The Bleeders, I think. I can't keep the gangs straight—all the same to me."

Graysen smiled to himself. The numbers were dwindling at the armory which would open up an opportunity.

"The mutants followed a group back, killed one of the men. John wanted me to be sure to tell you."

Coming from the man who refused to share his bullets and wanted someone else to deal with the problems? "Now you've told me. Anything else?"

"They have a new girl. I've never seen her before but...Church seemed to know her."

He thought for a long moment, finding the information interesting. "Did they volunteer anything about her?"

Roman shook his head. "They acted like she'd been there all along. I had to pry Church away from her. They were in a corner together, talking low. Obviously, they knew each other."

"Did you ask him?

"Yes, sir. Said they went to high school together, and he was excited to see someone he knew, someone he could ask about his family. Didn't give me her name. I'll keep working on him. He'll be more than happy to go to Icehaven again. I guarantee it."

"Good." Graysen exhaled and stood in front of him. "Have all our units returned?"

"Echo Team is still out searching for our missing vehicle." Shipley checked his watch. "Should be back soon. None of the other units had any problems today."

"Would you say we have a major Sprogg issue?"

"I would, sir. Permission to put a plan into action to remedy the situation?"

"Pending my approval, of course. I look forward to taking care of that annoyance."

"You didn't want me to put any of the newbies on the west gate, did you?"

"No," Graysen snapped, brushing by his subordinate. "Definitely not."

Roman put his hand against the door, stopping him. "You wanted me to tell you if I saw anything…strange."

A flash of adrenaline zipped through him. His thoughts switched quickly to his daughter, who lay, catatonic, in one of the bedrooms.

Only his number-two-man or others with a similar ability knew his pain and his plan. "What did you see?"

Roman lowered his voice, unnecessary in the private quarters, the only area in Liberty not under surveillance. "It's about Morgan Hill, Church's friend. He knew the gang was going to attack before it happened. He was inside with the rest of us. Couldn't see them coming. No one could."

Graysen took in the news, intrigued to learn another survivor with special abilities was at arm's length. He wasn't sure if Hill was a remote viewer or if he'd developed ESP after the experiment. Didn't matter. He'd be useful, either way.

"Oh, and that weird girl, Harper, started talking about how everybody was glowing red, like the Bleeders and Sproggs. Not the newbies, though. She's not subtle at all."

"Could you read her mind?"

"Not at all. Everything in her head is a muddled mess. No one even argued about the single-child mandate."

That surprised and encouraged him. Maybe some of the survivors did, in some abstract way, understand what the world's population was up against. Babies could be kept from starvation if there were no babies.

"Or maybe—nobody's thinking about marriage, sex, babies, and family just yet."

"Don't read *my* mind. Not if you know what's good for you," he warned. "They'll be keeping each other warm soon enough. Just so we're clear, the mandate applies to all of us. We must practice what we preach."

The man's eyes widened like saucers, which had been Marx's intended reaction. He knew full well you couldn't keep men and women apart, whether they liked each other or not, especially in a survival scenario. Internal population issues wouldn't look good when he took his message to other groups in the near future. Liberty needed to be the inspiration for all survivors to look at in the weeks, months, and years to come.

Graysen opened the door and ushered Shipley out. "Did anyone come back with you?" They walked together toward the guards' infirmary.

"No. A woman and two kids, girls, were going to until Harper opened her big mouth."

Too bad. He loved children. After all, they were the future. The day might have gotten off to an unexpectedly bad start, but all the news wasn't bleak.

Liberty was still on course, and he intended to do everything in his power to steer things on the right trajectory to keep him at the top of the food chain.

• • •

August stumbled into the armory, numbed by both the cold and the Sprogg attack. She stood quietly, watching the others, wanting to curse and throw a chair against the wall. She inhaled a deep breath and exhaled, trying to calm the adrenaline pulsating through her veins.

What on earth had happened out there?

They were more than brazen to attack the armory and Graysen's men in daylight. Brandon's friend had seen it coming. How? Another question that needed an answer and August didn't have one.

She'd been here for two days and had taken a life—killed another human being. Her empty stomach lurched, and she gagged. So much for ever returning to normal now. How many times could each of them bounce back before breaking? She saw no end in sight.

The group remained quiet, kept to themselves, nursing their physical and mental wounds.

August didn't know for sure if Brandon had made it back okay to Liberty after the fight. She hoped he had. Things always seemed to go his way. Straight A student, captain of the football team, prom king. He never had to struggle. Which was why she'd felt guilty, bringing her baggage to him after her mother died. He didn't deserve any kind of ugliness, then or now.

Her gaze settled on Noah, Snow's little boy, sitting on his mother's lap with his head bowed, his face void of expression. Kids didn't need to see the type of violence they'd experienced. Kids should be able to be kids. Considering the events of the past few hours, no one was talking about the one-child mandate, yet the topic stuck in her mind. Maybe because she needed something else to think about.

How did Graysen Marx have the power to make this kind of a decision? He was one man. The mandate went against everything women held dear—the ability to choose for themselves. Nothing had been said about what would happen if someone violated the mandate. Would the baby be aborted? Tossed off a cliff, like the Spartans did with those they considered weak? What about the parents? Would they be punished as well?

Brandon looked good, and she wished she could have had more time with him. August wondered if he remembered them sitting under the stars, making wishes in the backyard. She wanted to know where he'd been, how he'd survived, and how he ended up at Liberty.

A hand landed on her shoulder, and she jumped, ready to fight again.

John took a few steps back, forced a grim smile and motioned for her to follow him.

She gathered her coat, hat, and gloves and hurried to catch up. "Are they back?"

"No, not yet. Give me a hand outside before the sun sets." He shouldered his rifle and led her up the stairs and through the tunnel, moving like a man on a mission. "Take this."

She flung his military duffel bag over her shoulder, relieved to have something to do, even in the painful cold.

Once they were outside, he slammed the door shut. "This is bullshit! We're sitting ducks out here, getting picked off one by one."

"What can we do?" August asked, wondering what he had in his bag.

"We can't waste explosives on alarms." John took the bag from her and unzipped the big, middle section and pulled out an airhorn. He frowned. "It's the best I can do. We found them at a school not far from here. They'll give us an early warning for uninvited guests."

August raised her eyebrows. An alarm system. "Great, let's do it."

John nodded. "Fish that roll of wire out of there, and the box of four-inch pins. We'll use them to secure the wire to the ice, about two inches above."

She dug into the bag and found the items he'd asked for, plus a hammer. Then John set her to the task of pounding the metal pins into the ice. Her hands ached after two pins, but she continued, unfazed, focused.

"About eight inches apart," he instructed and maneuvered a cement block into place near the entry. He stepped over to inspect her work. "Perfect, no longer than the length of your forearm."

Puffs of breath appeared and hung in the air as she worked her way around the approach points to the main entry of the armory. He followed, stretching the wire between the pins, winding a loop around each one until he reached the cement block.

"Now what?"

He handed her the air horn. "Bury the horn under the cinderblock. We want the top sticking out. We'll put one horn on each side, two at each entrance."

Shit. They'd be out here all night. Using the claw of the hammer, she chiseled holes into the ice, dropping in the can of air every now and then. When everything was ready, she signaled to John.

Ice had already accumulated in his beard and eyebrows. "This is the tricky part."

She wiped her watering eyes and watched him. He looped the wire through eyelets screwed into short slabs of wood and propped the narrow block on the wood, so it appeared to hover over the air horn. No one would notice the gap or the wire.

All it would take was one tug on the taut cable to pull the block and sound the alarm. Simply genius.

John finished and turned to her. "Got it?"

She nodded and carved out the next hole. Then they went to the next entrance and did it all over again. Unable to feel her fingers or her toes, she bit back any complaints before they came out of her mouth.

A small price to pay for security. No one in the armory would have to endure another loss. At least not tomorrow. A tide of protectiveness rose up her spine. These people had done nothing wrong. They'd taken her in, given her food and a bed when they didn't have enough for themselves. They didn't deserve the pain they absorbed on a daily basis.

She'd do whatever she could to make sure they stayed out of the cross-hairs of gangs like the Sproggs and make the armory a better place to live. Lydia was right, they didn't have to make life harder than it already was.

While they worked, anger gave August the illusion of warmth. After completing two more traps in determined silence, John stopped.

"We need a rest. The cold will wear down our bodies quicker than you think. We've all been through so damn much. I was here when it happened." He pulled his hat down, to cover his eyebrows. "I was supposed to meet my wife and daughters at St. Bonaventure for the carnival after drill."

"What kind of drill?"

"I'm a staff sergeant, Army National Guard. At least I was. Doesn't mean much now. The climate change thing was the last thing on my mind." He paused to clip the wire. "I got to the church right after the big boom and found my family with about fifty others, huddled in the basement. I thought we still had time. Hell, I knew we still had time. We had cars and fuel, and nothing was frozen yet."

His silence prompted her to ask, "What happened?"

He turned to look at her, his face etched with pain. August felt silly. Obviously, his wife and daughters weren't inside the armory. She shook her head and went back to hammering a pin into a chunk of dirty ice.

"They wouldn't come with me."

The mournful tone of his voice broke her heart.

"Why wouldn't they go with me?"

Her shoulders slumped, and she stilled, recalling how she felt that day. "They were afraid. No one knew what was going on, much less what to do."

"That's what I tell myself. What I have to say to get out of bed every day."

"John," August started, then realized she didn't have any good words.

"The building collapsed. A damn two-hundred-year-old stone church crushed them. There has to be a reason. Why would God allow this to happen?"

Of all the thoughts she had entertained, his question wasn't one she could answer. In a family focused on science, God didn't enter the conversation often, less since her mother's death. "I don't know."

"I found three survivors and I sent them here. Only one made it. He died scavenging the first night. I have to believe there's something better, but most of the time, I just do what needs to be done and hope for the best."

"We've all lost people we love," she offered, letting go of her anger to try to comfort him and herself. "I don't know what became of my family. Even though everyone tells me they couldn't have survived, I survived. No matter how or why I'm alive, whether I died and came back to life or not, couldn't they have survived, too?"

John sighed and set the trap. "Who am I to tell you no?"

Her heart fluttered with the possibility. With the sun slipping below the horizon, they fell back into silence to finish their work.

Afterward, four entrances were fully equipped with trip alarms. She felt a little safer and hoped everyone inside would sleep better tonight. When John was satisfied, they shuffled back into the armory to thaw out next to the stove, their conversation and the attack playing over in her mind. She had a difficult time eating her dinner of boiled rice and pork from the frozen pig Ian and the others had found. As she choked down the food, little by little, her body warmed. August leaned back in the chair and closed her eyes. With the chance meeting with Brandon, her mind turned to happier times. Their first date, her first kiss. Everything had changed between them when her mother died. She hadn't meant for anything to change, but losing loved ones can easily change your direction.

Her life had changed course, flung her into her father's world, and she became more of a student of science and a parent to her siblings. What she wouldn't give to see them again, even one more time.

Her mind grabbed at memories, random moments in the kitchen with her mother, rocking her baby sister and holding hands with Brandon. Memories turned to her father, to an excited conversation they'd had about a breakthrough in the project.

It was all coming back to her now. Her eyes popped open, and she jumped out of the chair. "Where's Lydia?"

"Sleeping, I think," Snow said as she put a spoonful of rice into Noah's mouth. "Are you okay?"

August nodded and headed down the hallway. She found the still-mourning woman, her new friend, already in bed, the Christmas lights twinkling above her. She didn't look at August.

"I fell asleep out there and had this dream about my father."

Lydia swung her legs over the edge of the bed and sat up, her face hopeful, a welcome sight.

"He came home really late—he was always late. I was still up because I was working on university applications." She sank onto the bed beside Lydia, recalling the sparkle in her dad's eyes as he burst through the door.

"Hey, kiddo, guess what? Our project is one, no two, steps closer to reality. We found a way to produce the sulfur dioxide particles coated with Amexotrate. Do you know what this means?"

No, she hadn't known what it meant. She remembered drinking in every word about how the new compound would protect the environment from pollution.

She looked at Lydia. "The compound was going to be pumped into the upper atmosphere by thousands of airplanes."

Lydia's brows creased. "Why? What would the particles do?"

The idea had taken August's breath away when her father had described it, and again as she relayed the concept to Lydia, "They were meant to increase the amount of sunlight reflecting away from Earth—basically creating a cooling effect. The temperatures were supposed to drop by six to eight degrees over the course of the next couple of years."

Lydia placed a hand on August's knee. "It's safe to say, things did not go according to plan."

"What I don't know is what went wrong." August's heart ached for all the loss and destruction caused by good intentions gone awry.

A silent war began within her heart and mind. She valued the new, protective feelings she had toward Lydia and the others who'd helped her, had saved her life. But August wanted more than anything to know what had happened to her father, to Luke and Chloe. Brandon had lived, maybe they had, too. And she wanted to understand what had happened to her. Why was she alive, again, when others had perished? If she'd died, why was her heart beating right now?

Holding Lydia's hand, her eyes misted over. August would be forever grateful to the woman and the rest of the group. She would do all she could do to repay their kindness, to defend them like she had today. But if even the slightest opportunity presented itself to get the answers about the event, about her second chance at life, August had to take it.

•••

Brandon scarfed down his supper, a hearty meat stew with fresh vegetables, a salad, and a slice of bread with butter. The stew was delicious, the tastiest he'd had in a long time, the meat incredibly tender with an interesting savory sweetness to it. In a way, the meal reminded him of his grandmother's pork stew, except it was spiced differently with seasonings he could only assume were grown here.

Afterward, he left the chow hall and drove through the underground tunnel to meet Morgan where their security detail was posted. This was their first working shift. They'd been pretty much confined to their living quarters, other than joining the rations convoy. He was still in shock. August was alive. More time to talk to her would have been great. The Sproggs messed that up. Having Shipley peering over his shoulder, listening in on their conversation didn't help matters. He could have just read his damn mind. Did she know anything about his parents, if they were alive? With his gut full, guilt washed over him, and he wondered what she had for dinner.

Why didn't she come back with him?

He needed to convince her to come to Liberty where she'd be safe, where he could protect her. Not that she looked like she needed much protection the way she had handled that gun. Brandon shook the thoughts from his mind and stared through the windshield, focused on not missing the sign to the west sector. Shipley had drawn him a map, but map reading wasn't his strong suit, unless it was a nautical chart. The Jotti brothers were posted on the east side with a quarter of the ship's crew. Shipley had made sure they were divided up.

As he drove, the tunnel was strangely quiet, other than the echo of the truck's engine. He instinctively turned on the radio then shut it off when he realized there were no longer any radio stations. He was astonished by how large the settlement was, and he'd only had a sneak peek at its vastness during Shipley's rushed tour. Brandon spotted the sign to the west entrance. He slowed the truck to a crawl and turned into a room with several other vehicles and parked. He opened the door and got out.

He had a feeling Marx was disappointed with him and Morgan for not recovering the vehicle the Sproggs had hijacked. Oh, well. The guy would survive.

After going up the two dozen stairs, he opened the heavy metal door and found Morgan waiting for him. "Ever notice there aren't any people with disabilities or old people here?"

Brandon shrugged. "Maybe that's just the way things worked out." It was odd. At least if people were sick, they would be probably in medical. But when he and the rest of the crew had been processed and medically cleared, the infirmary was empty except for Lt. Kelly.

"There's more than one medical facility here."

He heard Shipley's voice behind him. Brandon turned, and his muscles twitched. The mind-reading gig was getting old. "Do you have to keep doing—?"

Shipley grinned. "Every chance I get."

"Have you always been like that?" Morgan asked and added, "Irritating?"

The man laughed. "No. It happened right after the event. It's kind of fun reading minds." He winked. "I can keep tabs on things. Shut down situations before they happen."

There was something about him that Brandon didn't like, besides his mind-reading skills. A deep arrogance, as if he was better than everyone else because he came off as Marx's right-hand man. Brandon was putting up with Shipley only because he had to.

"Don't forget to check each area listed on your detail, including Mercury living quarters." Shipley took a couple of steps then stopped. He spun and glared at Brandon. "I'm not arrogant, but I *am* Marx's right-hand man as you call it, and I'm only putting up with you because I have to—until Marx tells me differently."

Brandon's heart stopped, and he swore his face turned red.

"Yeah. It's bright red." Shipley shoved a clipboard and keycard at him. "Get to work. I want a detailed security report of west sector completed before your shift ends. Make sure you do random searches of the living quarters for prohibited items."

"Prohibited?"

"They're listed on page two."

Brandon flipped the page and read. "No personal weapons, alcohol, recreational drugs, cigarettes, tobacco, computers, video game consoles."

"Talk about taking away all the fun," Morgan said.

"The computers and gaming consoles we like to have on hand in case we need parts to fix something to keep Liberty running." With that last statement, Shipley walked away.

Brandon sighed. He waited until the man was out of sight before saying anything. "I guess I shouldn't have opened my mouth or had a thought."

"He's an A-hole. I don't like him one bit. He's up to something."

"Still getting a bad vibe from this place?"

"Even more than before."

He handed Morgan the clipboard as they walked to one of the golf carts parked a few yards from the entrance.

"I'd flip a coin to see who drives, but I don't have one," Morgan said with a grin.

Brandon hopped in the driver's seat. "I drive. You read the map. Where are we off to first?"

Morgan got in and glanced at the map. "The aquaponic fish farm. Cool. You can fish here." He pointed. "A quick right then another right."

"I don't think you can actually—never mind." Brandon started the cart and drove down the extra-wide corridor.

A golf cart passed them carrying four people: three men and a woman. They all appeared to be young, teenagers and some in their twenties or early thirties. A golden retriever ran behind the cart.

The people all wore long-sleeved black work coveralls, their hair buzzed short, even the women. Their eyes quickly shifted from him when he made eye contact. Brandon did a double-take, not because of the dog, though it was nice to see something normal. One of the men looked familiar. He wasn't sure. He looked a bit like Luke, August's brother. He looked again and blew it off as hopeful thinking.

Brandon had to admit it was a bit odd. Why was everyone's hair cut like that? He understood having to wear uniforms if they were working. The guard had to wear uniforms. But the haircuts threw him off, and the people appeared nervous. He took his right hand off the steering wheel and glanced at the black emblem stamped inside of his wrist. Did everyone have one, or just the guard?

• • •

When they arrived at the fish farm, Morgan jumped out first. "That smell is enough to gag a maggot."

"It's ripe." Brandon handed him the keycard and shut off the golf cart. He grasped his rifle and followed.

Morgan swiped the card and pushed open the door. Strong fishy-smelling, moist, warm air rushed out. They walked inside.

The structure was huge, shaped like a glass pyramid, built with the same steel and panels like the rest of the settlement. Rows of long metal troughs were crowded with perch and other species of fish. Every few feet above the troughs, rows of stacked grow trays were stuffed with lettuce and herbs. At the far end of the space, twelve males in black coveralls, their hair buzzed short, fed the fish. Morgan checked out the area while Brandon approached one of the workers.

When he drew near, the man glanced at him then lowered his head.

Brandon shouldered his rifle. "How's it going?"

"We aren't supposed to talk when we're working." The man's sunken eyes glanced to one of the cameras across from him and continued tossing scoops of fish food into the trough. The other men did the same, as if in a trance.

"It's okay. You can talk to us. What's your name?"

He didn't look up. "Paul. That's not what the other guards said."

"Where does all the fish poop go?" Morgan asked as walked up beside Brandon.

"The water is piped through a filter then pumped back into the close-looped system. The solid waste is used to fertilize the vegetable gardens and crops."

The way Paul spoke sounded like he'd been forced to memorize the information. The whole thing felt and sounded rehearsed.

Morgan dipped his hand in the water, and the fish swarmed and splashed around his fingers. "What are you feeding them?"

"Corn and soybeans." Paul's gaze moved to the cameras again. "I can't talk anymore." He tossed the scoop into the plastic bucket and walked away.

Brandon watched him disappear around a corner with his shoulders slumped and his head lowered. The no talking thing was extreme, downright strange.

Morgan shifted from foot-to-foot, antsy to get moving. Either that, or those bad vibes he'd been experiencing had gotten stronger. "Man. That was weird."

He brushed off the weirdness, for now, hoping it was a one-off, not fully convinced either way. After getting back into the golf cart, he looked at Morgan and turned the key. "Which way to the living quarters?"

"Back the same way, then left at the west entrance," he said with his eyes glued to the map.

Five minutes later, Brandon steered the cart past the entrance. He had never been to the residents' living quarters before and was curious to see if he knew anyone. They had been told there were six five-story domes surrounding the assembly hall that housed workers who had already been here, plus survivors.

"Maybe we took a wrong turn." Morgan scratched his head and checked the map. "This doesn't look right. I don't see the auditorium."

Brandon peered ahead and noticed the corridor came to a dead end.

First night on the job and they were already lost. He slowed the cart and stopped in front of double metal doors with a white sign handwritten in bright red lettering that read: *West Entrance - Sick Survivor Processing Only.*

Morgan looked at him. "I suppose it's logical, under the circumstances."

All it would take was one sick survivor coming in and the settlement could have a pandemic on their hands. Enough people had been lost during the event and in the aftermath. Segregating the ill from the healthy made sense.

Morgan climbed out of the golf cart and held up the keycard. He grinned. "Want to take a peek?"

Brandon glanced up and down the corridor, searching for cameras, then up to the dome ceiling. He didn't see any. "Why not? We're lost anyway."

• • •

Brandon looked around. The entrance was set up the same as the guard's entrance in the south, except it was smaller and no one was around. It was nothing fancy. Basically, a check-in area inside an oval dome with a door leading to the outside, another door on the right, and one on the left which was marked, *Restricted.* There was a small wooden table, two folding chairs in the center of the space, and a cluster of lofty plants and trees in huge clay pots. At this point, incoming traffic would be close to non-existent.

"Someone's coming." Morgan pointed to the door on the left, his voice low.

Brandon's head snapped to the door then to the greenery. He pushed Morgan, almost tripping over him. "Hurry. Get behind those plants."

Both men scurried, their boots squeaking against the floor as they rushed to crouch behind one of the trees. A fly buzzed and landed on Morgan's cheek. He viciously swatted it away at the same time the door opened.

A short and stocky guard member emerged first, wearing a white medical mask, followed by a man and a woman in their seventies dressed in ragged heavy winter coats. The man coughed violently in high-pitched agony, barely able to catch his breath. It was obvious he was sick. Then Graysen Marx appeared with a second guard member, both wearing masks. The guard had his rifle pointed at the backs of the man and woman.

Brandon's heart pounded. He exchanged glances with Morgan. Good thing Shipley wasn't around. Otherwise, he'd be reading their minds. If they got caught, there was no telling what Marx would do with them.

"Where are you taking us?" the woman asked with a shaky voice.

"No need to worry. You will be looked after. Our medical facility is through there. My men will take your husband to see the doctor." Marx pointed to the door marked, *Restricted.*

The woman grasped her husband's hand. He continued coughing. All he could do was give her a quick nod.

Morgan shook Brandon's arm, trying to get his attention.

"What?" Brandon mouthed.

Morgan whispered, "It isn't on the map—the medical facility—it isn't there."

He had to be wrong. Why would Marx be lying to these people? They were old, sick, had braved the unrelenting elements to get to Liberty, looking for shelter and much needed medical care.

Morgan quietly slipped him the map. He lowered his head and studied it. He looked up. Worry worked through him. Morgan was right. What was going on?

One of the guards opened the door, and the survivors were escorted inside.

Marx turned and walked to the same door they had entered where the golf cart was parked. Brandon held his breath. They were busted, and there wasn't anything they could do about it.

• • •

A half-hour later, inside Graysen Marx's living quarters, Brandon stood in one place, waiting to face the music. Getting caught didn't feel good. His heart hammered in his throat. From what he'd seen back at the survivor entrance, he needed to either justify his curiosity or bring Marx's modus operandi into question. He debated the second option, considering the trouble he was in already.

From what he'd seen so far, everyone in Liberty lived humbly, though Marx had more space than he imagined anyone else did. His quarters were decorated in black, white and silver including leather furniture. The space looked bleak and blah. With the natural light not being even close to what it used to be, Brandon felt boxed in and depressed.

The man had a few material things on display, which made sense if, as he claimed, he'd been here at the time of the event. A stack of books on the far corner of the desk indicated an interest in philosophy and politics, while outdated financial magazines littered the coffee table. Everything else—if he had anything more—was tucked away in the one closet or the chest of drawers just inside the doorway of the bedroom. A silver picture frame atop the drawers glinted as he turned his head, daring Brandon to step into the room and take a look. He hesitated, not knowing when Marx might appear to read him the riot act. He'd been caught snooping around once already. The man would have more trouble writing off Brandon wandering through his personal space.

The door opened, making up Brandon's mind for him. He stood at attention, a habit hard to break.

The door closed. "Mr. Church."

Brandon swallowed the words rising in his throat, reminding himself talking would only dig a deeper hole. He waited.

"I've spoken with your colleague. He claims the two of you got lost." He came around and stood in front of Brandon. "I find that hard to believe from two trained sailors. Such activities will send you before the Infinity Council for disciplinary action."

What kind of discipline? A slap on the wrist or something else? "You weren't aboard the *Eagle* for long, sir. We navigate the grid. It becomes second nature. Land travel is a whole different animal. Ask any of the crew."

Marx raised an eyebrow, and Brandon didn't blame him for being skeptical. "I will. Also, the maps your guys are using aren't drawn to scale. Now with a larger population and more going on, there hasn't been time to appropriately mark and map the area better. Even so, *that* area was clearly marked. We don't need anyone going in and out of the survivors' gate that isn't properly approved and vaccinated. This is how contagion spreads. It risks all of our lives and will not be tolerated."

"Understood, sir." It still didn't explain why the area meant to receive the ill or wounded didn't have any medical equipment or staff. Or anything at all. "May I recommend the maps be updated since there are so many of my crew now stationed throughout the settlement who may have issues?"

Marx's expression hardened. "Let me remind you that we've been very generous with you and your crew. There have been no such incidents with any of the others who have arrived, only you and Hill."

"It won't happen again."

Stepping forward, inches from Brandon's face, Marx let his intense gaze bore into his. "If it does, you will go before the Infinity Council and accept their punishment. I will interpret any insubordination from your crew as coming from you, so it's in your best interest to keep your people in line, which should take up the majority of your time."

"Yes, sir." Marx could learn some tactics from drill instructors, yet the force fueling his words was real and deep. He didn't mistake them for idle threats. Something more lay behind his words, and Brandon had only glimpsed the tip of the iceberg. "Permission to return to the armory in Icehaven tomorrow to make sure the area is secure to protect the next ration's convoy from future Sprogg attacks?"

Marx stared at him, considering the request. No doubt Brandon was skating on thin ice. He'd have to watch his step from this moment on.

"Yes, granted. For now, I want you working with Hill doing inventory in our armory until your shift is done. Meet back here at eleven pm. I have something else I want to talk to you and Hill about." He waved his hand. "Go."

Brandon didn't take a breath. He turned and exited the living quarters, glad to be free of such an intense personality. As he quick-stepped through the corridor, he realized he needed to mind his manners, at least for the time being. Secondly, he had to find a way to shield his mind and thoughts from Roman Shipley. The man was a living, breathing radar. He didn't know how far away he needed to be from him to avoid detection. Everyone, especially Morgan, needed to be on alert.

As Brandon walked, he passed a large number of guard members and Petty Officer Jackson Moss from the ship, who winked and smiled. Brandon only gave him a nod in case Marx or Shipley were monitoring the cameras.

• • •

South of the comm-center, Brandon entered the armory nestled between Marx's living quarters and the Liberty Guard entrance. He wasn't surprised Marx would keep the munitions close to him.

Morgan caught his eye from the far side of the room.

Brandon motioned him over to the corner of the room. "You met with Marx?"

"He's not playing around. This place is not what it seems."

"Are you having some sort of metaphysical insight again?"

"No. Just a big case of the willies."

"Then why were you all gung-ho to come here when we were on the ship? You made these guys seem like the second coming of Christ, like we had nothing to fear but fear itself."

Morgan kept his voice quiet. "Because that's what it seemed like. I'm not Roman Shipley. I can't read minds. I'm seeing things that happen five or ten minutes before they do."

"What are you seeing about the next few minutes?"

"Dude, don't make me count all these bullets."

With a laugh, Brandon slapped him on the shoulder. "That's what you get for dragging my ass where we shouldn't have been. Marx wants us to meet at his living quarters at twenty-three-hundred-hours. Wants to talk to both of us."

"About what?"

Brandon shrugged. "You tell me ten minutes before we meet."

Nearly two hours later, buried in paper with a pencil tucked behind his right ear, Brandon supervised fifteen men as they inventoried the ammunition stores. Echo Company had returned with an assortment of armaments from somewhere. The contents varied, odds and ends left behind, things needing to be merged with the existing stockpile.

Brandon looked at the wall clock. His anxiety grew as the meeting with Graysen Marx approached. He took a deep breath and cleared his mind. Nothing he could do about Marx since he couldn't figure out what else he might want to discuss. He focused on tallying the numbers brought to him. With a few minutes to spare, Morgan appeared beside him. "He wants to know about me, about how I see and know things."

"How does he know about you?"

"Shipley," Morgan said shaking his head. "They are coming together."

Brandon slammed his clipboard down on the table. Perfect. They had nowhere to hide.

"Did your mother teach you nursery rhymes when you were a little kid?" Morgan asked.

"Sure. What does that have to do with anything?"

"Get one in your head and keep repeating it to yourself. Over and over, no matter what Marx says."

Worth a try. Morgan retreated to the back of the room, where he resumed his count of loose .22 caliber bullets. While Brandon couldn't really recall a complete nursery rhyme, he could easily remember the Pledge of Allegiance. He ran through the phrasing once in his mind, satisfied he could focus on the words even under stress.

Five minutes later, the door swung open, and Roman Shipley barked, "Church and Hill. Come with me."

The pair glanced at each other then followed Shipley to a smaller room off the short hall.

"I thought he wanted to meet in his living quarters?" Brandon asked.

Shipley opened the door. "He changed his mind."

• • •

Graysen Marx was waiting inside, seated on one side of a plastic folding table. The door closed behind them, and the mind-reader motioned for them to sit in the two chairs across from Marx. Shipley slid in beside them.

I pledge allegiance, to the flag...

"I wanted to talk to you together," Marx started. "There's something odd going on since the event. It's come to my attention that you've noticed the change, that one of you might be a part of it."

Of the United States of America...

Neither Brandon nor Morgan answered, so Marx continued. "You've noticed—and commented on—Shipley's innate ability to know what you're thinking. Let's talk about it."

They both shrugged, and Morgan said, "He's the one using it as a weapon. If you want to know what people are thinking, maybe he should just ask."

Marx shot a withering glance at Shipley, studying the top of the table. He returned his attention to Brandon and Morgan. "Be that as it may, I'm here to have an honest conversation. A couple of your crew have mentioned that you, Hill, can see events before they transpire. Is that true?"

And to the republic, for which it stands...

"I've always been able to do that like my grandmother. On my father's side," Morgan added.

Marx furrowed his brow. "Then this is not new?"

"No. I mean, I don't go around talking about it. People think you're weird and don't want to hang out with you anymore, right?"

"He's lying," Shipley said in a flat tone.

One nation, under God...

"Nice try." Marx grinned. "You knew we were coming to the ship."

Morgan sighed. "Yes."

Indivisible, with liberty and justice for all...

Shipley raised his head and met Brandon's gaze. His small smile sent a shiver of warning down his back.

"What else have you seen beforehand?" Marx asked.

Morgan answered honestly. "The attack at the armory in East Haven—Icehaven a few minutes before it happened. I don't get a lot of details."

Shipley turned his head and looked at Marx. "We would have lost more men if he hadn't alerted us. I'm certain of it."

"This is a new phenomenon since the event. I have encountered others with paranormal abilities, what we're calling them for now, coming into Liberty. Right now, it's impossible to know the ratio. We simply don't have a large enough sample."

I pledge allegiance...

"Okay, now that you know what's up with me, what do you want from us?" Morgan asked, motioning to Brandon. "Why are you telling us any of this, especially since you've cautioned us both about asking too many questions?"

Marx glanced at Brandon, who hadn't spoken at all. "Because I need to know if you've seen or experienced anything else. Or if you know of anyone else with these types of abilities."

Of course, he did. He and Morgan both shook their heads, Brandon unwilling to give thought or images to the suspicions in his mind.

To the flag of the United States of America...

"There's a member of our research team, a physicist, who sees music in colors, visually. It's called synesthesia, something usually found in autistics, who have other talents, like perfect pitch. But that's not the case here. He finds music distracting now and must work in complete silence. The pitch of someone speaking to him is overwhelming to the point we're having to communicate in writing."

And to the republic for which it stands...

"Wow," Morgan said, "I can't imagine."

"Then there's that girl at Icehaven." Marx leaned his hands on the table.

Brandon's heart jumped into his throat, and he beat it back into submission. "Which girl?"

"The one who can see colors around people?" Morgan asked immediately. "Yeah, I didn't know what to make of her. She seemed super angry."

One nation, under God...

Marx rubbed the back of his neck. "Any idea what that means?"

Morgan leaned back in his chair, cool as a cucumber. "Not a clue. But hey, I can alert you when she's ten minutes away."

Marx scowled at Morgan, and Brandon laughed out loud. How were they supposed to know what any of these things meant? Liberty had all the scientists. They should figure it out.

Again, Shipley's gaze shifted to his, but he said nothing.

Brandon smiled. *With liberty and justice for all.*

Marx stood. "We're done here for now."

The pair left without another word or any additional fanfare, leaving Brandon mentally exhausted and wondering about the meaning of the conversation. Marx chose carefully what to share with them. He must have really needed their intel, no matter how marginal.

Morgan's tip had worked perfectly. "I don't think Shipley could break through my chatter into my internal thoughts."

"Good. I just focused on the words he was saying, not trying to go anywhere else in my mind. Like, I didn't want to give up an image of that girl you know at Icehaven."

The girl he loved who said she'd died and come back to life. "Thank you."

• • •

Inside the quietness of his living quarters, Graysen handed Roman a bottle of beer from one of the dozens of cases Echo Team had discovered at a home in Little Compton with a personal fallout shelter. Even though alcohol was prohibited as far as the general population was concerned, the rule didn't apply to him or the Liberty Guard. He needed the workers in tiptop shape to get through their shifts to keep the settlement running, for all their sakes. He took a long swig, savoring the taste of home then put the bottle down on the small table beside him. "Hill is full of it."

"No doubt," Shipley said. "He knows more than what he's willing to give up. It might be wise to separate him and Church, for the time being, sir."

Separating the two would help. Although, having the men together, he could keep an eye on them much easier. "I do believe they did get lost. A simple wrong turn, but they're too nosy for my liking. Put extra security in the area, of course, no one from the *Eagle*, in case Church and Hill decide to make a return visit."

"Yes, sir."

"How are the repairs coming in the north sector?"

He knew it would be a challenge to get the ecosystems up and running again after part of the dome's roof collapsed days ago from the heavy ice.

"On schedule. Everyone is working extra hours, knowing how important it is for us to save what's left of the cattle. They aren't happy about working five hours past their three pm shift."

"They'll get over it. Whatever it takes to get it done. We do have another small problem." Graysen paused. "Eve Petty is becoming an issue. She gave me a hard time when I took Church in front of the council."

"Don't we need to keep the mayor of Providence around to show the population there is still some type of formal government, along with the Infinity Council?"

"It's neither here nor there at this point. She might have been a governmental force in her day, long before the event. The only reason she was here to begin with was because of the opening of the third steam plant and all the fanfare." He paused and took another drink of his beer. He didn't like the woman and he didn't need any roadblocks. "She got lucky. Nothing more." He contemplated for a few minutes, studying the man.

At six-foot-one, Roman was strong as an ox, with a solid backbone when it came to doing what was needed to protect Liberty. He was thirty-five, older than most of the military men and women who'd shown up looking for refuge from the devastating climate change, and the only person he trusted. "If she gets out of hand again, then you know what must be done."

"Of course, sir. What about the others?"

"They're fine." He stood to stretch his legs. "The rest of the council fully understands what we're facing. I want you to go with Church to the armory in Icehaven tomorrow morning."

"He wants to see the girl he knows?"

"Yes, I'm guessing. He did say he was concerned about the armory after the attack. However, we should be worried, as well. If the Sproggs get a hold of their weapons stash, the consequences could be deadly for all of us here. Afterward, head to the barracks in Newington and finish offloading the rest of the weapons, if the gang of thugs hasn't sucked the place dry. Get rid of anyone who gets in your way—for the safety of Liberty." He walked to his desk and picked up a piece of paper. "I'm sending the mobile health unit with you to the armory." He handed Roman the paper and waited for the man's reaction, knowing there would be a big one.

Shipley's eyes went wide, his face tight with concern. "Are you sure about this?"

"It is not your job to question my decisions. You know how important it is to weed out the ones with special abilities."

"I'm sorry, sir. I didn't mean any disrespect." Roman downed the rest of his beer, setting the empty bottle on the coffee table, careful not to touch the financial magazines. "How is your daughter?"

He appreciated the man's concern, another show of his allegiance to him, to what he was trying to accomplish. "She's still sedated after the last outburst." He glanced at his watch, cuing Roman it was time to leave. "It's quarter to eleven."

"Yes, sir. I need to make sure the next security team is ready to go to Providence to look for more medical supplies."

After Roman left, Graysen walked into his daughter's room. Kenna was sound asleep on her back, her long brown hair flowing across the pillow. Sweat gleamed on her forehead.

His stomach clenched.

He hated having to keep her sedated, but the sixteen-year-old needed it for her own safety. He pulled up a chair next to the bed and held her hand, caressing it softly.

It had been a year since they'd received the devastating news—craniopharyngiomas at the junction of her spine and brain. The doctors estimated the benign tumor had been growing for years. Last year, the mass had grown enough to push upward into her brain, causing periodical seizures, migraines and changes in her personality. His sweet child had become angry and violent. With it came outbursts and trance-like states followed by crazy talk about future events. He'd blown off her ramblings, blaming them on the tumor pressing on her brain. As she continued to rhyme off events and they happened, Graysen took notice.

Kenna knew the climate change experiment was going to fail, the horrific shift in the temperature, weeks before it became reality. She was scheduled for surgery with the top surgeon in Boston in three weeks. Now, surgery was no longer an option.

His eyes misted over. The thought broke his heart. There was nothing left of her, only a shell of the person she once was.

He was lucky they had some of the best scientists at Liberty, as well as doctors who could administer some basic care to keep her comfortable and safe. His choice to come here was the right one.

Once he learned some survivors had developed special paranormal abilities after the experiment, he needed to find a healer. Someone who could save Kenna and Graysen would do whatever it took to find one.

CHAPTER NINE

"You need to learn to use this in stages." John placed the crossbow on the table in front of August.

Sure, crossbows were sexy, and lots of television and movie characters used them, but now that she got a good look at the contraption, she had her doubts.

She raised an eyebrow. "What stage is this?"

Rounding the table, he held up his index finger. "Stage one. Looking at the crossbow."

August laughed. John reminded her so much of her father, a kind man with dribbles of humor when you'd least expect it. "Is this where you tell me which part does what?"

"Don't be glib," he warned with a dose of sarcasm. "Respect the crossbow. Respect the process. When the bullets have been spent, this bad boy will still be firing on all cylinders, if you take good care of her."

Imagining a world without bullets seemed impossible.

"I wanted to start inside, without the wind. Lots of time for the wind later. You ready?"

Ready as she'd ever been. Without ever touching the crossbow, John went over all the components with obvious names like stock, cable, string, and trigger. After he finished, he quizzed her until she flew though the names with no effort.

"Let's talk about stance. How do you think you should hold it?"

August picked up the bow and set her right foot well ahead of the left then brought the bow into her line of sight. Like she'd seen it done on the big screen.

John immediately shook his head. "Pretend you have a bolt coming through. Pull your right arm back and imagine where the bolt goes when it's released. See the problem?"

"Yeah, I have no aim."

"Right. Instead, you'll want to keep your feet almost parallel, the left just slightly in front of the right, like using the shotgun." He watched as she adjusted her stance and brought the crossbow to her shoulder. John put his hand on her back. "Don't be timid. There's no bolt in there, so you can't hurt anyone, least of all yourself. Now, bring her back down and hoist her up a few times. See how you can aim straight down the stock through the scope?"

She squinted into a perfect line of sight. "Yep."

"Move your right hand up to the trigger, just like a rifle. You want to keep your trigger finger outside the circle. No accidents."

Glancing down, she followed his instructions. The bow felt remarkably light in her two-handed grip, even as he adjusted her hold to distribute the weight more evenly. "What's this made of?"

"Fiberglass and carbon fiber. It just looks heavy, and they used to be. It's light enough to carry on your back with minimal effort, even if it is a little more clunky than a rifle." He took the bow back from her and pointed the nose at the ground. "You know how to hold it, how to fire it, and here's how you cock it."

August stepped back, and John slid his foot into the metal loop at the tip of the bow, then stretched the string back to hook it on the trigger mechanism. With one hand. She couldn't lie. "Looks difficult."

He shook his head and pulled the trigger to reset the string and handed the weapon back to her. "Nah. You might need two hands. Give it a go."

She emulated his efforts, holding the bow against the floor with her right foot, but she couldn't pull the string back with one hand. She looked to John for guidance. "Feet shoulder-width apart, pull up with both hands, like you're putting your hands in your pocket."

Two hands made things easier. "How fast can you reload it? I mean, in a fight, you're kind of screwed."

"You'd be surprised," John said. "You'd want to use this almost like a sniper, or in the open only when you know your adversary is unarmed."

"Now what?"

"Practice cocking the bow a few times until you have a good feel for it, pull the trigger to release. Then we'll load you up and you can shoot." He stepped back and took a seat to watch her practice, correcting her a bit at first, then settling back with an appreciative expression. "You're a quick study. Must be the fancy Yale education."

She started laughing. Yale had nothing to do with any of this, except for the event that started it all. They certainly didn't have any classes on how to use weapons on campus. Now she thought they all would have been better off if they had.

Regaining her focus, August went through the motions a few more times before John stood and picked up an arrow. "Pretty simple, these are twelve inches. You can use up to fifteen inches in this particular bow. The sharp end goes away from your face, genius."

He slid the bolt into the mechanism and secured it in place. "Aim then fire when ready."

She lined her shot up with a target on the wall. "What's behind the wall?"

"Storage."

August pulled the trigger. The rig had amazingly little kick and the arrow flew straight into the middle of the target. Bullseye on the first shot. Outside, the wind gusted up to a hundred miles an hour. Aim wouldn't matter quite as much.

"I'd have to aim for the biggest part of the target and hope I made a hit."

"Exactly. Already thinking ahead—"

"Can you keep the noise down? I'm trying to sleep," Harper yelled from her room across the hall.

August glanced at John, somewhat put off by the woman's behavior, like she was the queen of the castle. "What's up with her?"

"Don't mind her. She's not adjusting well to our new lives."

"None of us are. That doesn't give her the right to act that way."

"Give her a break, August. She's had a rough life, being tossed into foster homes most of her childhood. That has to take a toll, I would think." His gaze moved to the bow. "Tomorrow, we'll practice outside, and you can start to get a feel for wind direction, speed, and how to make adjustments. It affects bullets the same way, the farther the object needs to travel, the more likely something will change the direction."

Her thoughts veered to Brandon. She was missing him, wanted to see him again.

"Let's go over everything one more time."

She submitted to his redundant-method training, understanding repetition would train her muscle memory and in due time, she'd be able to do this effectively with her eyes closed.

By the time the others started coming in to prepare lunch, they'd burned through nearly three hours of training. August wouldn't be satisfied until she was able to put in the work outside and not think about what she had to do next in order to fire an arrow.

•••

A quarter mile from the National Guard Armory in Icehaven, the rolling landscape shimmered in the ruby-red drenched light as they traveled past a set of collapsed ice-encrusted buildings. Brandon would never get used to the bleached-out sunlight, the way it always looked and felt like twilight, even though it was late morning. He sat quietly in the passenger seat while Shipley drove. The man had put Morgan in the other truck, probably because Marx wanted them separated after they got caught where they weren't supposed to be. He figured they were lucky they hadn't been dumped outside of the settlement to fend for themselves.

He glanced in the side mirror and watched the large black vehicle following them. His heart beat faster the closer they got to the armory. He hoped August was okay. "Why are we bringing the mobile medical unit?" He didn't know there was such a thing until they were ready to leave Liberty. Apparently, the extended-length box van had been sent out the day of the event to supply immediate care. "Is someone ill at the armory?"

"Your girlfriend isn't sick, if that's what you're asking," Shipley said in a flat voice.

Brandon cursed under his breath. "She's not my girlfriend. We're just friends." He figured there was no point in thinking anymore around the man. He might as well say out loud exactly what he thought. "Morgan's right. That really is annoying."

"It's not a whole lot of fun for me at times. Imagine being in a room with ten people and you're bombarded with every single thought. Now that's annoying."

Brandon had never thought of it that way. Why were only certain people affected after the experiment with strange abilities and not everyone?

"That's what Marx wants to figure out."

Brandon shook his head and gave up.

The truck slowed and stopped about ten yards from the back door of the armory. Shipley shut off the engine then got out.

Brandon released the seatbelt and opened the door, keeping his thoughts to himself for the time being. When he climbed out, a strong squall of wind battered his face. With his rifle over his shoulder, he used both hands to push the door closed against the burst of air.

He spotted August next to a man near the treeline. He smiled to himself. She looked much smaller in the baggy navy parka she wore. The tips of her blonde hair, partially tucked under a pink wool hat with a giant pom-pom on top, waved in the breeze. He did a double-take. Was she shooting a crossbow?

She never ceased to amaze him, the way she had always been able to pick up something new, determined to learn it. A crossbow was the last thing he figured he'd ever see in her hands, or a gun for that matter.

"Looks like your girlfriend is just fine." Shipley smirked and slapped him on the back, giving him a friendly push toward the armory door. He turned to two of the other men. "Get them all out here. The kids, too."

The guards disappeared inside the armory at the same time as August and John approached.

Brandon grinned, happy to see her again.

She put the loaded crossbow in her other hand and smiled at him for a long moment. Then her expression turned serious. "What are you doing here? I thought the next delivery wasn't coming for two weeks." Her eyes shifted to the medical unit then back to him. "What's up with the big truck?"

Brandon couldn't answer because he wasn't sure why they brought it with them. "I don't—"

Shipley stopped him. "We'll talk with everyone, once they're out here."

"What's going on?" John asked, his forehead lined with concern.

"When everyone is outside," Shipley repeated with a bite of irritation.

Once all the survivors were at the back of the armory, Shipley held up his hand to get their attention. "Each of you need to be checked out for any immediate medical concerns in our mobile medical unit."

"No one is sick here," John said.

"I'm sure you're right. Imagine what would happen if someone was—and contagious. After that, you will all be taken to Liberty for further evaluation by our medical staff. There's only so many tests we can do here. Basic bloodwork will be done at the settlement."

John laughed. "Not a chance. We're not leaving. What if the Sproggs or Bleeders show up and break in? You can check us out here or forget it."

Shipley's eyes darkened.

The woman with the injured leg limped closer. "You can't make us go with you. You're glowing red for a reason. Don't listen to him. He's lying to us."

Shipley exhaled long and slow, causing bursts of white to surround his face. He ignored her and shortened the space between him and John. The rest of the guards followed suit, except for Morgan, and formed a circle around everyone with their rifles raised higher than when they had arrived.

Brandon's gut tightened. He hung back, stunned by the development. This was ridiculous. He understood it was necessary to not have unchecked illnesses and diseases coming into the settlement for the population's sake. He had a bad feeling what his unit leader was telling them was a façade, and so did Morgan. He didn't have to be a mind-reader. Brandon could see it on his face.

"I have a message from Graysen Marx," Shipley said, his voice rising, becoming louder with each word. He pulled out a piece of paper from his pocket and unfolded it. He handed it to John.

Brandon craned his neck to see what was on the note, but one of the survivors was blocking his view.

"What does it say?" a man who looked like a big brown bear in an oversized coat asked.

After reading the paper, John raised his gaze. "Basically, if we don't obey, the rations will stop."

The woman with white hair, holding a little boy, shook her head. "You can't do this to us. We have children to feed."

"Then do what has been asked, and the rations will continue. It's that simple. You're making this harder than it has to be," Shipley said.

The little boy started to whimper and cry. The woman held him tightly, jostling him on her hip.

Shipley walked over to the boy, reached into his pocket and pulled out a small truck. "Look what I brought for you." He gave the toy to him. The boy instantly stopped crying and grinned.

August's eyes narrowed, her gaze settling on Brandon, as if he had been the one who had delivered the message. She was partially correct, except he wasn't aware of what was going down. He noticed her death grip on the crossbow.

"Marx can't do this to us. That wasn't the deal," another woman with two young girls said.

August settled between John and Shipley. "Who made Graysen Marx the boss?"

Brandon had a sudden urge to go to her, but decided to stay put, not wanting to make things worse than they already were.

Someone shouted out, "Yeah. We have rights."

Shipley shook his head. "We're trying to stay one step ahead of any potential medical problems that could affect all of us. There aren't that many of us left. We need to be diligent. The quicker we get this over with, the sooner you can get on with your lives."

"The usual rations will be delivered on time, not half?" August asked, pursing her lips and staring him down.

Shipley stared back at her just as hard, his eyes barely open. "Yes."

Brief chatter broke out between the survivors before their leader spoke up.

"Fine," John said. "We'll do it, and afterward, we don't want to see you again until ration delivery day. Fair enough?"

"Agreed." Shipley turned and pointed to the guards, his eyes shifting to Brandon. "Get them lined up outside the medical unit. Let's get this show on the road."

John looked at him. "Before we leave, I have to lock up and set the alarms."

"Alarms?" Shipley asked.

John stepped away from the man and muttered under his breath, "For people like you."

Brandon grinned and stopped himself from laughing out loud.

As the survivors were rounded up and escorted to the medical unit, Brandon met August halfway.

"What's really going on here? This doesn't make sense, and you know it."

She was right. There was no reason for Marx to be worried about these people. They were far enough away from the settlement, and anyone who entered Liberty was subjected to a battery of medical tests before being moved into the general population. He and his crew had gone through all of them.

"Honestly, I don't know, August. I'm just as surprised as you are."

She looked at him like she was determining if he was telling the truth, and that hurt him.

A guard, maybe eighteen years old, who looked much younger, came up beside August and grabbed her arm. "Get moving."

"Let go of me." She squirmed and yanked free of his grasp.

Brandon eyed the guard. His muscles tightened, anger brewing inside him. "Don't touch her again."

The kid straightened and puffed out his chest through his suit. "What are you going to do about it?"

August kicked the kid in the shin. He tripped backward and almost fell.

"One for the good guys," Harper yelled from behind the medical unit.

Another guard seized Harper by the shoulders and shoved her back hard against the mobile unit. "Shut the hell up."

Brandon's heart pounded. He couldn't believe what he was witnessing. This wasn't what he'd signed up for. These people were harmless. They weren't the Sproggs or some other group. They weren't going to hurt anyone.

August planted her feet and raised the crossbow, aiming in Harper's direction.

Before Brandon could say anything, an arrow landed an inch from the foot of the guard who'd pushed Harper. Ice sprayed into a mist up to their calves.

Cheers erupted on the other side of the medical vehicle.

Shipley pointed the barrel of his M16 squarely at August's chest, his eyes traveling to Brandon. "Take that crossbow from your girlfriend before she kills someone, or I will."

Brandon looked at August. He didn't want anything to happen to her. He held out his hand and saw hesitation in her eyes. "Give it to me, August, please." If he had to take it from her, he would.

Long seconds passed, and she finally lowered the weapon and handed it to him. He breathed a sigh of relief.

"He deserved it," she said.

"I agree. He did."

As they walked side by side to the others, Brandon said, "I'm really sorry. I didn't know this was going to happen. I had no clue."

She didn't answer, her gaze fixed on one of their trucks.

John came up behind them and stood next to August. He winked at her. "Good shot."

Pride shone in her eyes. "You saw that?"

Brandon had to admit he was proud of her, too.

John grinned. "Sure did."

"I should have put it through his leg."

John patted her shoulder. "Let's get this over with." He looked at Brandon. "You've got a great girl here. Don't screw it up." Then he hurried ahead of them to check on Harper.

He didn't know his affection for August was that obvious. If it wasn't so cold, Brandon figured he probably blushed.

While the survivors entered the medical unit one by one, Shipley sent Brandon inside to keep an eye on them—punishment, he figured for August's actions. The man would do everything he could to keep them apart now.

The mobile unit was a modern, glorified ambulance, ten times larger, filled with medical equipment and supplies. An older male doctor with a white beard and squinty eyes was taking Harper's temperature. He removed the thermometer and recorded the results on a notepad at the same time as an engine roared then faded.

Shouting came from outside.

The door flew open, and Shipley appeared. "Church. Go after her. That's an order!"

And Brandon knew August had stolen one of the Liberty Guard's vehicles. He also knew where she was heading.

• • •

August arrived in New Haven after a twenty-minute harrowing drive dodging rubble, damaged buildings, and vehicles. This was her city, a city she knew like the back of her hand. Yale University should be exactly where she stood, the same campus she could walk in the dark. She tied a knot in the wool scarf covering the lower half of her face and blinked away tears from the afternoon's searing wind.

Nothing remained.

Buildings had been leveled as far as she could see. Automobiles crushed and abandoned. Layers of snow and ice masked any landmarks or main routes. She couldn't tell Woolsey Hall from the faculty parking lot. With the wind at her back and a ski pole she found in the truck clutched in her hand, she ventured into the hills of ice. Her heart pounded, and her pulse sped up.

She wouldn't hit anything alive.

Regardless, August kept poking the humps, if only to relieve her frustration. Her feet slipped and slid out from under her on a solid sheet of ice. She landed flat on her back, wiping a thin layer of crusty snow off the ice.

Groaning, she stayed there for a few minutes, peering up at the dirty red sky, wondering if the old world she knew would ever return one day. She flipped over onto her stomach then climbed to her hands and knees. A scream burst from her throat.

Below her, dozens of convoluted bodies of young people pressed against the frozen barrier. Frantic, August cleared the area of the crusty snow with both hands.

The students were frozen in hideous shapes inside the Women's Table, a sculpture commissioned to mark the date of the first women who attended the School of Fine Arts. The oval rim of the water-filled basin formed a boundary for the few who had attempted to find shelter inside it. They clearly didn't know what was coming or how quickly the temperatures were going to drop.

Pressing her gloved hands against the outstretched hands of the young women suspended in animation below her, she felt both blessed and horrified to be alive.

"August?"

She gasped and sat up straight. Her gaze landed on Brandon, standing at the edge of the clearing she'd created. "These people…my God!"

He walked to her, taking quick, cautious steps. He grabbed the sleeves of her coat and pulled her to her feet. "You can't help them."

"What are you doing here?"

"Looking for you. I need to bring you back."

She frowned under her scarf. "You don't understand. I have to try to find them. My father, brother, and sister. We were all here that day."

Brandon scanned the area. "No one could have survived."

"I did. Maybe they did, too."

Silence bounced between them.

"All right. I'll help you look, but then I have to take you to Liberty."

After an hour passed, August knew in her heart no one would be found alive. Nor were their any clues about the fateful day. Nothing but rubble and terrified frozen corpses.

Brandon took her by the arm and turned. "It's useless. We need to go back."

She shook free, disappointed not only by her fruitless search but by how Brandon had come after her not as her friend, but as a member of the Liberty Guard. "No way. You're not taking me back there to be bagged and tagged like everyone else. I can't believe you're working for him."

He walked ahead. She stood her ground. "You don't understand what's happening at Liberty. I've seen how things work. We can be together there."

She pulled him back by the arm, her heart thumping. She hoped he wasn't deeply involved with someone like Graysen Marx. Maybe he didn't grasp the things the so-called ruler was doing outside of Liberty. "The others at the armory don't like him or trust him. I trust their judgment. He's not a good man."

"I won't let anyone hurt you. I'd rather die myself."

The urge to be near him was bigger than anything else. August didn't want him to be in trouble for not bringing her in. "I trust you. I don't trust Marx."

Brandon closed the gap between them, his blue eyes still sweet after all these years. He reached up and gently pushed down her wool scarf with one finger.

"What are you doing?"

"What I should have done a long time ago. I never should have let you push me away. If it wasn't for this crisis, we might never have been in the same place at the same time again. I won't let this moment pass because we might not get another."

August considered the forces pulling them back together for the first time. "Maybe you should kiss me, then."

His lips pressed against hers. His kiss felt like home and happier times. Her eyes filled with wishful tears, and when he pulled away, she buried her face in his Ghillie suit.

He wrapped his arms around her and kissed the top of her head through her hat. "It's always been you and me. Come back to Liberty, and we'll figure everything out together."

"Wait." She turned and looked in the direction of where she'd left the vehicle she'd stolen. Two guards stood next to it, rifles in their hands.

He glanced over his shoulder at the guards then back to her. "I have to bring you back, August."

She took a big step away from him and shook her head slowly. Had he meant what he'd just said? You and me against the world? It sure didn't feel like it. Anger took over. "Your mission, should you choose to accept it, is to bring me in like a common criminal?"

"You did steal the truck. I'm already up to my eyeballs in crap. I've been nosing around, trying to get answers to my questions, and have already been called on the carpet more than I'd like. It wasn't hard for them to guess we know each other. Bringing you back is a test. I can't fail, August, or I'll be punished."

Her head swam with the revelation. Was he joking about being punished?

"Look, I don't know what tomorrow looks like, but I do know I'm not going to let you slip away again."

With what had happened at the armory earlier, getting some insight into Graysen Marx and his operation could mean the world to those who didn't line up with his mandates. Could she turn her back on the opportunity to go and find out the truth herself?

She looked up at him with clear eyes, her duty to her family complete, new intentions set in her mind. "As long as we're together."

They piled into the truck she'd left on the edge of campus. Brandon turned up the heat, checked in with his team by walkie-talkie and put the vehicle into gear.

August studied him as another truck with the two guards followed their vehicle. He was older, more serious than she remembered. He had grown a beard, probably to combat the cold. She peeled off her gloves and touched the rough facial hair with her fingertips.

"Bet you wish you had one," he joked, taking her hand in his. "How are you really?"

Her mind wandered through the ruins of the past couple of days. "I don't know. I can't stop fighting long enough to think about how I feel. Where were you when it happened?"

"On a coast guard cutter. The ocean froze solid around us. We couldn't make it to the dock. Graysen Marx's men bailed us out when we had little food left. Not like we had any other choice. We were either going to go with them or start eating the dead."

His crew had chosen what they'd believed to be the lesser of evils. "I get it, I do. But Brandon, I was dead."

"We all thought we were."

Her mouth dried. "You don't get it. I woke up in a bank of snow. I don't know how I got there or how long I'd been there. When I opened my eyes, a woman was stealing my boots. She's a nurse. She told me I was dead."

"She could have been mistaken."

August shook her head. She'd considered all those things. "I can't remember anything between the time the ceiling caved in at the auditorium until I opened my eyes in this hell. No one thinks I could have survived the event. They believe I died and came back to life. I felt my body going back online. Like I had a superpower."

Brandon glanced at her, his eyebrows meeting in the middle. "A superpower? Are you sure?"

"As sure as I can be without killing myself again to find out."

Silence echoed throughout the truck.

"There are others, August."

"Others? What are you taking about?"

His hands strangled the steering wheel. "Marx pulled me aside yesterday to talk about it. One of his guys can read minds—and it's annoying as hell because there's plenty to think about when you're in Liberty. And one of my guys? He can see things, ten, fifteen minutes before they happen."

August shivered, remembering how Harper claimed she could see people glowing around her. "Do you think there are more?"

"Not sure yet. I want to find out."

August fell quiet. Even though she felt sure about Brandon, she didn't know what his relationship with Graysen Marx was. What if Brandon had bought into Liberty? Stranger things had happened. "Tell me about the settlement. No one who goes in ever comes back to share anything about it, I'm told."

"It's amazing in a lot of ways. It was built as the prototype for the first Mars colony, able to withstand the elements unleashed by your father's experiment. Everything is domed, from the utilities to the various farms and research facilities. Lots of underground tunnels. It's warm. No more wind, no sub-zero temperatures. No kidding, I'm still walking around in a daze."

August tried to visualize the place. It did sound awesome, too good to be true.

He sighed, feeling her apprehension. "They've got a leadership group called the Infinity Council supposedly running Liberty. I'm pretty sure Marx handpicked them, and he doesn't take any opposition. I haven't got it all figured out yet. A guy like Marx always has an end game."

Graysen Marx had his settlement and resources, his Liberty Guard and enough influence to tell everyone else how many kids they could have. What else did he need?

"There's one other thing," Brandon said, catching her eye. "He has medical facilities and all survivors who are sick come in a certain entrance, but..."

The hair on August's arms stood on end. "What, Brandon?"

He shook his head. "My best advice? When we get there, stay away from Roman Shipley, the redhead who pointed his gun at you at the armory."

He was scaring her. Liberty obviously wasn't all rainbows and puppy dogs, which in a way was expected, considering their new world. She wondered if they'd be separated. She hoped not, but it would probably be in their best interest not to spend too much time together, which would be difficult.

As they continued traveling across the bumpy frozen landscape, August leaned against the headrest, taking in the warmth inside the vehicle. She wasn't sure how much time had passed when the truck slowed and came to a stop about a hundred yards from what she assumed was the entrance. Four guards stood outside a normal-looking building, carrying rifles, two on each side of a large metal, garage-type door.

"This is it," Brandon said, pointing ahead to the concrete building.

Behind it, dome structures in different shapes, some reaching high in the sky, others round and oval, lined up as far as she could see. Fear and excitement filled her body and mind at the unknown.

His hand slid into hers and tightened. "Now, watch this."

A net of turquoise sparkled, the blue glow twinkling in the red world around them. The famous geofence she'd heard about was a beautiful sight.

Brandon put the truck into drive and inched forward slowly. The garage doors opened as they approached.

He steered the truck inside and shut off the engine. "Don't talk to anyone about coming back to life, even me, okay? Stay under the radar. Can you do that?

"I'll do my best," August said, even though she didn't know what her best would be inside the domed settlement of Liberty.

• • •

In the darkness, forty minutes south of New Haven, Brandon's team of eight exited the four vehicles and huddled around Roman Shipley. Morgan had been left behind to continue counting bullets in the armory.

Brandon eyed the facade of the cracked and crumbling Army Barracks store, the entrance scarcely visible, blocked with ice. "What are we doing here? I thought we were going to the Army National Guard base."

"We are. The base is only a few minutes away." Shipley said. "A quick stop to see if anything is left that we can use. You're about to get your first real taste of a scavenger run. Put your night vision on, in case anyone is inside. Keep your eyes peeled."

Wearing Ghillie suits, the men lowered the helmet-mounted goggles, and Brandon stepped behind his unit leader. Their boots crunched against the ice with each rushed step. He kept his hands tight on his M16 as they ducked through the doorway below the wooden green and yellow sign precariously dangling.

Shipley glanced over his shoulder. "Clear out whatever you find."

"Looks like the Sproggs have already been here. Didn't leave much behind," one of the men said.

Brandon had no interest in getting to know any of the men he'd been teamed up with after what had gone down at the armory. He'd witnessed the true colors of who the Liberty Guard really was. It was one thing to protect, another to act the way Shipley and the two men who'd manhandled Harper and August had. Pushing women around was not who Brandon was, and never would be, regardless of what this new world threw at him.

Shipley pointed. "Load what we can use, and let's get out of here before anyone knows we're here."

The men quickly broke off in different directions and searched through what was left of the store's military surplus inventory. Strewn on the floor were three BDU's, mis-matched pieces of men's and women's military clothing, four backpacks, some tactical gear, knives, ammo boxes, flags, and footwear. Empty metal shelves and wire racks were overturned and cluttered the aisles. The large gun display on the wall behind the counter was empty. Even the Airsoft and paintball guns advertised on sale had vanished.

They gathered everything they could and stuffed the items into the back of one of the trucks. Brandon hoped August and her friends were okay at Liberty. He couldn't wait to see her.

"Stop worrying about her. She's fine," Shipley said, hopping into the truck and slamming the door shut.

Brandon pulled on the seatbelt and glanced at him, frustrated. "Stop reading my mind."

"Just saying. Thought it would actually make you feel better."

"Thanks, but not answering everything I'm thinking about would make things a lot better." Brandon stared out the side window. "What's your story? How'd you end up at Liberty?"

The truck jerked forward, the tires spitting chunks of ice when they finally caught.

Shipley unzipped his camouflage suit partway and flicked on the heat. "I was at the military base in Warick when things turned ugly. I'm an Army National Guard Special Forces operator, second in command. I've trained guerrilla armies, executed missions behind enemy lines, conducted counterterrorism, that kind of stuff."

"So, you're a soldier."

"Forty-third Brigade. Anyway, when the event happened, I gathered up my men and sent them to Liberty, since I was familiar with the place, basically a hop-skip-and-jump from the base." He rubbed the back of his neck. "While the men were heading to the settlement, I rushed home to get my wife and son. By that point, the temperature had started dipping. The highways were backed up for miles with terrified people trying to do the same thing. I didn't get far, totally gridlocked. I ended up walking five miles. Better than sitting in traffic, at least I thought." His voice broke. "I didn't want them—to be alone."

Brandon could tell it was killing him to talk about his family. He wanted to stop him, but Shipley continued.

"I was a block away from the house when an airplane fell from the sky—just dropped. It took out our house and most of the block. They were gone."

Brandon blinked numerous times, his eyes moist, and stared through the windshield. Minutes went by before he found his voice. He swallowed the lump in this throat. "I'm really sorry. What was his name, your son?"

"Logan. He was three." Shipley turned his head then changed the subject. "I pretty much know where almost all of the National Guard bases are in Rhode Island and Connecticut. We're almost there."

The next few minutes droned by in silence.

"There are others," Shipley said.

Brandon glanced at him, confused. "What do you mean others?"

"Like me. Hill. That girl, Harper. There are more at the settlement, kept together."

He wasn't sure why the man was offering up the information. Brandon was intrigued on both fronts.

"Your girlfriend—"

"She's not my girlfriend."

"Whatever." Shipley laughed. "She died and came back to life."

Concern hijacked him and didn't let go. Brandon didn't know what to say. What was he supposed to say?

"I didn't tell Marx."

"Why not?" It wasn't as if the man didn't tell his boss everything.

Shipley was quiet then said, "I don't know. Thought I'd wait it out and see if it's confirmed to be true somehow."

"Why is it so important to Marx? I mean, what business is it of his?"

Shipley shrugged. "I don't know. Believe me. He'll find out, regardless. Thought I'd give you a heads-up. She really died and was resurrected back to life?"

Brandon was afraid to answer. He wasn't sure if Shipley was playing mind games and this was some sort of trap.

"So, it is true. I won't say anything."

Moments later, Brandon got out of the truck and inhaled the icy air, feeling like a black cloud hovered over him and August. He pulled the hood of the suit over his head. A blast of tiny icicles pelted his face.

There wasn't much left of the building standing in front of him. The once rectangular, multi-floor gray brick structure looked like a bombed shell of destruction. The floors had caved into one another, pancaked together, flattened from the ice.

"We go in through the back," Shipley said, standing next to him.

"It doesn't look very safe."

"It's fine. This is the last time we'll be inside. Watch your step." He pulled down his goggles. "Be warned. There are a lot of bodies inside."

That was the last thing Brandon needed to see. The sense of doom took over again. He grasped his rifle and followed the team to the back of the building, nervous as to what he was about to witness inside.

When they came around the corner, gunshots rang out, filling the night air.

Brandon crouched, so did Shipley and the rest of the team.

Sproggs. It was hard for Brandon to tell which direction the shots were coming from.

Shipley leaned against him. "They're behind us. Spread out. Time to take care of these assholes."

The rest of the team dispersed cautiously.

Brandon gawked through the night vision lenses and noticed movement a hundred yards away, between two abandoned cars.

More shots sounded.

He flattened to the ground and looked beside him. Shipley was gone.

Zaps of heated adrenaline thrust through his body as two of the team members sprinted along the right side of the vehicles. He fired in the direction of the cars to make sure whoever was behind them didn't spot them.

Another gunshot.

Brandon ducked, expecting more.

They didn't come.

When he popped his head up slowly, two boots came up fast. His eyes traveled upward at a man wearing a gasmask, his chest heaving in and out through his heavy winter coat. A gun pointed directly at him.

Brandon's heart thudded in his chest. He squeezed the trigger.

The shot bored into the center of the man's forehead, stopping him in his tracks. His head snapped back, his arms flailing in the air.

Another shot came from Brandon's left. He turned his head. Then four more gunshots boomed in the direction of the cars.

Sudden silence except for the small shards of ice in the air, tinkling gently against anything they came into contact with.

He relaxed the grip on the M16 when Shipley and the others hoofed to him with grins on their faces. "We've got all three of them. Damn Sproggs. There must still be munitions inside. They wouldn't be here if there weren't." He stopped and glanced down at the dead man then directed the others to go inside. Holding out his hand to Brandon, he yanked him to his feet. "Guess that makes four."

Brandon couldn't help but look at the lifeless body in front of him. It was the last thing in the world he'd dreamed he'd be doing—staring into the blank dead eyes of someone he had killed.

CHAPTER TEN

August's fingers curled into fists. She had expected she and Brandon would be separated, but wasn't prepared for it to be so immediate. As soon as they'd parked, one of the guards stepped in front of the truck while another hauled her roughly out of the passenger seat. Pretty much the way a car thief would have been treated. She certainly hadn't made a good impression by taking the truck in the first place, if she decided she wanted to stay at Liberty for any length of time. With Brandon living here, her decision would be more difficult to stay or to go. He was a piece of her past and home.

August had returned from New Haven with something after all, something she didn't want to give up again. On Brandon's advice, she offered no resistance as they hustled her into a small, cinderblock room with no windows, the scent of lemons lingering though the space that might have been some sort of janitorial space. Could always be worse.

The absence of the shrieking wind hit her immediately, though, funny how she'd gotten used to hearing the awful sound.

A young square-jawed man in his twenties, wearing a tight military uniform, sat beside her at a worn table with a clipboard in his hand. "Name?"

"Willow." She used the name John had given to Birdman then made up the last name. "Willow Monroe."

He scribbled down the information. "Age?"

"Twenty-two."

"Gender?"

She stripped off her hat and scarf. "That's kind of obvious, don't you think?"

Sparing her a quick glance, he muttered, "You never know. Really."

True enough for the last civilization. Now, people worried about their next meal, instead of arguing about how they were identified. Except for maybe those outlaws who dressed like deadly steampunk creatures. Maybe the Bleeders and Sproggs wanted to confuse and disorient more than cross-dress.

"Place of birth?"

"New Haven, Connecticut."

He scribbled some more. "Blood type?"

"AB negative." She bit her lip. Maybe she shouldn't have volunteered that information so freely. As a rare type, they might drain her dry before she could argue.

"Number of pregnancies?"

"Number of what?"

"Pregnancies."

"None."

He drew a zero on the form and made her feel like she should have had a more interesting answer. She remembered how in movies about aliens they always wanted fertile women, so they could cross-breed. In this case, with the moratorium on children, maybe the opposite won out.

"Do you have a high school diploma?"

She nodded, glad to be away from the personal questions. "Yes."

"Did you attend college?"

She nodded again. What did any of this matter? It's not as if she could order up some school transcripts to demonstrate her knowledge.

Thinking quickly, she added, "I didn't finish, though."

"What did you study?"

She lied just a little to help stay under the radar. "Biology. I only did two years, so I didn't get into it much."

Square-face didn't care; he kept firing questions her way. "Any remaining family members?"

The query sent an arrow into her heart, and she lost any playful sarcasm. "No, you?"

Finally, he looked up from his clipboard. His eyes were gray, heavy-lidded and looked exhausted. "No, ma'am."

August saw tears pool in the corners of his eyes. "I'm sorry."

He offered a quick nod before he looked back at his questions. Jesus, what were they doing? She struggled against the urge to hug the young man, who looked to be about the same age as her. Instead, she sat on her hands.

"Do you have any special certifications or skills, which might be useful in Liberty?"

She shrugged. "Anything like office work or teaching some basic things to kids. I guess lab work if someone could show me the ropes?"

"Did you ever farm or participate in assembly lines or other manufacturing activities?"

"I can't even keep houseplants alive or change a tire."

"Okay," he said, putting his pen down, apparently finished with the form. "You missed your medical screening earlier, so we're going to take you over to the medical clinic then afterward, assign you a room for the night."

It all sounded straightforward. Then why was her heart hammering its way out of her chest? Brandon's reminder to stay under the radar looped through her head. She stood and followed the guard out of the room.

Goosebumps skated over her skin, and she took a deep breath. She detected the scent of greenery, grass or moss, and water, almost as if there was a creek nearby.

While the color of the sun kept the horizon relatively dim, she noticed a large cluster of gnats hovering around her. She celebrated the strange normality. Weeks ago, bugs would have annoyed her to no end. "Are there still cockroaches?"

Her guide grinned. "They'll never die."

• • •

August reluctantly entered the large dome with a guard on either side of her. The medical facility wasn't unlike any of the small hospitals she'd seen. Not knowing what kinds of tests to expect, she fidgeted with her hands.

"I'm Dr. Northridge," an older man in a white coat said as her escorts disappeared. "Please come in. You seem apprehensive. Let me assure you, I'm not here to hurt you, pressure you or anything of the sort."

August didn't believe a word of his well-rehearsed speech. He appeared frail, thin, with graying hair receding from his temples. He read through her questionnaire, then looked up and smiled. "We have to ensure we do all we can to eliminate any illnesses since we have a limited amount of medical supplies. We'll draw some blood, run some screens, do a complete physical and gynecological exam, as the latest mandate requires."

Shivering inside her parka, August shook her head. "I don't like this one bit."

The doctor peered over the top of his bifocals, his expression not as soft. "We can always sedate you if you prefer."

Her thoughts turned to Brandon. Even if she only stayed for a few days to be with him, she'd have to agree to the medical exams. Sedation sounded far worse and God knew what they would do to her. "Fine. No sedation. I'm at least going to know what's going on."

"As you wish."

He directed her to a chair and cordoned off her arm with a blue rubber band, sanitized the vein on the inside of her elbow. He didn't speak, which she appreciated, and the near-painless blood draw took less than a minute.

After Dr. Northridge gathered the four vials, he labeled them and passed them to his nurse, a round woman in a white lab coat. Next, he invited August to follow him behind an orange and blue curtain.

He handed her a gown, a two-toned blue-checked one that closed in the back. "If you'll change quickly, this shouldn't take long."

She snatched the gown from his hands. "Great. Because I have some important dinner plans."

Snapping the curtain shut, August shed her clothes and tried to tie the gown, an impossibility for any human being. She couldn't remember the last time she'd seen a doctor, even though she'd been religious about keeping up her annual eye and dentist appointments.

"Okay. I'm ready," she said.

The doctor pushed the curtain aside, and the nurse followed him. He smiled. "I appreciate your humor. I know these exams are stressful."

"Especially when you don't expect one."

While the doctor inspected her ears, nose, and throat, tested her reflexes and listened to her heartbeat from the front and back, August became more uncomfortable at the thought of having a gyno exam.

"Are there any genetic issues? Has anyone in your immediate family had any chronic illness or disease?"

"No."

What about mental health issues?" He motioned for her to lay back on the cold-looking metal table and began poking and prodding her abdomen. "Any depression, bi-polar disease, schizophrenia?"

"I don't think so." She tried to ignore the nurse pulling out the shiny stirrups. As the doctor began, August counted the ceiling tiles and blocked out the invasion of the pelvic exam, quick as it was.

He withdrew and turned to the nurse. "Bring me the portable ultrasound."

Images of her mother again flooded her head. August lifted her head. Panic drove through her. "Is something wrong?"

He smiled. "No. Not at all. It's part of our examination. It's my job to be diligent."

Minutes passed, and the small off-white piece of medical machinery was wheeled into the room. She had seen an ultrasound machine before, when her mother was in the intensive care unit fighting for her life. The thought wasn't making her feel better.

The nurse plugged in the cord.

Snapping on a new set of latex gloves, the doctor turned on the machine. August went back to counting the ceiling tiles since they were the only thing to look at.

When the examination was completed, he rolled his chair back and tore off the gloves one at a time. "You can get dressed now."

She sat up, his unreadable expression making her anxious. As August pulled on her layers of clothing, her hands trembled. Once dressed, she sat on the edge of the table and waited.

From the next room, she heard subdued voices, a male and female, the doctor and nurse. She slid off the table and tiptoed to the slightly ajar door.

"Find her a magazine or something to keep her occupied until the blood results are back. It'll be at least half an hour."

The nurse's voice faded in and out. "What about her GYN results?"

"She can't have children. Endometriosis. Both fallopian tubes are completely blocked and part of her uterus. She's excluded from the mandate."

August felt the blood leave her face. The news pushed her back from the door, and she tripped over her own feet, almost losing her balance. Quickly she resumed her position on the edge of the table before they caught her eavesdropping.

Surely, she'd heard wrong. She couldn't have children?

The doctor had to be wrong.

Having kids was something she wanted when she got married. Doom washed over her. That fairy tale wasn't going to happen. August wasn't sure how she should feel.

While the wall clock ticked, each minute dragging on, she swung her feet back and forth, fantasizing about seeing Brandon. She needed to focus on something good to avoid facing the horrible news.

Minutes later, voices were outside the door. This time, she heard them clearly.

"It's just odd," the doctor said.

"What's her blood type?" the male voice asked.

Pages shuffled. "She said AB negative, but this is...different. Just like the others."

A member of the guard opened the door and met her troubled gaze. A redhead, taller than average. The man Brandon had warned her about. Roman Shipley.

Dr. Northridge greeted him, not taking take his eyes off her. "Here's her file for Mr. Marx."

August eyed the manila file folder. "What does he need that for?"

"Helps him decide where you best fit in, Miss Monroe," Roman Shipley said, tucking the file under his arm. "Or should we use your real name?"

August's heart skipped a beat. She knew she wouldn't be able to hide her identity for very long. She narrowed her eyes. Reading people's minds without their permission constituted a severe invasion of privacy. "When you meet new people, do you introduce yourself as the mind-reader or use your name?"

"I'm just doing my job."

"Well, your job sucks." August hopped off the table and came toe-to-toe with him. "Who am I, then?"

When he stepped back, she felt a small victory...until he said, "August Madison."

•••

The songbirds' chatter had vanished hours earlier outside the Liberty Guard's living quarters, their cheerful chorus silenced by the early morning darkness. Brandon wiped the sweat from his brow, something he never thought he'd be doing after experiencing the bone-drilling cold. His new home was warm, comfortable and reminded him of one of those tiny houses he'd seen during an infomercial on the TV, basically a small apartment for two, maybe three people. The guard's units were designed efficiently, modern and compact, each separate unit stacked five levels high, curving toward the sky.

He was housed in the Alpha section, named after the military phonetic alphabet along with Morgan, the only other member from the *Eagle* and, of course, with Shipley who was probably creeping about somewhere. The guy was determined to keep an eye on them at any cost. Brandon wasn't sure why the man had mentioned there were others with odd new abilities since the experiment. Why had he said he wouldn't tell Marx about August coming back to life? Maybe it was a trap. Maybe it wasn't. He couldn't be sure. But why was Marx keeping them segregated from the other citizens?

The rest of his crew had been divided as expected into other living sections: Bravo, Charlie, Delta, Echo, Foxtrot. Each of the phonetic alphabet also coincided with the Liberty Guard security teams.

They'd finished their shift at exactly seven am, and Brandon found himself still in awe after seeing what he had during their rounds.

After the incident in the restricted area near the west entrance, their security detail had been stationed in the far northern sector where he had taken a good look at one of the dry steam plants supplying electricity to the settlement. With water in a large reservoir, the plant used geothermal steam to churn the giant turbines that produced electricity to Liberty's power grid.

Next door, the drinking water was processed using ultraviolet light and a peroxide water treatment system. The peroxide would eventually run out and Marx would have to look for another solution. It was a problem they would all face together.

The crops, agriculture designed to be regenerative and non-polluting, took Brandon's breath away. Fields stretched tens of miles, covered with dome structures in various shapes and sizes. Potatoes, apple orchards, corn, soybeans, nut trees, and vast plots of regal-looking sunflower plants, the seeds used in the biofuel for the exterior security vehicles, was breathtaking to view. Rows of golden plants swayed in the biodome's air and reminded him of running through his uncle's wheat fields when he was small. He'd even seen where the cows and chickens were kept and talked to a parrot in the apple orchard. He'd also witnessed the awful destruction of miles of the dome structure immediately after the event.

It was as if he had been tossed in a dream world, compared to being outside the settlement. Then he was jarred awake to the true reality of Liberty.

For the majority of the population, living quarters were sparse and overcrowded. Most citizens didn't have a bed, left to sleep on the floor or forced to take turns, sleeping in shifts. The units were messy, smelly and unclean. Complete chaos. They certainly didn't have many of the perks the guard had.

With a full belly, Brandon felt bad he was living the high life while others were barely getting by in what felt like cluttered cages. He still hadn't seen any children. Where were the children? Did Marx have them isolated, too?

"You want to play Xbox?" Morgan asked as he walked into the main living area after taking a shower, his hair slicked back and wet.

More benefits the Liberty Guard had. Lots of hot showers and video games, even though gaming consoles were prohibited for the rest of the population.

Brandon wondered why his friend hadn't been secluded with the others. Perhaps, Marx found Morgan's new ability useful at the moment. Strategically, it would come in handy, knowing if the Sproggs were going to attack the settlement or anyone else beforehand.

"You go ahead. I think I'm going to get some sleep."

Morgan grinned. "Your loss. I'd beat you anyway. Did you find out where August is?"

"Not yet."

"I'm sure she's fine. She's in out of the cold, safe for now," Morgan said, picking up the game controller.

Brandon didn't like his disguised warning. "For now? Is that your professional opinion? Do you know something?"

Morgan shook his head and flicked on the small flat screen TV then sat on the floor cross-legged in front of the screen. "I've got no heebie-jeebies at the moment, just saying."

At least his friend wasn't seeing anything bad as far as August was concerned. If he could sneak out and find where she was housed, he would. The cameras and Marx's threat of having to deal with the Infinity Council if Brandon or any of his men got out of line again stopped him. He'd try to track her down after breakfast, when they had their "free" time. He wanted to see her, make sure she was okay. After a quick shower, he crawled into his single bed.

Within minutes, Morgan burst into the room, panicked, talking a mile a minute. "They killed them! Strangled them!"

Brandon dropped the paperback in his lap and sat up straight. "What are you talking about. Who was killed?"

"The old couple, you know, the old man who's sick. I can't believe it."

He'd seen something. "Who killed them?" A shiver raced up Brandon's spine at the same time as Shipley's face came into focus in the doorway. He was standing behind Morgan, the butt of his M16 raised.

"Oh God, I saw it. We have to stop them. They're going to..."

Shipley smacked the end of the gun into the back of Morgan's head. He went down hard in front of him.

Brandon jumped out of bed. "Why the hell did you do that? Jesus." He bent down and checked Morgan's pulse. He was breathing, but unconscious.

"He's crazy as hell." Shipley bent and grabbed Morgan's feet. "Help me get him to medical. The event did something to him, screwed with his head. He's losing his mind. Nobody killed anyone."

•••

Early the next morning, after a well-needed shower to wake her up, the first in weeks, August entered the expansive assembly hall sporting short hair and an odd-shaped black tattoo stamped on the inside of her wrist that looked like an angry snowflake with spikes.

She had been told everyone had to have their hair chopped off to ward off any possible outbreaks of lice, which could be true in such tight quarters, or it was Graysen Marx's way to strip the population of any individualism. August guessed the latter.

Running a hand over her hair, she swallowed her insecurities and marched past the thousands of inhabitants. Her eyes roamed over the thick sea of black coveralls, the exact same dull clothing she'd been forced to wear. The only available seats were in the front rows like in church and lecture halls. The hall reminded her of the university's auditorium, but much larger and with more rows of seating stretching high into the dome.

Where was Brandon? Looking over her shoulder, she searched the room. Armed guards stood at each exit. Brandon wasn't among them. Where was he?

Passing rows of people, August suddenly realized there were no older people, disabled or children in attendance. She wiped her sweaty palms on her clothing. While she could dismiss the lack of small children, the demographics made her uneasy. None of the citizens met her gaze as she took a seat, front and center. Doors slammed shut from various directions and reverberated against the walls.

In front of her was a large stage, the width of the hall. Seconds later, a tall man strode on the stage, looking remarkably healthy, considering the events of the past days. Despite the dark shadows under his eyes, they twinkled, like he knew the secrets of the universe everyone else could only imagine. He wore business casual attire with a black sports coat for an added touch of authority and leather shoes.

No one applauded.

August had only seen Graysen Marx a handful of times in person when she had tagged along with her father for the day. She'd endured endless business meetings with the two because they'd go to dinner afterward to her father's favorite Italian restaurant.

Five others followed Graysen and took a seat at a long, conference-like table behind him.

His gaze met hers as he positioned himself behind a wooden podium embossed with a bronze cross below a microphone. He probably had appropriated the cross from a church in the area. Or he thought he was God.

"Good morning, people of Liberty. Since the day that everything changed, I promised I'd give you updates and share new information. As you know, Liberty was formed as a self-sustaining environment. We're lucky to have housing and food." He paused and took a breath. "As more survivors trickle in, we must be flexible to find new ways to share our space and food."

August shifted in her seat. Being one of those new survivors with a bed, meals, and an assigned job, if she chose to stay, she felt the eyes of the crowd on her back.

"Because of this," Graysen continued, "we are adding additional hours to all essential job categories to ensure we're making the most of our resources and our population. Increased production will help meet the demands for food and alleviate the strain of shared housing."

In other words, work harder longer.

A ripple of disgruntlement clattered through the hall in the form of gasps and sighs.

He held up his hands. "Life here is better than anywhere, even if we have to work hard to maintain what we have. We've learned of a settlement in Icehaven situated inside an Army National Guard armory. They have suffered nearly daily attacks from marauders who have stolen their supplies and killed some of their friends. When my men were there nurturing an alliance, they came under attack. We also suffered casualties. One guard member was killed, another seriously wounded. The outside threat is *real* and should not be taken lightly. If you go outside, you *will* die. We must provide a haven for those who wish to come in out of the cold, who support our mission and provide resources to help us live and grow in this trying time."

A few people murmured in agreement.

August found nothing to argue with, other than Graysen sounded less like a humanitarian, and more like a politician the longer he spoke.

"As you know, food is in short supply. It could take months or years to get to where we need to be. Our means of production, farms, and our sheer numbers need to be controlled. With this in mind, the Infinity Council," he motioned to the five sitting silently, "have mandated that all women of childbearing age must be sterilized immediately."

August's jaw dropped open. She'd barely absorbed the idea of limiting the number of children per family or thought through the revelation she couldn't have children herself. To force the population to sacrifice this particular freedom seemed extreme.

"Who do you think you are?" All the air in the room seemed to vanish the moment August said the words.

Behind her, women gasped and chatted to one another. No one else in the crowd said anything to support Marx, or her.

She hadn't planned on speaking her thoughts out loud. Now that she had, August stood, hoping no one could see her knees shaking.

Marx glared at her like a lion watching his prey, waiting for her to make the next mistake. "Miss Madison—yes, I know who you are—you are a guest in my house. Would you care to explain yourself?"

He really meant, would she like to keep digging a hole so he could bury her?

Her father's words echoed in her head. *In for a penny, in for a pound.* Taking a deep breath, she leapt into the deep end of the pool and said what she assumed most of the population was thinking. "You can't make these decisions for people. I know who you are, too. I don't know why you think you can play God with people's lives, relationships, and families simply because you happened to be here at the right time."

Applause broke out around her.

Marx walked around to the front of the podium, his body language stiff. "Do you think they should gradually starve to death instead? Is starvation more or less humane?"

"It's a choice," August said, her blood pressure and voice rising with her anger. "Using threats to control people isn't right. Chopping off our hair, so we all look the same isn't right. Forcing us to undergo medical procedures isn't right."

Marx sneered. "You know it's chaos out there. You've seen it. The only real choice is to stay. All the rest is just details."

Details that mattered. How would they repopulate if they sterilized all the women? No one had any information about how many had survived the event. They couldn't possibly know. "You know nothing after such little amount of time. These people are scared and you're just keeping them there, which makes you a terrorist."

"It makes me a prophet." He stepped to the end of the stage. "All the information your father and I had access to tells me what I need to know and what can be done. I can keep everyone in the settlement safe, but there are limits. Limits you don't fully understand."

August shook her head. "Then share your vast wisdom. Let us all decide for ourselves what we think is best."

"You have no idea," Marx barked, gesturing to the crowd. "None of you have any idea what's really happening in the world. This isn't going to end. It's not going to revert back to what used to be. We're never going back—we have limited food, medicine, you name it. We must ration it. Don't be fooled into thinking you're still in a world where you have an abundance of anything, including choices."

Turning a full circle, August took in the faces in the room, then lastly, Graysen Marx. His cool, professional demeanor had vanished. His face contorted, displaying his anger and disdain to all who cared to see.

He reverted in the blink of an eye and smoothed his jacket. "This meeting is over."

As he stormed past the still passive Infinity Council and out of the room, August collapsed in her seat. If she thought the citizenry of Liberty would converge around her and celebrate her small rebellion, she'd been mistaken. No one made a sound as they filed out of the room, scared and defeated, exhausted and probably hungry. August felt hollow inside. She'd said what everyone had to be thinking, and all the bluster had gotten her nowhere. Had gained nothing for anyone.

Alone in the hall, she forced herself to opt out of the spiraling emotions threatening to drag her down. She needed something, anything to help her to feel human again.

"August? Is that you?"

She twisted in the seat at the man's voice.

Two familiar faces stared at her, smiling.

"John. Lydia." The warmth of their friendship surged through her. August jumped to her feet and gave Lydia a hug. "I'm so glad to see you."

"Me, too. Are you okay? We heard you were the last one through."

"I'm fine."

"I'm glad to see you, kid," John said and gave her a bear hug.

When he let go, she looked around. "Where are the others?"

"They're scattered all over the settlement. We don't know about Harper. We haven't found where they've taken her yet."

August looked at him, reality beating at her. "We aren't getting out of here, are we?"

John shook his head. "Not too likely, unless we make a break for it."

"Clear out," a guard said from one of the exits. "Madison, come with me."

Barely able to remember Brandon's warm hand in hers, his gentle, hopeful kiss, August felt anger. She needed to figure out what to do next. He had brought her to a place that looked like Heaven but was, in fact, a new kind of Hell.

CHAPTER ELEVEN

"Right there," Brandon said, pointing to August's name on the intake list. He'd just finished breakfast, an omelet with fresh vegetables, toast and two pieces of bacon. He yearned for her company, not wanting another minute to go by. Shipley had sent him to the east guard station while everyone was in the assembly hall for a meeting of some sort. Nothing surprised Brandon anymore, at least when it came to the mind-reader.

"Does it say where she's been designated to live?"

Thankfully, his old crew member, Asher Jotti, had no qualms about sharing the information. "Um, looks like she's in the Mercury unit, Pod 1. It's in the opposite direction to where you're housed, right off the—aquaphonic fish farm? We have a library, too. I didn't know that."

Neither did Brandon. "Thanks, man. Can I see the list one more time? I want to see if my parents came in. It's worth a try." He knew the chances were slim and had accepted they probably hadn't made it.

Asher looked at him and pushed the list to him. "Don't tell anyone."

He slapped the younger man on the shoulder. "I owe you one."

"If you happen to find any smokes…"

"They're yours," Brandon said, knowing the cigarettes were something the guards were allowed but only smoked in the concrete confines of the Liberty Guard entrance.

He scanned the first few pages and didn't see his parents' names. When he flipped to the next page, he spotted Morgan's name, but the housing unit entry was blank. Morgan Hill had disappeared and that worried Brandon. He'd look for him after he found August.

He continued searching the names. One caught his attention. He couldn't believe his eyes. *Luke Madison.* August's brother. Brandon knew he wasn't seeing things when he thought he'd seen Luke in the golf cart. "He's alive."

"Who? Your father?"

"I have to go. Thanks, man." Brandon grinned and ducked out the door.

•••

Brandon smelled the place long before laying eyes on it, surprised the Mercury living quarters was located next to the fish farm. The stench permeated the dwelling areas, which were far more open and communal than those of the Liberty Guard. Bunkbeds lined the walls. Metal shelving found in industrial kitchens or garages ran from floor to ceiling, stuffed with belongings.

As he wandered through two such areas and entered a third, his mind buzzed with the inequity he saw. No video games, no televisions with movies playing, no books or magazines. The first dome had been lights out, and the bunks had been filled, the second had been completely empty, and the third, quiet at first, now buzzed with people coming back from the meeting.

Brandon hung back from the entrance and stayed out of everyone's way. They all gave him a wide berth without meeting his eyes. Were they afraid of him because he wore a guard uniform?

About fifty women entered the quarters. They all appeared to be getting ready to go to sleep. It dawned on him the quarters were arranged by work shift, first, second and third. This would be the second shift. His attention moved to a woman with short, blonde hair and blue eyes. It was her.

August pulled him into a corner—if a round room could have a corner. "You shouldn't be here."

He reached to touch her spiked hair, and she knocked his hand away. "Can you leave?"

She grabbed his hand and pulled him outside the living quarters.

Brandon glanced around, searching for Shipley or anyone else who would get in their way. "I want to show you something."

She didn't protest and followed his steady pace through the corridor. Above the dome panels, the russet sun had turned the world the color of red wine. He didn't know much about wine, but he knew where he was headed this time around. He paused before leading her inside, excited to tell her about Luke.

•••

August's eyes lit up at the sight of the countless rows of sunflowers. "This is amazing. It's beautiful." She glanced at him. "Are we supposed to be in here?"

He shrugged. "It doesn't matter. We're here now." The cameras couldn't see them once they ducked within the rows of stalks, couldn't see them at all if they timed it right. "We can safely talk in here." He brushed her bangs out of her eyes. "August, Luke is alive. He's here."

She grabbed his arm and her eyes widened. "I can't believe it. Really? What about Chloe? My father?"

"I didn't see their names on the list."

Her eyes teared up.

He held her hands. "It doesn't mean something bad has happened. There are more lists at the other entrances."

She released his hands and walked away. "We have to go and check them right now. I have to find the rest of my family."

He grabbed her by the shoulder and spun her around. "You can't. Marx will catch you. No telling what he'll do to you. Or Roman Shipley. I'll check tonight during my work shift." He stared at her for a long moment, sadness and concern heavy in the back of her eyes. "I'm sorry for the way things went down—I didn't know they'd..." He touched her hair again.

"You didn't? Look around. Everyone looks the same. Even you guys with your uniforms. The hair, the clothes, it's meant to take away our identities. These people in here are like zombies, still in shock over what's happened, what they've lost."

How could he tell her he had his own concerns? He opened his mouth then detoured into another question. "Did you go to Marx's meeting?"

"Yes. It's horrible what he's doing, making it mandatory for all females of childbearing age to be sterilized. What happened to freedom? What happened to choices?"

In his mind, he heard the answer. The choice was between the outside and Liberty. No other choice mattered. That really wasn't true. Marx made himself and his word law without having the support of the people he ruled, which made him a dictator. "He thinks he's doing the right things, given the situation."

"Don't tell me you've drunk a pitcher of the Kool-Aid too?"

"No, I'm just seeing different things than you. A different perspective."

"Don't you want to have children one day?"

The question almost knocked him off his feet. Of course, he did. But not like this. Not under these circumstances. He didn't want to bring a child into the world, this world. He didn't have the heart to say it out loud. "Maybe, one day."

Silence stretched between them before August said, "I think I'm in trouble with Graysen because I challenged everything he said at the meeting. He didn't handle it well. I'm sure I'll get called to the principal's office."

Brandon knew the feeling all too well and was concerned for her. "Just keep your cool. He likes to talk. *Loves* the sound of his own voice. You might get some useful information out of him instead of the other way around."

A fleeting smile graced her face. "You might be right."

"Did they give you a job?"

August moved through the flowers, looking up at their bright golden petals. "In the Research and Development lab. I start in the morning."

"What do you think you'll be doing there?" He trailed behind her as she wandered in and out of the stalks. Even with her short hair, she was stunning.

"I was told data entry, assisting with experiments, that sort of thing. What kind of things have you seen since you got here?"

He stopped, and she walked through the rows between them until she was at his side. The words to explain what he'd seen felt jumbled and confused. "My buddy, Morgan, and I got lost, ended up near the west entrance where they have the sick survivors come through. We saw this older couple come in. The man was really sick, needed medical attention." He stopped again, not wanting to be the one who killed her spirit, making her see the bad in the world.

Her hand rested on his forearm. "Tell me. Nothing is going to shock me. It's a crazy world, and people aren't the same anymore. Graysen Marx is a perfect example. I doubt he was this way before the event. They are doing things they wouldn't have normally done, and so are we."

He couldn't argue with her assessment. "There wasn't anything there. No medical center on the map. No equipment, no personnel. Nothing. We didn't see what happened to the couple, but Morgan claims he did. He sees things before they happen. Last night, he lost it, freaked out, started screaming about how they were going to kill them, how we had to stop them."

August's face turned white, and her hand flew to her mouth. "My God."

"Shipley knocked him out and ordered me to take him to the medical to be assessed, that he was crazy."

"That's horrible. Is he okay?"

"I don't know. I can't find him now, August. He's disappeared."

She ran her hand along the side of his face. "I'm sorry about your friend. He has to be somewhere in the place."

"I think Marx has him hidden from the rest of the population. He had asked Morgan some questions and told us about how Shipley could read minds. If you see or hear anything about other people able to do weird things, you have to let me know somehow."

"Of course, I will."

He took a deep breath and told her his worst fear. "I think Marx is studying people with those strange new abilities."

"You didn't tell them about me, did you?"

He heard the panic in her voice. "No way. Something else is bothering me. I didn't see the full extent until now."

"What is it?"

"It's the way you live versus the way we live, the guard." He tried not to feel guilty about the good life they had. After all, they did dangerous work. "We're aren't stacked into our space like you. We have entertainment for our down time: video games, movies. We get three meals a day and long hot showers, clean clothes, basically whatever we need, including cigarettes for those who smoke."

"Lucky guy. We only get two meals. Only one of them has any protein, usually, mystery meat that tastes like a mixture of beef, pork and something sweet made into stew, patties, meatloaf, that type of thing."

She had just described the flavor of the stew he had days ago.

"When I start working, I was told I'd get some fringe benefits, like access to whatever video instruction might be helpful, and I'll be able to use the library."

Brandon's heart dropped, and he felt a stab of fear. "I'm sorry I brought you here."

"I'm not." She stepped in close to him, her beautiful eyes tying him in knots, as usual. If he could, he always wanted to feel this way. "Nothing is ideal, not here, and not out there, either. At least we have each other, a way to remember there used to be something better, and I don't just mean the climate. Human beings used to be better."

He wrapped his arms around her. They had to find their way, or the world would never find its way. They had a lot of work ahead of them. They needed to find Morgan, and August needed to see Luke and find her sister and father.

She quickly stepped out of his embrace and pulled down the zipper of her coveralls. After undressing, she stood in front of him in only a sports bra and panties.

"What are you doing?"

"What does it look like? I'm going to run half-naked through a sunflower field. I might not get another chance." She took off running, zigzagging through the crop, giggling.

Brandon grinned and ran after her. "You're crazy, August Madison."

• • •

Graysen Marx pointed to one of the chairs next to the couch in his living quarters. "Have a seat, Miss Madison."

Her behavior in the assembly hall was worrisome and needed to be shut down immediately. The last thing he needed was a mutiny on his hands.

August looked at him, defiance frozen in her stiff limbs and straight back. "I prefer to stand."

Roman seized her by the back of the shoulders and shoved her down into one of the two white leather chairs behind her. She turned her head and glared at him. "Touch me again and you'll find out how much I've learned—"

"Enough," Graysen said sternly, then nodded at Roman to leave.

After the man left the room, Graysen peered at August, intrigued by her tough talk, and wondered if she had been like that before life had been altered by the weather. He didn't remember her that way. "Again, Miss Madison. Manners, please. Do I have to remind you? You are my guest."

She laughed. "This is how you treat your guests? Forcing people to stay here even if they don't want to? Chopping off their hair, shedding them of any dignity or individuality, requiring women to be sterilized. Sounds like a dictatorship. Who died and made you God?"

"We have all died a little since the event. Don't you agree?" He took a seat in the chair across from her, his gaze never leaving hers, reminding her he was in charge. "This is a difficult time and requires strong leadership if we're all going to make it in the long run. You may not understand why things are the way they are. You're young, inexperienced in the old world, and in this one. Your father always said you were a firecracker. A firecracker is not what is needed at Liberty."

August stood and put her hands on her hips. "Then I can leave and go back to the armory."

He made sure his tone was harsh enough to ensure she got the message. "Sit down. You're not going anywhere."

"You can't keep us here like prisoners."

"You wouldn't survive twenty-four hours on your own on the outside. You're far from being a prisoner here. You're free to move throughout the settlement in the areas you are authorized to use during your free time and before the eleven pm curfew." The woman was testing his patience. He crossed his arms over his chest and stared at her, hoping to knock her down a few notches. In the past, her type of spunk would be welcomed, especially in a business sense. Not now. "I'm going to assume you didn't find what you were looking for in New Haven when you stole one of our vehicles?"

August shrank into the chair and kept her chin high, her defiance never wavering.

"That's strike one. Let's not forget your performance during *my* meeting. Those types of outbursts will not be tolerated for the good of the population. Strike two."

"You mean, your agenda, to make yourself look good. The almighty Savior. This place is a safe haven for everyone, anyone, not your private dictatorship."

"If we have to deal with a strike three scenario, the Infinity Council will choose your fate."

She laughed again. "Get real. This isn't a movie. It's real life. Okay. I made a mistake by taking the truck. I should have asked, but I doubt I would have been allowed to use it. I wanted to go back to the university to look for my family. I needed to know if my father, brother, and sister were alive."

"Did you find them?"

Her eyes lowered, and she shook her head.

Part of him felt sorry for her. He'd heard the same story over and over from so many. Emotions he'd felt before the event didn't register anymore. He was fully aware her brother and sister were at Liberty. He wasn't going to tell her after her public display of defiance. As for her father, Graysen assumed the scientist was dead. Everyone had lost someone important to them.

He'd lost his wife, Alexis, because she wouldn't listen to their daughter's warnings, didn't take them seriously. He forced the thought from his mind and continued, "I know you died during your father's experiment, or after. No one can be sure. I'm also aware that you resurrected, if you prefer to call it that."

She remained silent and stared at the wall.

Graysen knew she was taking in everything he had said so far. He stood and walked to the flat screen TV mounted on the wall, separating the spacious kitchen area. He kept his back to her for a couple of minutes, wanting to let things sink in a bit more before saying, "Did you ever wonder how it was possible to suck in your last breath then feel a gasping rush of air filling your lungs days later? I'm sure you've thought about it a lot. It would only be natural to question something as unusual and miraculous."

"People die and come back to life all the time, so I've been told. It's not rare at all."

He cocked his head to one side, amused by her argument. She did have a point, except the situation was different, a reason why it had happened to her and why other survivors had developed strange powers. "Stop lying to yourself, to me, August. You know it happened."

"I guess you know what's going on since you claim to have been so close with my father. How much do you really know?"

He pondered her question and tried to form an answer she would believe. He couldn't reveal everything to protect himself and his daughter. "It's true. I was close to your father while he was working on the experiment, since it was my company's money backing it. I have to be honest. I don't have any idea how this happened to you, or the others, for that matter."

"Then why are we having this conversation? You gave me a slap on the wrist for standing up for what I believe in and now I'd like to leave."

The twenty-two-year-old was gutsy and reminded him of his daughter. Even at sixteen, Kenna had the same stubborn streak, defiance, passion to fight for the underdog, and was extremely intelligent. It was those traits that would create problems at Liberty if not controlled.

"Not quite yet. You told Dr. Northridge your blood type was AB negative."

"Because it's true."

"When he checked, the result was different."

Her eyes searched his and she laughed. "A person's blood type doesn't change. That much I do know. He obviously made a mistake."

"The sample was double-checked then verified in the research lab. There is no mistake. You have golden blood. RH-null."

August straightened in the chair, her eyes wide and her jaw slack. "How can my blood suddenly lack all sixty-one antigens in the Rh system?"

He took a seat again and waited for her to figure out the mystery, at least part of it.

"Oh, my God. The experiment. It did something to my blood." She shook her head. "That's not possible."

"Apparently, it is. You're living proof and so are other survivors with newfound paranormal abilities. Roman is another example and your friend, the young woman at the armory." Graysen knew there was a connection to the experiment and possibly how it happened. Telling her would ruin his plan, and he wasn't about to do that. Too much was at stake. He stood. "Come with me. I want to show you something."

She looked at him unsure, trying to decide if she should trust him or not. August finally got up and followed him.

He opened one of the bedroom doors. His daughter was asleep, her features peaceful and relaxed. Beside her, an IV stand pumped a bag of fluids and nutrition into her. "This is Kenna, my daughter."

"What's wrong with her? Was she injured or something?"

"A brain tumor. She's sedated for her own safety. Although the mass is benign, it's rapidly growing and causing tremendous pressure on her brain. Kenna knew the experiment was going to fail. We left Boston and came here, the only place where we'd be safe from the horrendous climate change."

"Is—she going to die?"

Her words stabbed him in the heart, and anger reared its ugly head. "Eventually, yes."

August looked up at him, the angst in her eyes and voice evident. "Why are you telling me all of this?"

"It's fairly simple. My daughter is why you aren't going to cause any more problems at Liberty. You will keep your mouth shut, do your job and become a model citizen of this settlement." He took a deep breath and puffed it out, his muscles tight beneath his clothing. "Mr. Shipley will escort you to medical lab where you will undergo more elaborate medical testing. No more outbursts, Miss Madison. Do you understand? Because I will do *anything* to save Kenna." He waved his hand toward the door, unable to rein in his anger. "Get the hell out of here."

• • •

Leaving Graysen Marx's living quarters, August felt like she walked a slow death march. The hair on her arms stood at attention when she came face-to-face with Roman Shipley. He turned and walked briskly ahead of her. She followed without a word, forcing a lid on her thoughts about her meeting with his boss.

Even though it was a straight shot, she paid close attention to the route between her living quarters and the medical facility. Getting around the settlement's maze took concentration and alertness to detail. No one was about to give her a map. She wanted to know more about her change in blood type, seemingly instigated by her father's experiment.

On the trip over, she wracked her brain about the experiment. One component stood out, the Amexotrate. She needed to learn more to understand if its effect on humans had ever been considered. It wouldn't be the first time an altruistic mega-idea suffered unintended consequences.

"We're here," Roman said, his first words to her.

Assuming he'd been listening in on her thoughts, August cursed a few times mentally for good measure.

He grinned and shook his head.

Outside the medical unit, a single-file line snaked from the entrance, overlooked by another guard. August realized there was only one man among those in line. The rest were female. She kept her head down as she approached, where she was pulled to one side.

"Medical testing to the right." The familiar, oval face of the nurse bobbed into view. "Sterilization to the left."

August's heart dropped. Only she and the man stood on the right. She counted twenty women of various ages huddled together on the left. Their expressions told a story of fear, defeat, exhaustion and hard choices. None of them met her questioning gaze.

The medical staff dealt with the women first, taking them in pairs. Roman pulled them inside when the nurse called their last names then disappeared from her view. August walked a slow circle around a clump of floor plants. When she looked up, she saw John loitering next to a towering flowering tree. He motioned her over.

"What's going on? I thought you were processed already."

"I was. They said I have a rare blood type and need to do more tests. Why are you here?"

"One of the workers got hurt at the steam plant. I brought him over."

Thank God John wasn't being picked apart. "Have you found Harper?"

He shook his head. "The rumor is they're housing survivors with the odd abilities in a different area. I'm trying to find out where. We don't know why they're being separated unless they're in some kind of danger."

To Graysen, perhaps. August had a sinking feeling in the pit of her stomach that she might end up there, as well. "John, everyone with weird abilities have the same rare blood type. It's not the type I was born with, it changed somehow."

His eyes widened. "That's strange. How can that happen?"

"Inside," Roman barked, pointing at her.

August waved John off and trudged into the medical facility, sick of Roman Shipley's mind-reading skills.

• • •

The first round of medical testing began immediately with more blood panels. August counted twelve vials of blood. Then, a full body x-ray—that couldn't be good for anyone—followed by a head and neck MRI, both with and without contrast. The tests gave her plenty of time to reflect, something sorely lacking.

Lying inside the MRI tube, the monotone tapping of the machine beat doubled her heartbeat. Tears welled in her eyes. She couldn't believe how much things had changed since that moment in the auditorium at Yale. They'd lost their safety, their freedom, and family. Her heart had more difficulty catching up.

Brandon had changed from the innocent boy she remembered, and he shouldn't be the same. He'd been in the coast guard, had men under his care and direction, which equaled responsibilities. Her attraction to him endured, underlying everything else, and she wondered if they might have ended up together. If they did, how would he feel about her inability to have children?

The monotone noise stopped. Seconds later, the table slid out of the machine.

"Everything looks good. The doctor will double-check everything," the nurse said.

That meant nothing, given the situation. Her blood type hadn't been addressed, at least not in her presence. Golden blood was beyond rare, and to have peculiar abilities along with the same blood type was impossible, something out of a movie. There weren't even fifty people on Earth with that typing. If her suspicions fell in line, Marx could have intentionally or unintentionally instigated the change.

"We'll take some blood every two weeks," the nurse said. "With this extraordinary type, having a few bags on hand is important, as you can imagine."

"What I can't imagine, is how my blood changed overnight, to begin with."

Their eyes met, and August caught a glimpse of fear, quickly hidden. The medical realties the nurse had witnessed scared her. The woman had no idea what was going on, either.

"From your test results, you are very healthy."

Except for being able to have a baby. "I know I'm not the only one with golden blood."

Her exhausted eyes indicated confusion. "There are about eight of you in the settlement right now. There could be more..."

Based on her meeting with Graysen, August wasn't sure what his threat meant, why his daughter living or dying would have any effect on her behavior and decisions. Did he think her ability to die and come back to life somehow changed his daughter's sad circumstance? It was odd how his daughter displayed the foresight prior to the experiment.

"You're free to go." The nurse shot her a small smile and closed her file. "A cart will be by in a few minutes to take you back to your living quarters."

August hated the woman a little less because she'd shown some humanity.

Moments later, August climbed aboard the next golf cart, taking in the route and markers along the way. Every now and then, they passed small work teams. None of the people appeared happy, and maybe they wouldn't be, even if they weren't inside Liberty.

How long until the shock of the climate tanking wore off and they realized they'd become little more than servants to a man with no right, except what he took from them?

She disembarked in front of the Mercury housing unit, relieved to see Lydia waiting for her inside the entrance. They hustled off to a quiet, yet still crowded space, where they could talk privately.

"How are you?" Lydia asked. "I saw John for about five seconds in passing. What are they doing with you in medical?"

August shrugged, not wanting to alarm her. "Something about my blood. What's going on here?"

"They brought in about twenty women so far today," Lydia said. "There's not enough room for everyone."

Food would obviously be an issue. She took a brief look at the room stuffed with the meager personal remnants of previous lives. Inevitably, things would be stolen or lost, and fights would break out. August thought about how Brandon and the Liberty Guard lived and grew irritated by the difference.

Lydia grasped August's arm and brought her attention to two guards circling the room. One of them had a photograph in their hand.

"Someone is probably sick," Lydia said. "They were in here earlier and took a woman out, one of the new ones."

The guards moved into a group of about ten survivors and plucked a woman forcefully by the arms. The woman held a teenaged girl to her chest. She screamed as they ripped the young woman from her grasp.

August closed her eyes for a second then opened them, the shock of the scene too much to comprehend, the latest in a long string of outrages. No one stepped in to help, which she understood. She wanted to help but couldn't after Graysen's threat. She had to lay low and stay out of trouble, at least for now.

As the guards dragged the teenager from the area, her mother's painful cries continued. Women circled her to provide comfort, to no avail.

No. The word repeated in August's head. This was not the way. The old world had been destroyed and the stress of the new environment affected them all with shortages. Everyone had suffered. Did the stress have to make them monsters? No matter what happened, there had to be more humane ways to deal with one another. She looked at Lydia, knowing she agreed. August gave her hand a squeeze, a silent pact between the women.

They would come up with a plan to make life better for everyone. Even if it meant dethroning Graysen Marx.

CHAPTER TWELVE

Outside, clouds scudded by, the red-hued daylight beginning to disappear along with August's energy. She sat next to Lydia in the dining area attached to the Mercury living quarters and stared at her dinner: a bowl of meat stew with chunks of potatoes, carrots, and peas with a slice of stale bread on the side.

"Protein. Looks yummy, doesn't it?" August said sarcastically. Her stomach twisted, thinking about how hungry she was and would be until things changed.

"Better than doing without, I suppose." Lydia gazed down at her meal and frowned. "I heard the Liberty Guard are having fresh fish and a tossed salad tonight."

August ripped the bread into pieces with anger and dipped one into the stew then popped it in her mouth. "They're the privileged ones who get three meals a day and other benefits. Graysen Marx's Golden Boys."

"I'm not surprised there aren't any women in the guard. Graysen's speech was a long-winded rant. Good for you for standing up against him. I wish I had the courage to do the same. If food needs to be rationed, then his soldiers need to give up a meal, like us. Especially with the new survivors that came in."

"Do you think our life at the armory was better? I mean, in here we're warm, fed, though it's nothing special, and I don't have to empty buckets of poop like at the armory. We have toilets that actually flush."

"It's better in some respects, I suppose. Not by much. John wants to leave. So do I. I'd rather take my chances on the outside than live like this. Look at all these women with bad hair cuts, including us, and the way we are treated. Like animals."

August scanned the room. Lydia was right. Their hairstyles made them all look like young boys. "What job did they give you?"

"I'm stuck in laundry doing the guard's uniforms and ours. At least I'm not in front of a sewing machine making these hideous uniforms. You?"

Things could be worse. Like being in the kitchen. August couldn't imagine washing the ton of dishes. "Research and Development." She paused. "He knows I died and came back to life. There are other survivors who developed unexplained superpowers since my father's experiment. That redheaded guard, Roman Shipley, reads minds. Another survivor sees things before they happen. Graysen said there were more. The nurse in medical said so, too."

Lydia placed her spoon down and leaned back in the chair. Her gaze traveled to a guard pacing the dining room with his rifle pointed at the floor. She kept her voice low, slightly above a hushed whisper. "Harper sees those weird auras. I'm worried about her. They took her away. Everyone else is accounted for."

A shiver drove through her. "Marx is studying people with abilities, keeping them hidden from the main population. Why? Where are they?"

Lydia shrugged. "They could be anywhere. At least we know where the others are. John is housed with Ian and Davis, in the Pluto unit. They're working in one of the steam plants in the north part of the settlement. It takes them almost an hour to get there through the underground tunnels. Snow and Noah are with Maggie and the girls living in the Saturn housing unit where all the children are kept." She looked at August. Worry wrinkled her features. "There aren't many children. With the sterilization order in effect, there won't be any more babies. How can he do this?"

Population control. "He believes he's doing the right thing to feed everyone who is already here. Instead, he's playing God."

"It's not right."

No, it wasn't right. There had to be another solution. August wasn't sure she wanted to tell Lydia about discovering she couldn't have children. Brandon had made it clear he didn't want to bring children into this world. She understood completely under the hostile conditions, inside and outside of Liberty. But what if things changed for the better? All she knew for sure was the whole situation sucked. "What about Henry? Is he with John?"

Lydia shook her head. "He got sick last night. It might have been something he ate. Guards took him to get checked out by a doctor. At least that's what they told John. No one has seen him since."

Uneasiness channeled through August. Had they taken Henry to the restricted area Brandon had told her about or somewhere else? She needed to talk to Brandon and see if he could find out anything.

As they continued eating, two more guards paraded into the dining area. The soft chatter in the room quieted, and heads lowered.

She was surprised to see more guards, considering there were only forty to fifty women eating. It wasn't as if they could make a break for it and walk out of the settlement. It was overkill, but Graysen Marx liked to show who was at the top, in charge—and it wasn't the Infinity Council after their compliance and silence in the assembly hall. They even appeared scared of the man.

Lydia bowed her head when one of the guards circled behind their table.

August did the same and lowered hers. She waited until he moved on before saying, "I found my brother. He's here. I'm going to see him tomorrow after my work shift. I don't know yet about my sister, Chloe—if she's alive."

"I'm happy for you. Not everyone has been lucky when it comes to their loved ones. The majority of the women in my housing unit have lost their children. Their stories are heartbreaking. It's a gift that you have your brother." Lydia blinked and looked away. "I would do anything to have Dax with me right now. Take what you can get. Cherish what you have left."

"Keep your head down in our presence," a guard yelled, standing behind a petite woman with doe-shaped brown eyes sitting at the table across from August and Lydia. He looked like a teenager, maybe sixteen or seventeen at the most, lacking any facial hair.

He snatched the woman by the hair and pushed her face down into her bowl of food. "That will remind you not to forget next time."

The guards burst out laughing, humiliating the woman more when she lifted her head and her face was covered with brown liquid.

August grasped the edge of the table with both hands, ready to get up and fight. A hand clamped down on her wrist, and Lydia shook her head, stopping her from drop-kicking the smirk off the guard's face.

"Clear the tables and get out of here. You are all done eating," he said, holding up his rifle as a show of power.

The men laughed again.

Was this the new normal? Men disrespecting women? This was Graysen Marx's new world. August felt sick. She didn't want any part of his world. She wanted to go back to the armory, wishing she had never allowed Brandon to bring her to Liberty. She should have fought harder, regardless of how she felt about him.

After filing one by one, putting their dishes in a large plastic tub filled with soapy water next to the kitchen, she followed Lydia out of the dining room. When they were outside of August's housing unit, screeching screams came from inside one of the pods. Lydia's face creased with disgust.

August turned to her, knowing the guards were about to drag someone else out and take them God knew where. She had an idea but first, she needed to speak with Brandon to make sure he was on board. "Can you find out from the others what time their work shift ends?"

Lydia smiled. "Sure. What do you have in mind?"

"We're going to stop this craziness together—all of us. Graysen Marx isn't going to know what hit him."

• • •

Inside the assembly hall, Graysen cracked the knuckles of his right hand, the tiny cuts on his fingers burning as he stretched the skin. He winced. Nothing he could attend to now. The Infinity Council filed past him and took their seats.

Citizens filtered in quicker than usual, due to the rather unfortunate circumstances surrounding the unscheduled gathering. He watched how they grouped together, took mental notes on who seemed upset versus who appeared more passive. Ever on guard, he watched for anything...unusual.

They all dared to grumble, the ungrateful lot.

The council would deal with offenses swiftly, and this particular problem involved individuals who'd banded together to pilfer food from crop storage. Catching one led to two, then four and soon, he had six thieves on his hands. Justice needed to be swift and effective. Everyone available needed to witness, even at the most inconvenient times. Missing the morning meal or an hour of sleep would reinforce the message they were about to receive.

Still, he didn't want to slice too deeply into productivity. More pressing, personal matters required his attention. His daughter needed him.

Ten minutes later, the guards closed the doors when the last resident had been let in, directing him to step onto the stage from behind the dirty-white curtain. He strode to the podium, the microphone already on and tested.

"You are here today to witness the judgment and punishment of six of your neighbors who were caught stealing food, literally *taking* food out of your mouths when there is precious little to spare." He waited, letting the understanding spread through the crowd. Some appeared shocked. Others stared at him with dead eyes. He had to reach them. "Bring out the thieves."

From the corner of his eye, he noticed Eve Petty squirm in her seat. If he could find a way to link the former mayor to the six lined up in front of their peers, he could put a new face, a more compliant personality on the council. He slid the idea away to mull over later. The six arrested stood, facing him and the council. Roman handed him a folded paper, detailing the criminal acts the four men and two women had been accused of.

Nodding, Graysen unfolded the paper and read the charges. "You are charged with theft of property from the food supplies of Liberty. Based on the testimony of those charged and witnesses to the act, you have been accused of theft. Turn and face your peers to hear your verdict and sentence."

The frightened individuals turned.

Mr. Wallen, the chairman of the Infinity Council, rose and stood next to him, to read the decision. Graysen took a deep breath and ingested the whole scene. The thieves could be anyone. There were undoubtedly more out there, who would do the same thing given the same chance. This lesson needed to be branded on their psyches. None of them possessed the golden blood. He'd made sure of it.

"Sir?" Mr. Wallen nudged him with his elbow.

"Yes, proceed." Graysen stepped back to allow the man to read the verdict.

The older man cleared his throat and leaned into the microphone. A screech of feedback heightened the suspense. "By a vote of five to zero, we find the accused guilty of theft of perishable goods vital to the settlement. We have agreed to leave the verdict up to Mr. Marx, to be given at his earliest convenience."

Hushed static ran through the crowd.

One of the accused women began to cry, and it almost touched Graysen's heart—if she hadn't taken food out of the mouth of a more worthy citizen.

Wallen turned and left him alone at the podium. Graysen peered at the crowd and let the anticipation rise.

He gripped the sides of the podium. "The punishment is banishment to be carried out immediately. This is the fate of anyone who takes food from the mouths of their neighbors."

Even though his decision shouldn't surprise anyone, it sent a shockwave through the room. Everyone knew the odds of survival outside ran between zero and ten percent.

Banishment equaled death.

Graysen walked off the stage and entered the small room adjourning the assembly hall. Roman knew what to do next, didn't question, stumble, or interfere. He just did his job and did it well. Graysen stood in the shadows, waiting to hear any dissent from the survivors leaving the hall. Today, he heard some angry undertones. Discontent. He'd dealt with the beast as a business owner. He wouldn't be able to appear to act independently now like he had in the past. He didn't have to hear their words to know their issues: housing, food, jobs, amenities.

Most people didn't know how to do without. Without plenty, or even enough. And especially without instant gratification. They'd have to get used to the way things were.

• • •

Graysen headed back to his living quarters on foot, Kenna foremost on his mind. She'd somehow loosened her IV sometime in the night, the sedative dripping onto her sheets rather than into her vein.

Her screams could have woken the dead.

The cuts on his hand were from a broken mirror she'd slammed him into. He didn't understand how she had the strength to charge at him. It took three of them, himself and two nurses, to get her back into bed.

Nearing his quarters, he hurried inside, locking the other matters out while he attended to his daughter. While they didn't have the medical wherewithal to help her, a possible solution had come into sharp focus.

The survivors with the golden blood.

Early medical reports indicated none of them began life with this phenomenal blood type. Somehow, they'd evolved. He now had eight such people identified, each with varying degrees of strange abilities, like Roman and Morgan Hill.

As he sat beside his sleeping daughter, he knew the answer lay with someone like Roman, someone who could do things with their mind, body or a combination to fix Kenna.

He would test all he could find, both inside and outside Liberty, to find the one person who could heal his daughter.

• • •

Through the clear panels in the corridor, the sky was the same dull red it had been for weeks. Brandon wasn't sure if it would always be that way or not. He hoped it wouldn't, that one day the environment would be back to the way it used to be. At least they had real sunlight. He missed the warmth of the sun on his skin as he stared at the terrain stretching as far as he could see. So much damn ice.

Scientists had warned the world would be like this if climate change wasn't addressed in time. If it wasn't for August's father's experiment, he doubted he would have been alive to see the next Ice Age. Now they were stuck thick in the middle of it.

While citizens, as Marx called them, made their way out of the assembly hall, he leaned against the wall outside of one of the exits and waited for August.

An ocean of grim faces walked by him, trudging mindlessly like an army of the living dead, their vacant eyes not connecting with his. If he hadn't been late leaving the comm-center, he would have been inside to see what Marx was up to. Two meetings within days was a waste of time, even though Brandon couldn't imagine what it took to keep Liberty running efficiently twenty-four hours a day. The enormousness of the settlement still left him breathless at times.

During his downtime, he'd discovered areas he hadn't seen yet: food processing and crop storage as well as where they kept the cows, chickens, and pigs. At times, life inside felt like he was living on another planet. Maybe he was, and all this was a dream. If only it was that simple.

Taking a deep breath, Brandon saw August talking with a few people he recognized from the armory in Icehaven. He was grateful they had found her. If they hadn't... He took a long look at her as she headed in his direction.

She appeared to have lost weight, not that she was very big to begin with. Slender and perfectly proportioned, he could see the difference in the thinness of her face. Guilt sat like a ton of concrete blocks on his chest. She was going hungry, along with the majority of the population, while he had enjoyed a hearty breakfast.

Then he spotted Shipley marching up behind her. He rushed past her, elbowing his way through the herd funneling out of the hall.

He stopped in front of Brandon and glanced over his shoulder at August, a few yards away. "Make sure she gets back to her job. Marx's orders. There's a problem in the comm-center. I need to go deal with that."

"The geofence went down again?"

"The cameras, too. We're going to have to make a parts run to Icehaven if the teams can't locate what we need in Providence. We're not going to have a choice. We need to keep the fence up to protect Liberty from those crazy gangs and to stop citizens from walking out," he added. "I'll talk to you later, after shift." He turned and disappeared, weaving in and out of the river of survivors.

"Why is he suddenly all friendly with you?" August asked accusingly.

Brandon waited until the mind-reader was long gone. He rolled his eyes. "He thinks we're friends."

"Are you?"

Her questioning look hurt him. Did she truly believe he could be friends with Roman Shipley? "Definitely not. We're on the same side, you and me. I was told to escort you to your job." He flashed a grin and ran his fingers across the top of her hand. "I'm happily obliging."

She finally smiled. There was a hint of something else behind her smile. A dark unknown. It wasn't happiness.

They walked to the main corridor and remained quiet. After finding a golf cart, they drove northeast to the lab.

"I have good news for you," Brandon said. "I checked the intake lists last night—"

"My father?"

"I'm sorry, August. No. I found Chloe." Relief sprang in her face, and her features relaxed. "She's housed in the Saturn housing unit with all the other children. She's okay."

"Oh, my God. Thank you." She leaned her head against his shoulder then straightened when another cart passed in the opposite direction. "I can't wait to see her and Luke this afternoon. I'm happy she's with Snow and Maggie. I wish I could have seen them sooner."

He slipped his hand into hers and steered around a corner past one of the steam plants. "I know."

"What about your parents? Did you find them?"

Brandon shook his head, digesting and accepting his loss, as hard as it was. "They weren't on any of the lists." He felt her exhale a long, trembling breath.

"I'm sorry. I always liked your parents. They were always kind to me."

He didn't want to think about his parents or what had happened to them. He hoped they hadn't suffered. "I almost forgot. I found Morgan."

"Is he okay?"

"I think so. I haven't talked to him yet. He's in a restricted dome, east of the research lab."

"The nurse told me yesterday there are eight with weird abilities that she knows of."

"I'm sure that's where Marx is detaining them."

She was silent, and he could tell she was absorbing everything.

"It's horrible here. You don't see everything that goes on. You won't believe what happened at the meeting." August took another breath and blew it out. "Marx caught a few survivors taking food. He's sending them outside with nothing other than their coats to fend for themselves. Women. Young men. Then yesterday at dinner, a guard put a woman's face into her meal for not bowing her head. I can't take the way we're treated, females in general. I doubt the male survivors are treated the same way. I won't put up with it. Others won't, either."

"August, I understand, I really do. But this place is our best hope in the long run."

"Is it? Not like this. We're going to do something about it." She glared at him. "Are you with us, Brandon? Or are you with Marx?"

He didn't have to think about it. He said he'd die for her. He meant it. "I'm always with you, August. No matter what."

Her gaze locked with his, and she smiled. "I need you to find someone else."

"Who?"

"A friend from the armory. His name is Henry. The guards hustled him out because he was sick. We're really worried about him." She gave him the man's physical description and last name.

"I'll see what I can find out tonight. He might be in one of the medical units." He stole a look at her when they pulled up outside of the research and development dome where the lighting appeared brighter. She hadn't slept well, judging by her heavy eyelids and her dull blue eyes, lacking their usual sparkle.

The outside of the lab was heavily guarded, more than some of the food areas. Brandon was taken aback. It didn't make sense. He counted eight men, four on each side of the wide entrance. It made him wonder what secrets were hidden inside. "What do you think they're doing in here?"

"I don't know, but I'll find out." Her gaze drifted to the guards. "Kind of heavy-duty authority presence. It's the first thing I noticed this morning."

"It is odd." He kissed her hand when it was safe from human eyes, not caring about the cameras. "Be careful. Please don't do anything to bring attention to yourself." Brandon paused. He couldn't tell her how he felt about her in case she didn't feel the same way. "I don't want anything to happen to you."

"Don't worry. I'll be careful because we're going to make sure things change here. We have to," August whispered, then got out of the cart.

At that moment, Brandon had a horrible sinking feeling in his gut, as if they were jumping off a ship into icy water, about to drown.

• • •

After her day shift ended, free of the stifling, tense environment of the research lab, August moved through the slow-moving crowd, followed the lab workers into the tunnels, then boarded a bus. She broke away from them upon arrival and headed toward the Venus living quarters where the men were housed, wondering if they lived any better than the women, or if only the guards did. She kept her head down. With her chopped hair and baggy coveralls, she didn't look any different than the Y chromosomes heading through the tunnel. The natural light had declined, adding long shadows to her camouflage.

She'd been careful to stay off the grid, do her job, not asking questions while keeping her eyes open. Minutes before she'd left the lab, she had risked a lot by stealing a pen and a piece of paper then scribbling a message on it to give to Snow and Maggie.

Working on a plan to change things here. Be ready.

No one mentioned the golden blood or special abilities of anyone kept under watch. The research team she'd worked with today had been tasked with analyzing the corn production, searching for methods to improve growth and quantity since direct sunlight was a thing of the past.

If the general population felt pressure from Graysen Marx, he apparently saved his tantrums for the group of scientists who'd been at Liberty since the day it opened. Those people lived under both intense scrutiny and pressure. They only spoke to one another about work, nothing personal, and the dread in the air affected every second of the day.

They lived in fear.

John hurried across the room to meet her at the entrance of the housing unit. "August? What are you doing here? You can't come in."

"My brother's alive. I just found out he's housed here. Can you find him for me? His name is Luke. He's eighteen."

John's eyes widened, and a soft smile curved his lips. "I'll try. Wait here."

Her gaze followed her friend as he went bunk to bunk then up the stairs, disappearing somewhere into the five other levels.

The living quarters didn't vary much from where she lived. The men were just as jam-packed inside as the women. The only difference appeared to be the number of warm bodies. There were more men than women from what she could see.

Minutes passed, and John walked toward her with her brother in his wake. A little over six-feet, Luke could be one of the thousands wandering around the settlement. Then his eyes met hers.

August jumped on him the second they stopped in the shadows. Tears clogged her throat.

He held her so tight she thought her ribs would break. "I'm sorry. I'm so sorry, August."

She released him and put her hands on either side of his face. He'd lost weight, looked skinnier than before. His hair looked a lot like hers but there was no mistaking his eyes, gray like their mother's. "There's nothing to be sorry for. Not one damn thing. I'm so glad you're alive—and Chloe, she's alive, too. Did you know?"

He nodded and held her hands. "They wouldn't let us stay together, said I had to go to work, that I only get to see her once a week."

"Once a week?" If a child had a family, they should be kept together. "Why?"

He shrugged. "Why do they do anything they do?"

"Control," John said. "They keep track of us every minute of every day."

Her heart sank. Chloe must be so confused. "Where are you working?"

"Biofuel processing. Crappy job. People hate it."

"What happened, Luke? Where were you? How did you get here?"

"I was lucky we were late. We managed to hide under one of the stairwells with a handful of others. We stayed there for the better part of a day and eventually had to dig out, took clothes from those who'd died. We were picked up by some Yale students and holed up with them in the shell of a frat house on the edge of campus. When we heard on the radio before everything went down about Liberty surviving, we traveled out here. Only half of us made it."

August shivered, hating the ordeal they'd gone through, even though she had no memory of her own journey. She hugged him again. "Do you want to come with me to see Chloe?"

Luke looked at John. "I can't. If I go any other time than when I'm supposed to, they'll take my visitation away."

"It's okay," August said, consoling him. "We're all doing what we have to do." She forced a smile. "I have to go for now. Get to know John. He reminds me a lot of Dad. He'll get you up to speed on where I've been and what we plan on doing."

"Did Dad make it?"

"I—don't think so." When she hugged him this time, she felt his body shudder, and she swore he was crying. August held him tighter, then released him and walked away, her purpose clearer than ever. After locating Chloe, she had to make life better for them. Blinking away tears, she made her way to the Saturn unit, less careful now.

• • •

Roman Shipley's large arm barred her from entering the housing unit. "What are you doing here?"

Dumbfounded, August stared at him. "Can't you just read my mind? Might be faster."

"You've never been here before."

"I just found out my sister's in there." She tried to push past him and failed. "Are you kidding me right now? Please, I thought she was dead. I need to see her."

"You need to petition the council for visitation. No exceptions. Only mothers are allowed to be with the children."

From the other side of the room, Snow waved her arms. "August!"

Noah was sitting on her lap, and Maggie and her girls smiled at her with hopeful eyes. Before August could blink, Noah barreled toward her like a streak, yelling to her with the name he'd made up. "Gusty!"

Roman's expression changed, softened, at the sight of the little boy, his tough exterior cracking for the first time since August had arrived. He did nothing to stop Noah from throwing his small arms around her knees.

"You have to let me see my sister. By the look on your face, you know what it's like to lose someone like Noah or Chloe, don't you?"

His eyes moved to hers. August didn't blink or look away. She continued to run her fingers absently through Noah's soft, straight hair. She felt Roman's big, strong soldier's resolve crumbling the longer she held on to the child.

"Five minutes."

Thank you she thought, over and over. She pried Noah from her legs, leaving him staring up at Roman.

"Play with me?"

The redhead grinned. "Sure thing, little man."

Clearly, there was a connection between the two. Interesting. Snow met her halfway across the room and grabbed her hand.

"She's over here, August. I knew you had a little sister and when she told me her name, I knew she belonged to you."

Leading August to the far side of the area, to a lower bunk, a small girl lay curled under a blanket. Long blonde hair flowed from under the edge, and August teared up.

Her hair wasn't cut. The children were allowed to keep their hair.

August kneeled on the bed. "Hey, Chloe. It's me, it's your big sis."

The blanket edged down. Blue eyes stared at her, her father's blue eyes. "August!"

For the second time in half an hour, emotion gummed up her throat. "Hey, Chloe Bowie."

The little girl tossed the blanket off and bounded into August's arms. After hugs and tears, Chloe giggled. August laughed for the first time in what felt like forever. Over Chloe's shoulder, she saw the mighty Roman Shipley crouched beside little Noah, showing him how to do tricks with his fingers and a loop of string.

The housing unit had a surprising number of toys, games, and books for the kids. Had the children been able to keep things they brought, or did the security teams also bring back these types of things when they picked up food, weapons, and medicine?

Chloe put her hand on hers, jerking her attention back. "Will you come see me, like Luke does? Pinky swear?"

August kissed Chloe's round cheeks. "Pinky swear. I'll be here every moment I possibly can. I'm so happy I found you."

"I try to be brave like you."

"You've been very brave. We're all okay, that's what matters. We'll figure everything else out."

Her smile vanished, and she frowned. "Daddy's not okay."

"No." August exhaled a wobbly breath. "It's a really hard time. We lost Daddy, and a lot of other people lost the ones they love, too. So be kind to everyone. They all feel like you do about losing Daddy."

She nodded and perked up. "Your friends are nice."

August glanced at Snow, grateful she and Maggie had been looking after Chloe.

"We didn't know she was your sister at first," Snow said.

Maggie laughed. "She finally told us her name. We've been trying to figure out how to get word to you."

Overcome by emotion, August stood and hugged Maggie first, then Snow. "Thank you for looking out for her. I saw Luke before I came over here. He looks terrible."

"This is a terrible place," Maggie said. "The meeting this morning. That stupid council doesn't mean anything. It's Graysen Marx running things, making decisions for all of us. It shouldn't be like that."

August kept her eyes on Roman, still occupied with Noah. Carefully pulling the folded paper out of her pocket, she passed the note to Snow. She had to be able to communicate with the women without the mind-reader knowing her every thought.

The woman glanced at it briefly then stuffed the paper in her cover-all's pocket.

August turned and hugged Chloe tight. "I'm going to find out about how to visit you. I'll be back as soon as I can. Promise you'll stay close to my friends, okay?"

Chloe gave her a pinched smile. "I promise."

Laying her hand on top of her sister's head, she kissed her cheek. "Be good." August stood and walked back to Roman, busy playing with Noah at the unit's entrance. Filling her mind with thoughts about Chloe and Luke, August cleared her throat.

His gaze searched her face, and she knew he was trying to read her thoughts.

"Are you done?"

August forced images of her family to the front of her mind and nodded.

"I'll get you signed up for visitation."

CHAPTER THIRTEEN

An hour before the curfew, August strolled into the library next to the assembly hall, excited they had a plan. It would be dangerous. Winner-take-all. All they needed was enough people and weapons to take down Graysen Marx. After seeing Roman interact with Noah, she knew some of the guards would be open to change. She was counting on it. Graysen's number-two-man was nothing more than a pawn in Marx's game.

August wandered through the library, a welcome change compared to her cramped living quarters. Not your typical library like at Yale, more like a large great room in a sprawling futuristic mansion with a wooden beamed and metal ceiling. August imagined during the day, even with the low light outside, the room would be bright and cheery. Anything was better than the confined, untidy and uncomfortable housing units.

She walked past a rectangular garden stuffed with tall cacti and plants with bright orange and yellow flowers. To the left, modern metal shelves lined one wall, filled with books and magazines from floor to ceiling. She spotted Rachel and Lydia sitting together on one of two extra-long brown leather couches next to a winding staircase leading to the second floor. August watched survivors shuffle in, then out moments later with a book in their hand.

August smiled at Rachel, her once shoulder-length dark brown hair gone. She was one of the few women who could pull off short hair with her chiselled features. "It's so good to see you."

She hadn't gotten the chance to get to know the woman very well at the armory, but she knew she could trust her after Rachel had given her all when the Sproggs had attacked the facility.

"Good to see you, too. I've only seen Davis once so far, on my way to work."

"How is he?"

"Doing okay. He's sticking close to John and Ian. It's weird being separated from the men like this after everything that's happened."

"Where did they assign you to work?" August asked.

The woman's hazel eyes darkened, and she frowned. "In the kitchen next to my living quarters. I guess it was the only logical choice for a waitress. I've never washed so many dishes in my life. It never ends."

August's gaze traveled the room in search of the cameras. The two she discovered appeared to be obscured by branches from the terra-cotta pots with trees and plants adorning the boundaries of the space. She turned her attention back to the women.

Lydia touched her arm. "Did you see Luke and Chloe?"

"I did." August sat next to the woman, her family reunion fresh in her mind. She wouldn't be divided from her family for very much longer if all went well. "They're both doing the best they can under the circumstances, thanks to John, Snow, and Maggie. I owe them a lot—I owe you guys a lot, too. If it wasn't for..."

She felt a hand on her shoulder and August turned to see Brandon, grateful it wasn't Shipley or Graysen Marx. A smile crept across her face, the sight of him touching her heart.

Lydia sat straight up. "What is he doing here?"

"It's okay. He's with me," August said, hoping to calm her fear.

Rachel glanced at her worried. "He's not one of us. He's a guard."

"I can vouch for him. Trust me, he's on our side," August reassured both women. "This is Brandon. I've known him all my life. This is Lydia and Rachel from the armory."

Brandon gave the women a nod, acknowledging them. He lowered his voice. "I don't have much time before my shift starts. I couldn't find your friend, Henry. He was taken to the restricted area and hasn't been seen since."

"What restricted area?" Lydia asked, puzzled.

"Apparently, it's an intake area for sick survivors coming into Liberty," August added. "Brandon, we need to get in there to see what's going on."

"I'll see what I can do. I was able to get four guns out of the armory without anyone noticing."

"Where are they?"

"Buried in the sunflower fields for now. No one would think to look there, since the crops have another month to go before they're harvested."

Perfect. August admired his commitment to the plan, commitment to her. "I spoke to Snow and Maggie. I'm sure they will be ready if we need them."

"It's an enormous risk," he said. "It could get us all killed."

Concern brewed inside her, and August grimaced. "We don't have another choice."

"I'm game. It's worth a try," Rachel said.

Lydia nodded in agreement. "Things must change if we are going to stay here. We have to do this."

"I'll continue working with John and the others. Be ready to go within the next twenty-four hours. How many more guns do you think we need?"

"At least a dozen," Rachel said, her hazel eyes shifting to a small group of women entering the library.

They lowered their heads when they saw Brandon. The uniform was a dead giveaway and so was the rifle he carried.

Brandon walked away and took a book off one of the shelves then returned. He held up the paperback to make it look good. "I'll find a way to deliver the weapons to everyone. Also, anytime you're around Roman Shipley, sing a song in your head or recite something. It blocks him from reading your thoughts." He squeezed August's shoulder. "I need to get to work. Be careful. We'll talk again soon."

After he left, August wished he could have stayed longer. The separation was hard on both of them.

Lydia and Rachel both grinned at her.

"Why are you two looking at me like that?"

Rachel's eyebrows raised. "He's a good-looking guy."

August felt her cheeks warm.

"He's in love with you," Lydia said. "You can see it in his eyes, the way he looks at you. He has the same glossy-eyed look my husband had. Brandon has always loved you."

He loved her? Why hadn't she seen it when others could? Brandon and she were close, always had been growing up and when they dated. Not once had he told her he loved her. Maybe he was afraid to. Guys were like that sometimes.

"What is it?" Lydia asked. "You're staring into space."

Apprehension took over, and August was afraid to share her secret. Even if she ended up with Brandon, it would never work. Finally, she blurted it out, part of her relieved to say it out loud to her friends. "During the medical testing here, I found out I can't have children."

Both women looked surprised. Neither said anything for a few seconds, taking in the news.

"I'm sorry. I can guarantee that boy loves you with everything he has," Lydia said. "Do you love him?"

August thought for a moment. She'd always loved Brandon, from the time they were little kids. "Yes."

"Then it's not going to matter if you can have a child or not," Rachel said.

Lydia grasped August's hand and held it. "She's right. You know my story with Dax. We had a wonderful marriage without children. If Brandon truly loves you, then he'll accept you the way you are. But August, you need to tell him."

•••

Mornings always proved the hardest time of Graysen's day. Although he provided a separate medical entrance to Kenna's room for the doctors and nurses who looked after her, their arrival always woke him. This morning started no different. He groaned and climbed out of bed, details of the day's agenda already vying for his attention.

After showering and dressing, allowing enough time for the doctor to evaluate Kenna and administer the day's medications, he slipped into a pair of gray casual pants, a long-sleeved navy shirt, and his loafers. Graysen steeled himself to see if anything had changed for his only child overnight.

In her bedroom, he kissed her forehead and noticed she felt hot. "What's going on? How high is her temperature?"

The doctor sighed. "It's only slightly elevated, a hundred and one. It could be the exertion from her outburst. I don't want to panic yet. If her temperature rises this afternoon, I'll start her on some precautionary antibiotics."

Graysen held her pale hand and let the older man get back to work. His daughter wasn't going to improve on her own, he knew that much. Even if he had every second of the day to focus on her health, he would still come up empty. Every attempt he made felt like reaching into the unknown. His digital watch beeped, reminding him of his meeting with Roman. He let go of Kenna's hand and left her behind.

Stopping in the galley kitchen, he flipped on the coffeemaker, knowing the man never turned down caffeine. Roman needed to be wide awake. They had important things to discuss.

As the rich aroma of coffee filled the air, Roman knocked on the door and Graysen let him inside. "Coffee's ready. Help yourself. Then join me at the table."

He waited patiently while the redhead poured a cup of black coffee and sat across from him. "What am I thinking?"

Roman stared into his eyes and a broad smile grew on his face. "It's time to take care of the Sproggs. You had a chance to look over my plan?"

"Yes. Well done. Pick your team. I trust you to pull the right people together." Graysen sipped his sweetened coffee. "Be careful. You never know if any of them are...like you."

"Roger that."

He set his cup down and folded his hands around the warm ceramic. "Go early, be mindful of your time because I want you to make a stop at the National Guard Armory on the way back to get the stockpile of weapons in the basement. We need to bring as much as we can in one trip—I don't want any of the renegades getting their hands on anything that can ultimately hurt us."

"How much is at the armory?'

"I'm not exactly sure. No one will say. Ask August Madison or one of the others. It must be quite a haul. Expect the unexpected. Did you pick up my morning reports and read through them?"

"Yes, sir." Reaching into his back pocket, Roman pulled out a sheaf of folded, color-coded papers. "Do you want the short version?"

"Yes. Only what requires my immediate attention." He didn't expect there to be anything urgent until the man pulled out stapled green papers. He'd always used green for energy reporting.

"Crop production is steady at the moment. Due to the additional influx of survivors, supplies are likely to dip in the coming two weeks but," he slid the papers across the table, "biofuel supplies are dropping faster than anticipated."

Graysen skimmed the report. Numbers never lied. He hadn't been cautious about sending the guard out on missions because he wanted to accumulate manpower and munitions. Then there were the unexpected excursions, like the Sproggs stealing one of their vehicles and chasing after August Madison. He grimaced. "Ramp up hours and production and lower the working age from sixteen to thirteen. When you get back, we'll need to plan out a trip to Boston for early next week."

"Boston, sir?" Roman paused for a second. "Oh, I see. One of your companies has an underground biofuel storage facility near the harbor."

Graysen smiled. He almost didn't need to converse with him, except the kid respected him too much to dig too deeply. "We'll have to plan carefully. There's too much unknown between here and there. We'll also have to set aside enough fuel to make the trip. Staff the mission correctly to collect the fuel and protect the supply upon return."

"Understood."

Always cautious about broaching the next subject, he took a sip of his coffee. "Is there a report from research and development about the golden blood?"

"Not yet, sir. There are rumors running rampant through the living quarters, though. The best one I've heard is people like me are aliens, that the environmental change wasn't our doing. They're saying it's an invasion from outer space."

Graysen laughed, loving the imagination. He hadn't expected this kind of explanation. He probably should have. "People are so inventive. No, this disaster was definitely manmade. Something in the fallout caused biological changes, and I think we're only beginning to see them. Did they treat you well when you underwent testing?"

"Yes, of course, sir."

He treaded carefully and tapped his index finger on the tabletop. "Have you had any further interaction with Madison, or discovered any new information from Church about her?"

"Her siblings are here—which you already knew. She came to the Saturn unit last night to see her sister. I learned later her brother is in the Venus residence. He works in the biofuel plant."

His shoulders tightened. "Did you route her for visitation?"

Roman nodded.

"Control her access until we learn a bit more. Get the details of the arrangement to me once it's in—."

"Sir?" the redhead pointed. "Someone to see you."

Graysen craned his neck to see the doctor, then turned back to Roman. "We're done here. I expect a full report when you return."

He didn't sit long enough to see his second-in-command leave as he hustled toward the doctor. "Is she all right?"

"She's talking coherently. I thought you might want to hear what she's saying."

He pushed past the doctor and took his seat at Kenna's bedside. Ever since a fraction of what she rambled about turned out to be prophetic, he listened. The biggest hurdle was deciphering it.

"Through the tunnels...through the tunnels...like rats, rats dancing..." she rasped.

"Is someone writing this down?" he said, frantic he wouldn't be able to remember everything.

"Yes." The nurse showed him a recorder.

He leaned closer and continued to listen.

"Salute, salute all the king's men, all the queen's ladies...running in the tunnels...running for their lives through a river of blood."

Graysen had no idea what any of it meant, if it meant anything at all. All he knew was he hated the sounds, the noisy digital assessment devices, a constant reminder of the illness crushing into his daughter's brain. He sat beside her and listened to the insane ramblings, evolving into bits and pieces of the fairy tale *Cinderella* her mother used to read to her every night when she was small.

A light bulb went off in his mind. There was one thing they hadn't addressed. Did Kenna have golden blood? The last time her blood had been tested was weeks before the experiment. His pulse accelerated. Could she? "Take some blood and give it to Dr. Higgs in the research lab for testing. She'll know what to do." The doctor, who worked only with Kenna, didn't understand.

"Why?"

"Do it." Something strange had happened to his daughter beyond her illness.

The words she'd spoken before the event in her painful haze had proved true and ultimately saved their lives. Perhaps the tumor had started something that the dramatic change in climate had completed? Her life had to have been spared this long for a reason. It was a long shot. He'd try anything, unlock any door, peer around any dark corner, turn over any boulder if she could only be made well and whole again.

Tears formed in his eyes as she rambled on, unintelligible, writhing in her hospital bed. He again pledged anything and everything, including the lives of every man, woman, and child in Liberty, for her to rise from her sickbed, to hear her laugh again.

CHAPTER FOURTEEN

The ongoing foot traffic in and out of the Research and Development lab was staggering, as if Graysen Marx had suddenly lit a fire under everyone. August shuffled papers around on the desk to make room for a stack of newly delivered handwritten reports that needed to be entered into the computer. It seemed like a waste of time. If Liberty's infrastructure failed, putting a bunch of information on a computer or flash drive would mean nothing, if no one could read it—or if there was no one left to read it.

It was Marx's way of keeping his workforce busy and under his thumb. She had counted twenty other women in the lab doing exactly what she was doing, data entry. Their eyes never once connected with hers.

Now everyone knew who she was, thanks to Graysen, that her father was responsible for their loved ones' deaths. Would the people blame her? Would her life be in danger? August tried not to think about it.

Their pristine leader had already been in the lab twice before ten o'clock. The first time, he had talked with a couple of scientists about numbers and tweaking genetically modified plants for faster crop yields. During the second visit, he yelled at one scientist, Dr. Rida Higgs. Then the door slammed shut behind her, and August couldn't hear the rest of the conversation.

She had learned yesterday that Dr. Higgs had met her father at one of the climate change conferences held in Washington, DC. She was a nice woman, soft-spoken, who walked with a slight limp. She was around the same age as her father, fifty-five, with keen brown eyes. The doctor had been one of the first scientists at Liberty when the Mars prototype was in its beta stage. She spoke highly of August's father and his brilliant experiment, even though things hadn't gone according to plan. August missed him, wished he was here. She cursed God for everything he'd taken from her. Part of her still held out hope that her father was alive, knowing in her heart it wasn't true. Acceptance wasn't easy, tearing her down every day. He would never put up with Graysen Marx's idiotic games.

Determined to keep her mind focused on other things, August picked up a report titled: *Plant Microbiomes and Microfluidics-based Applications for Food, Agriculture, and Biosystems* and read it over before inputting the data.

She understood what Graysen was trying to do. It was ironic. Running Liberty with an iron fist, as if humans were his test subjects, at the same time he was behind the scenes working to find a way to produce food quicker, and more of it, to feed everyone. The man was a walking contradiction. August didn't care. The long-term impact of the climate change, personal losses, combined with his ridiculous mandates put enormous pressure on everyone, particularly the thousand or so women who were forced to give up their right to have children. It wouldn't be much longer before Graysen Marx learned he wasn't in charge anymore.

August saved the report and closed the document window. The mouse slipped and hit something else on the screen, a different icon.

The folder stared at her like an extra special gift, waiting for her to check the contents. She peered at the others busy keying in data like slaves. August double-clicked the graphic and kept an eye out by peering over the top of the monitor for anyone who might stop her. The icon opened into an image of a yellow folder. She double-clicked it. A password box popped up on the screen. Even if she could figure out the password, would alarms blare and she'd be tossed out in the cold, or worse? Her hand shook as she grasped the mouse and thought for a moment. On a hunch, she typed in the word *Liberty* and hit enter. Nothing. In a last-ditch effort, she typed in *Kenna.* Documents burst open on the screen. At first, she thought they were about Graysen's daughter until she skimmed through them. Instead, they were about the experiment. Her heart pounded and sweat beaded her brow as she read.

Everything about that day at Yale slammed into her full-force. The planet-hacking. *Millions of tons of sulfur dioxide particles coated with Amexotrate* to protect the environment had been *pumped into the upper atmosphere by thousands of high-altitude aircraft...particles that block the sunlight...* in a joint effort, coordinated by every country in the world. She kept reading. *Jeopardize crop yields...droughts...acid snow...extreme weather.* The scorching snow everyone had mentioned.

She found another report. Her heart thumped faster with each new tidbit of information. *Increased chance the aircraft dispensing the particles could crash...their electrical systems affected.* The high-pitched noise she had heard in the auditorium. It was a plane coming down, maybe multiple airplanes. A gasp escaped her lips. Her gaze lifted, and she made sure the women were still working. Keyboard keys continued to click at lightning speed.

Stunned by what she had learned, August searched the files for information on the chemical used to coat the particles when she discovered a scanned copy of one of her father's handwritten notes. *The Pentagon had attempted to alter Vietnam's weather for military purposes in 1971 by seeding clouds with silver iodide crystals.*

They had used weather as a weapon? Nothing surprised her anymore.

She kept digging and located a report about the Amexotrate manufactured by Paragon, the company owned by Graysen Marx. She skimmed the risks and rare side-effects to humans: *Can affect the liver...spontaneously change blood types in some individuals...deformities in unborn children...PML...a rare brain infection that usually leads to death or severe disability...death.*

The golden blood.

It was the chemical that changed her blood, the blood in others. But that didn't explain the odd paranormal powers or why it didn't affect everyone. Another thought hit her like a ton of bricks. Did he know what was going to happen before the world changed?

August glanced up again and noticed Roman standing outside the doorway to the lab, talking to another guard. The sight of him brought her stomach to her throat. She swallowed and quickly closed the folder, then backed out of the icon folder. Glancing at the report she'd already typed up, she read it mentally to keep him from reading her thoughts.

He marched to the front of her monitor. "What are you up to?"

Her heart stopped, and she tensed for a second.

He spun the screen around so he could see what she was doing.

"Working. What do you want?"

His eyes shifted from her to the screen. "How many truckloads of weapons are in the basement at the armory?"

"I don't know. Why?"

"Marx wants us to get them after we take care of the Sproggs. I need to know how many trucks to take with us."

She kept reading, not allowing him into her head. "Is Brandon going with you?"

"Don't worry. I'll look after him for you."

August looked up and wanted to roll her eyes at him, but didn't. He had a stupid grin on his face. "Ask John. He would know. I need to get back to work. I'm already behind." She snatched the next report from the pile and started reading and typing, ignoring him.

He got the message fairly quickly and stomped out of the lab.

It looked good on him, unable to read her thoughts.

August leaned back in the chair and exhaled to quiet her nerves. She stared out at the morning sky, the color of beet soup, through the lab's clear dome. Thoughts circled her head. Her father's experiment. The chemical that had altered her blood. If Brandon was going after the Sproggs, she hoped nothing would happen to him. She needed him, more than he knew.

They needed him.

Every single survivor at Liberty did.

All she could do was wait until Brandon returned. He was the only one who could get the weapons they needed to overthrow Graysen Marx. Without guns, they didn't have a chance in hell.

• • •

By mid-morning, the Liberty Guard team had finally rolled out of the settlement and headed toward Icehaven. Their mission: take out the Sproggs. Despite the simple plan the redhead had laid out, too many elements had been left to chance. Brandon would be lying if he said his butt wasn't clenched a little tighter. Always happened when they left the relative safety of Liberty. Not that *that* place was safe, either.

He rode shotgun beside Shipley. Eight vehicles trailed behind them, transporting an expert team of twenty soldiers, including two crew members from the *Eagle* Brandon didn't know very well. Time ticked by, ten then thirty minutes, the landscape scantly changing from the depressing bumpy whitish-gray dunes of debris and ice.

"I think I saw something—movement," Shipley said a half-hour later. He shifted forward in the seat to get a better view.

"How many?" Brandon skimmed the horizon for a speck of color or motion.

"Not sure." Shipley gripped his walkie-talkie from the dash and spoke into the receiver. "Possible detour ahead. Follow my lead."

A chorus of "Roger that" barked back through the static, everyone on high-alert.

Brandon blinked and saw a figure move on the distant ice hill. He tapped Shipley on the shoulder and pointed. "There. See it?"

After a moment, the redhead nodded. "Camouflaged and definitely moving. If we've seen him, he's seen us. Bleeders, I'm betting. They live in igloos. We need to circle the hill." He picked up the walkie-talkie again and directed the rest of the detachment.

Within ten minutes, their vehicles idled in a semi-circle at the base of what appeared to be a giant snowy ice drift. A small, shadowed hole was visible at the base. The entrance, Brandon figured.

"Check out those paths." Shipley shifted the beams of the truck's headlights to catch the indentations leading in and out of the structure.

Sweat dripped between Brandon's shoulder blades and sent a chilly blast through his body.

Shipley reached for his rifle in the back seat and said, "Let's go. You and me."

Brandon snatched his M16 and together, they cautiously climbed out of the truck, their eyes sweeping the area.

While the two cautiously headed down the tricky slope toward the entrance, the others exited vehicles and covered them from their positions.

Within a few feet of the hole, Shipley held up a fist. "They're watching us."

Brandon stopped. At the same time, a single gunshot rang out.

They dropped flat on their bellies.

Another shot. Two more semi-automatic bursts. Then deafening quiet.

"All clear!" one of their men yelled from behind them.

Shipley wasted no time getting to his feet. Brandon got up and followed him. They slipped through a short tunnel opening into a single, large room, guns raised at chest level.

The walls had been built with stacked manmade bricks of ice and snow. Brandon inspected a circular firepit, reinforced with steel plates and grates, like a barbecue grill. Flames would feed straight up into a hole in the top of the igloo, roughly the same size as the entrance.

Shipley kicked aside piles of blankets, pillows, and garbage. "See if there's anything worth taking. Make it quick."

While the redhead searched one side of the interior, Brandon picked through the other, pocketing a worn paperback copy of *Moby Dick*, a Coast Guard favorite, a stash of protein bars and an assortment of shot-sized energy drinks. They met in the middle. "There's nothing else useful."

"Toss everything into the fire pit. I'll light it up."

Refusing to think about destroying the items of the people who lived here, Brandon followed orders. When they were done, he exited the tunnel, smelling the smoke before he made his way back outside.

Without another word, they climbed into their vehicle. Brandon handed him one of the energy shots and a protein bar, then tore one of the bars open for himself. Nervousness filled him about the upcoming confrontation.

"I don't feel great about it, either," Shipley said, reading his mind. "Marx wants the Sproggs' leader out of the way. These guys are nuts. You never know what they'll do. As a military man, you know you can plan, but you can't account for or control everything."

His words didn't make Brandon feel better. All he could do was wait and see what was going to happen.

Forty minutes later, they parked about an eighth of a mile from the peak behind one of the snow-covered, ice-jutting hills leading to the summit, to the caves. They would have to go the rest of the way on foot.

When they arrived, they slung M16s over their shoulders and strapped a sidearm to their legs. They hoisted bulky black backpacks in place, filled with items they might need: climbing equipment, spikes for their shoes, MREs and emergency warming packs, in case they got stuck outside for a length of time.

Brandon rolled his fleece-lined ski mask down over his face and pulled the Ghillie suit's hood over his head. He fell into the second of four lines to maneuver up the face of the peak. While they stopped short of hooking themselves to lines, they stayed close, each man stepping in the previous man's footsteps.

Minutes into the climb, the wind howled, lashing snow and ice at them. Brandon squinted, scarcely able to see the outline of a man in front of him. He planted one foot in front of the other, leveraging his weight against the crosswind, only to have the direction shift throw him off-balance. They hadn't prepared for this, the slick dance with an icy beast.

A deafening explosion sounded to his right, on the far line of men. *A land mine or an IED.*

Chunks of ice and rock tore away from the side of the mountain, steamrolling down, pelting the team. Brandon stopped. Shouts then painful screams pierced the air and reverberated through the valley below.

A split second later, a hail of bullets rained down from the mid-level crevices above them. Large ammo, probably fifty-cals. Bullets lodged into the man ahead of him, slamming his writhing body backward, protecting Brandon as he fell. He lay under the lifeless form, the undeniable whistle of grenade and rocket launchers rattling his eardrums, one after another, sounding like a sick, disjointed symphony.

Then silence. Except for the wind.

Dragging in a breath, then another, he stayed still under the weight of a dead man.

"We're coming for you!" a booming male voice said, amplified by some kind of device, maybe a bullhorn. "You dogs run back with your tail between your legs—if you still got your legs—tell Graysen Marx we're bringing the show to Liberty!"

Brandon heard Shipley's voice.

Retreat! Retreat!

He grunted, hastily wriggled out from under his protection, and jumped to his feet, skidding down the mountain as if skiing without skis.

Another IED exploded. This time closer.

Panic rose in Brandon's chest. He zig-zagged, half-sprinting, half-sliding. Snipers took potshots at anyone they could see, ice spray spurting in the air in front of him. Once he was at the bottom, he ran to the back of one of the vehicles and squatted, keyed-up, his heart racing, wondering who else made it back alive.

By the time the men returned, stunned and scared, they'd lost half their number.

No one said anything as Shipley reorganized them into the vehicles. "We still have work to do."

Grieve quickly. Move on.

What little washed-out ruddy daylight remained wouldn't last long. They needed to haul ass.

Alone in one of the trucks, Brandon revved the engine then floored the gas pedal, following his unit leader in the lead vehicle. Tires spun as the Sproggs continued to snipe at the trucks.

Brandon ducked down in the seat enough to still see over the dashboard, the sound of spinning metal boring into sides of the vehicle.

He pounded the steering wheel with both gloved fists. What a goddamn suicide mission. Who in their right mind sent twenty soldiers, no matter how elite they used to be, up a mountain to overtake a force with advanced weapons?

Marx had planned this. The man had known the odds, sacrificing his men to see who had the bigger balls. A death mission. He didn't care about them, only how they could serve his needs. Exactly the reason he and August needed to carry out their plan immediately. Shoving his thoughts aside, Brandon drove, focused on reaching the armory in Icehaven in one piece.

• • •

Brandon and Shipley arrived at the armory before the rest of the team. They wasted no time heading inside, sidestepping the rudimentary alarm system, and kept their weapons readied, although they didn't anticipate anyone would be inside.

As Brandon made his way through the ice tunnels and down the stairs with Shipley at his back, he came face-to-face with a large man wrapped in layers of animal pelts, wearing a bird mask, the beak extending a half-foot from his nose. He growled at them like a rabid dog, catching both men off-guard.

Shipley charged past Brandon and rammed the intruder to the floor. Rolling back and forth, Shipley got the upper hand and used an armbar to choke his opponent.

Upstairs, two shots fired, followed by, "Clear!"

Shipley rolled off the man and jumped to his feet. "Nice mask." He slapped Brandon's shoulder, as if nothing had happened with the bird-looking man. "You take that room." He pointed. "I'll take these two."

Stunned by his unit leader's swift movement, Brandon walked through the concrete block hallway leading to a steel door. He pried it open then pulled his flashlight from his pack and shut the door behind him, fairly certain he'd found the stockpile.

Floor to ceiling heavy-duty military footlockers greeted him, the kind enlisted soldiers used to ship their gear to themselves on deployment. The containers weren't locked. He lifted the lid of the closest one and heaved a sigh of relief.

It was mainly small arms, not enough light to see exactly what he had. The pistols had been stored with the proper caliber bullet. Sliding his backpack from his shoulder, he hid four black 9mm handguns and equal boxes of fifty-count bullets inside. When he heard Shipley hollering for him, his footsteps nearing, Brandon added two cleaning kits and zipped his bag closed, heaving it back into place between his shoulders.

"In here. I found it," he yelled, pushing his plan full steam ahead to steal more weapons from the army at Liberty. Instead, he thought about how damn long it would take to get all of this out of here and how tired they'd all be once they returned to the settlement.

CHAPTER FIFTEEN

Seven hours after leaving Liberty, Brandon and the team returned, exhausted and shook up. The sky didn't look any different than the night before, still the same drab deep cherry-red, deepening to almost black. He helped unload the large weapons cache from the armory inside the guard's south entrance, his muscles aching from the heavy load of each wooden crate. Everyone was quiet as they worked, other than the occasional grunt and groan, their minds back at the peak. They'd lost ten men, a loss each of them needed to process in their own way.

Once the munitions were unloaded, they transferred the crates through the tunnels by trucks to the armory near Marx's living quarters.

"You start recording everything," Shipley said to Brandon. He looked at the rest of his team, their expressions sullen and strained. "We'll eat supper first and come back to finish the job."

Brandon knew he was the newest member of the team and had expected to stay behind. He removed his backpack and set it on the floor. "Sure." He started singing a song in his head to block the mind reader.

Shipley laughed and headed to the door. "You should sing that song out loud. I like that one."

"I would, but I can't sing worth a crap. Just trying to entertain myself until you get back."

After he left, it was Brandon's chance to grab some more weapons. The camouflage suit was comfortably baggy, two sizes too big to allow free motion under combat situations. The four weapons he'd stashed in the sunflower crops, he had to hide in his underwear and socks. At least this time, he could carry more to various locations in the settlement with ease for everyone involved in the plan to take control of Liberty.

The cameras were a huge challenge. He'd figured out they didn't record three feet of the perimeter of each of the domes. A little adjustment at the main panel in comm-center made it easier to hide in the shadows without being detected.

He lifted one of the smaller crates they'd just brought in and placed it on top of the other boxes at the edge of the wall out of the camera's view. With a clipboard and pen in one hand, Brandon pocketed one of the grenades and recorded the number left in the case. He moved to the next crate and found six M107 semi-automatic sniper rifles. The weapons wouldn't be of any help. After lifting another crate and setting it on top of the sniper weapons, he cracked the box open. Inside, he found a dozen Sig Sauer P229s, M-9 pistols, and ammunition. With his back to the cameras, Brandon unzipped his suit and stuffed two guns into the two inside pockets. Carefully, he turned, pretending to jot down numbers on the clipboard and pocketed another M-9 and ammunition. He pivoted back to the crate then faced right and slipped another gun into the other pocket next to the grenade.

He'd already talked to John before he'd left for Icehaven. A diversion would be set up east of the biofuel processing plant at nine pm, two hours before curfew. In the meantime, the cameras would go down for an hour, thanks to a supporter inside the comm-center. This would be a coordinated effort to help make Liberty what it should be. The majority of the guard would head to the diversion, leaving Brandon, August, and the others to grab the weapons from the sunflower fields and the guns he was going to hide in the library when he was done here.

They'd storm Marx's living quarters. From there, they'd have to play it by ear. All he could do was hope that once everyone realized what was going down, they'd jump on board.

His heart pounded as he bent and picked up his backpack, tossing it on a shelf where the teams kept their bags, next to the crates. Dipping his hand inside he pulled out the energy drinks and bars and then the ammo and weapons, unsure where he was going to put them. He dropped the energy bars and bent again to shove the guns and ammo into his boots, then zipped up his suit. He was risking his life for August...for everyone.

For the next thirty minutes, he busied himself tallying and recording the weapons until the door opened and the rest of his team walked in, looking full and satisfied.

"Get to work," Shipley said to the men.

Brandon handed the clipboard to him, his stomach in knots. "What's for supper?"

"Fish, salad, potatoes."

"Chocolate chip cookies, too," one of the men said. "Bravo team had a good run."

"Great. I'm starving."

Shipley passed the clipboard to another team member. "Get lost. We'll finish up then I'll report to Marx. He isn't going to be happy."

Repeating the word "cookies" over and over in his mind, Brandon pointed to the stack of boxes on the other side of the doorway on the way out. "Those haven't been counted yet." He wasn't a foot outside the door when he heard the redhead say, "Hey, Church."

With his pockets weighted down, he felt his pulse ramp up like a jet engine. He couldn't get caught. His legs froze, and he closed his eyes for a second then opened them. "Yeah?"

"Don't tell anyone about the cookies," Shipley said. "We don't want to cause a riot."

Brandon's shoulders slumped as he exhaled the breath he was holding. "No problem."

After getting into one of the golf carts parked outside the armory, he drove to the underground tunnel, hoping the cameras hadn't picked up anything inside the armory or anyone stopped him with metal clanking inside his suit.

• • •

August paced in front of the bookshelf in the library, waiting for Brandon to return, her stomach a tangled mess of worry. Raising her arms in the air, she stopped and shook the nervous tension from her shoulders. Lydia and Rachel sat quietly at a small round table next to the staircase, thumbing through outdated fashion magazines.

"What time is it?" August asked Lydia.

The woman checked her watch. "Quarter to nine. Don't worry, he'll be here."

The plan was going down in fifteen minutes. She needed Brandon. They couldn't do it without him.

Seconds later, he stopped inside the doorway, freshly showered, his light brown hair still damp, with the paperback he'd taken earlier and his M16 in his other hand. He walked inside as if he'd just dropped by, a ruse for the cameras, for Graysen Marx.

August met him at the bookshelf, happy to see him.

He smiled at her.

"Did everything go okay?"

"Not really. Tough day. Talk about it later. The guns and ammo you need are all in here. I delivered the ones from the sunflower fields to John, Ian, and Davis, as soon as I got back. I couldn't get in to see Snow and Lydia. Too heavy a guard presence for some reason. There are weapons in the flowering plants and..." He pointed to the garden in the center of the room. "...in there."

"Good," August said while they both pulled out a book and looked at them then put them back. "I'm glad you're back. I missed you."

His hand slid into hers. "I missed you, too."

"Hey, Church?"

He released her hand and turned.

A tall, thick-set guard with cropped black hair stood in the doorway.

August's body tensed. "Who's that?"

Brandon's eyes lit and he grinned. "A supporter of the cause."

While he met with the man, August hung back, not wanting it to look like they were all in cahoots for whoever was watching. As the men talked, her gaze traveled to Lydia and Rachel who continued to flip magazine pages, glancing at her and then to Brandon.

Brandon said something to him, and the man disappeared.

August pulled out a book and met him by the staircase so the women could hear.

"That was Petty Officer Jackson Moss from the *Eagle*. Good guy. Works in the comm-center. He destroyed two computer chips in the main camera system, replaced them with non-functional ones. As of now, the cameras are dead. Will be down for quite some time until they can locate new parts."

"Are you sure you can trust him?" Rachel asked.

"I trust him with my life."

Concern buzzed through August. The more people involved who knew what they were going to do, the odds increased of getting caught.

As if reading her mind, he said, "Don't worry. We've got this."

She hoped he was right. One word to anyone who worshiped Graysen Marx, and they'd all be in a lot of trouble.

"Moss also gave me this." He handed August a keycard. "It's a master. He scooped it from one of the higher-up guards."

August stared at the thin black and silver piece of plastic. *The key to Graysen Marx's kingdom.*

"I want you to keep it. If anything happens to me—"

"Don't be silly. Nothing is going to happen. We stick to the plan, and we'll all be fine."

"If it does go south, free Morgan and the others. Take care of Marx, then find out what is going on in the restricted area."

The thought of anything happening to Brandon tore her up inside. She couldn't deal with another loss, not after her father. Reluctantly, she slid the card into her coverall pocket.

He checked his watch then looked up at her and blew out a lengthy breath. "Should be any time now."

August's pulse sped up. Rachel and Lydia stood, prepared to get the weapons.

An alarm blared throughout the settlement. August covered her ears. She didn't know there was an alarm system. By the startled look on Brandon's face, he didn't, either.

On cue, he helped everyone get the guns and ammunition, speedily digging into the plant's moist dirt with both hands.

With bullets and pistols in their pockets, they were ready.

Brandon ran first to the door and looked left than right.

Golf carts whizzed by, filled with Liberty Guards.

Two guards on foot stopped in front of him. "You better hurry. We've got trouble."

"What's going on?"

"A fire east of the biofuel plant. A note was found a few minutes before in one of the housing units. A possible rebellion."

"Get going. I'm on my way. I'll head up from the west side, try to get behind the fire," Brandon said to the men.

The guards turned and high-tailed down the corridor.

Three more carts sped by, filled with men.

August's heart dropped, and so did her jaw. Someone had found the message she'd given to Snow.

Brandon turned and looked at her. He shook his head. "We can't go now. Not with the note they found. They'll be on high-alert, know we're coming."

August frowned and saw the disappointment in everyone's faces. This was her fault. She cursed under her breath.

"Bury the weapons. Make it look like nothing's been touched. Go," Brandon said.

After hastily hiding the guns and ammo, they regrouped by the bookshelf, the alarm still wailing, giving August a headache between her eyes. "You and Rachel might as well go back to the living quarters."

Lydia raised an eyebrow. "What are you two going to do?"

A long pause ensued.

"August and I will go to the restricted area while everyone is busy at the fire. We might as well take advantage of the situation with the cameras down and most of security in the east section of the settlement. We'll try again tomorrow. Meet here. The same time. If you can, tell the others."

"Be careful," both women said and left the library.

"Let's see if we can find a cart."

August's stomach knotted like a hard rock. She followed Brandon, feeling the weight of the world on her shoulders. If she hadn't messed up with the note, right now they would have Graysen Marx and be on the verge of starting a new life at Liberty, one they could be proud of.

• • •

Twenty minutes after leaving the library, August and Brandon raced up two flights of stairs, two at a time. Shoving the door open with both hands, August noticed the empty west corridor. "There aren't any golf carts."

"We'll have to walk it," Brandon said, shouldering his rifle. "It's not too far."

"I shouldn't have given Snow the note. Now, she and Noah could be in danger. Maybe I should have taken the chance and talked to her with Roman around when he was playing with Noah."

Brandon stopped and put both hands on either side of her face, his palms warm against her skin. "It's not your fault, August. If anyone is to blame, it's Marx. Things wouldn't be this way if it wasn't for him. Stop blaming yourself. What's done is done. We'll figure it out."

"What if we don't?"

"We will."

She was quiet for a few seconds, wanting to believe it wasn't her fault. If anything happened to Snow and her son, August would never forgive herself. The woman had saved her life. "Okay."

He kissed her forehead. "Let's go. I don't know how much time we have."

The closer they got to the fish farm, the stronger the horrible stench filtered through the corridor.

Brandon shook his head. "Man, that stinks."

"You get used to it. Like a woman in my housing unit said, 'It reminds us we're still alive.'"

"I wouldn't want to smell that all day." Following the corridor for another ten minutes, he pointed. "Down there. The entrance for the sick survivors is at the end."

Hurrying, they finally made it to their destination in front of scarred metal double doors.

August reached into her pocket and handed Brandon the keycard.

He swiped it through the reader. The lock made a loud click.

He pushed the doors open.

Once inside, her gaze roamed the area. It wasn't much. Another dome reception-like area with a small table, two chairs and plants, and trees like every other area in Liberty. She noticed the door marked, *Restricted.* Her heartbeat took off, anticipation beating at her.

Brandon swiped the card again then pocketed it.

Another click.

He edged the door open this time, unsure what they would find. August followed him in.

They were hit by a wall of heat and the sickening smell of something acrid like ammonia and reminiscent of human rot. The putrid odor stopped them in their tracks.

"What is that godawful smell?" She covered her nose with her hands.

Brandon coughed. "I don't know, but this sure isn't a medical area like Marx told that old couple."

Ahead, two dozen stainless steel vats towered at least forty feet high and just as wide. Each one had a narrow ladder leading to the top. The room was pristine with whitewashed walls and a glossy white floor, so clean you could probably eat on it. The cleanest place August had seen inside the settlement.

Brandon took a few steps and put his hand against one of the vats then jerked back. "It's hotter than Hades." He walked past the vat and slid his rifle off his shoulder.

August stayed close on his heels, her gaze searching the rows between the large tubs.

He stopped at another metal door. "Stay back. I'll go in first."

She watched him edge inside with two hands on his weapon.

Minutes passed before Brandon barreled back, his face white as a bleached sheet. He heaved for breath.

"What is it?"

"The...old...couple."

She pushed him aside and flung open the door with all her strength.

Rows of meat hooks stared at her with naked bodies dangling, the puffy, ashen faces of humans glaring at her.

Henry. The survivors Marx had exiled from Liberty. Old people. Children...

August let out a sharp cry at the grisly scene, worse than any horror movie she'd watched, unable to get her feet to escape. "No."

Forcing her legs to move, she scrambled backwards until her back slammed into the door. Her hand searched for the handle. Finding it, she threw open the door.

Brandon was crouched, his head in his hands, his M16 on the floor next to him.

Her eyes traveled to the vats.

People who didn't fit into Graysen Marx's plan had become food—stew.

Bile raced up her throat without warning, and she threw up on the floor. When she was done, August gulped gasps of air, tears streaming down the side of her face, barely able to find the words for what she'd witnessed.

"Brandon. Oh, my God! We have to stop him."

• • •

Graysen Marx shut his eyes then opened them as the assembly hall filled to standing room only. Awake for nearly twenty-four hours, his body burned with fatigue and adrenaline. Circumstances inside and outside of Liberty had left him no choice than to call the pre-dawn meeting.

Roman's report of their losses in Icehaven, the camera system going down, and Kenna's ongoing nightmares coupled with news of an internal fire killed any chance for rest. Then he'd learned about the possible rebellion. The members of the Infinity Council took their assigned seats, each of them glaring at him.

At the podium, his arms braced his weight. The ungrateful citizens grumbled because they'd been pried from their beds. He caught sight of a middle finger from the back row. Another closer to the front.

Fine. He'd make it short and sweet.

He tapped the mic repeatedly to get their attention. "Yesterday, in close combat in Icehaven, we lost ten of our best defenders to the Sproggs. Their leader, a man called Witness, vowed to bring violence to Liberty. He has more than enough weapons to attack our settlement."

"What are we supposed to do about that?" a female voice screeched.

A man yelled, "That's your problem!"

His head pounded at his temples, and he had a hard time suppressing the rage coursing in his gut. "We'll take appropriate precautions on the perimeter. Everyone needs to be aware of their surroundings, anything out of place, anyone out of character."

More shouting.

He gestured to the guards at the back of the hall. Movement behind him made him turn.

Eve Petty stood with a frown on her face. "This is a security issue, Mr. Marx. Something you need to look after."

A chorus of discontent rose from the crowd. "Yeah!"

He should have gotten rid of the pesky woman days ago. Holding his perspiring hands up had no effect. "The Sproggs may already be working with a group inside Liberty. There are traitors among us right now."

Not completely true. At least the statement quelled the noise for a moment. "We found evidence of people inside—maybe someone sleeping right beside you—plotting violence against us." He took a deep breath and held up the sheet of paper he'd been given and read it. "Working on a plan to change things. Be ready."

A man in the front row jumped to his feet and faced the crowd. "That doesn't mean anything. We don't have to listen to him. Wake up!"

Graysen took a step back and searched for the survivors from the armory in Icehaven—August Madison and her lot. He picked her out sitting with another woman on her right, near the front, with their arms crossed.

He waved, and two guards entered the stage, dragging a woman named Snow to the center. She dug in her heels, fighting every step of the way. He gestured again and a third guard brought in her boy, depositing him beside her, out of her reach. The kid gulped back tears and stared at Graysen with hate in his eyes.

Some citizens jumped up. Guards in the back of the room sprinted into position, ready to remove them on his orders.

"This woman, Sandy Globe, received the message," he shouted into the microphone.

A woman in the center of the crowd stood. "Get your damn hands off that child. Have you lost your mind?"

"These two received the message." Looking over his shoulder at Eve Petty, he had an inspiration. "And council member Petty has been implicated, as well. Bring her forward."

Another guard appeared and tore her from her seat, shoving her across the stage to stand with the others.

"Get your damn hands off me! You have no proof of anything!"

Along the aisles, a handful of protesters pushed the guards. Punches flew. When they were subdued and about to be removed, Graysen raised his hand to stop them.

He wanted everyone to hear the verdict. He didn't need the Infinity Council. They knew it.

He banged the podium hard with his fist. "The sentence for treason is immediate banishment."

Most of the crowd erupted to their feet.

Pushed back by their volume, he locked eyes again with August Madison, sitting calm and collected.

A second later, a group of men near the back of the hall charged one of the exits.

The guards blocked them, using their rifles. More people stood and followed, receiving body blows for their effort. His men struggled to keep the doors closed, forming a human wall to keep the chaos at bay.

Headed by Madison, a separate wave surged toward the stage.

He stepped back behind his men holding the accused. Sweat beaded his forehead, the crowd's response worrying him. He needed more time. Time to ensure his daughter would be safe if things spiraled out of control.

A single gunshot rang out, a blank but they didn't need to know that.

Everyone stopped, including Madison.

Graysen returned to the microphone. "Please, take your seats. I know this has been difficult. There is good news. Our food runs have brought in luxury items, like soap and chocolate, to be distributed today. Our next crop of greens and apples will be ready for you by the end of the week."

And with all the protesters he planned to banish, meat would be plentiful.

"Shifts today are reduced by two hours. We all need the rest to be at our best."

Most of the grumbling stopped. Graysen felt a small change in attitude, more compliant because they wanted what he offered until they demanded more than he could give.

"Dismissed." He walked away from the podium feeling as if he'd regained some control.

Roman was already beside him. His green eyes bored into his. "Sir?"

"Post guards outside my living quarters and escort the traitors to be processed out. Immediately."

"Are you serious? Even the boy?"

"Yes. Then sort through the protesters and figure out who's involved in the plot. Their fate is the same."

"I just received word there's been an accident at the biofuel plant, sir. Several serious injuries."

Things needed to calm down, not ramp up. Everyone would blame him, think he hadn't provided the appropriate safety measures.

Roman gripped Snow by the arm while another guard dragged a still-struggling Eve Petty and the little boy behind.

• • •

After the meeting, August and Lydia headed into the library to meet Brandon, horrified by what had transpired. "We need to stop him before he kills Snow and Noah. We know exactly what banishment means," August said, pacing, on the verge of a panic attack.

"I can't believe it," Lydia said. "I'll never eat stew again."

Rachel gagged a couple of times. "Me, neither. It was good to see people finally stand up to him. They would help us, I know they would. I can go and start asking around."

August shook her head. "It's too risky."

"We can't," Brandon said. "If Marx catches wind we're going to come after him, we might not get another chance."

"He really thinks handing out a few bars of chocolate and soap is going to make up for what he's done," Lydia said. "Unbelievable."

"I'm going to find Shipley and stop him." Brandon squeezed August's hand. "Stay here."

"Graysen Marx is going to be coming for us," August reminded him.

"I know. It won't take him long to figure where the note came from, if he hasn't already."

"I'm betting he already knows."

"More than likely," Rachel said.

"Even a better reason to stay put. You know where the guns are. Get them and have them on you just in case. I'll be back as soon as I can." Brandon turned at the same moment Roman Shipley strolled in.

Pent-up anger exploded inside her. She marched to the mind-reader, her hands balling into solid fists at her sides. "Where did you take Snow and Noah? What did you do with them? Kill them and use them for food, too?" She searched his eyes and wasn't going to give him the chance to answer. He knew exactly what had been going on. Everything John had taught her at the armory took over, the vision of dead bodies hanging like slaughtered animals imprinted in her mind. You're "*Hit*hard.

The redhead opened his mouth. "I took—"

August raised her right hand and throat punched him, just like John had taught her.

His rifle dropped to the floor. His hands flew around his neck. He staggered, gulping for air.

Brandon grasped her arm and dragged her away from the man.

"Bet you didn't see that one coming. You killed kids. You're a sick sonofabitch. You're no better than Marx."

Roman dropped to his knees, wheezing, fighting to catch his breath. "I...didn't... kill...kids."

She twisted, trying to get out of Brandon's grasp, prepared to go at Roman again, but Brandon stopped her. "Give him a minute. I know he doesn't deserve it."

No, he didn't. She forced her muscles to relax and worked on slowing the tide of adrenaline revving through her body.

A few minutes passed, and Roman raised his head. "The kids were sick. Most had cancer and other untreatable diseases, conditions that couldn't be treated here, or anywhere, not anymore. They died of natural causes. I didn't kill any kids. I wouldn't do that."

Lydia planted her hands on her hips. "What about Henry, the others?"

"I was following orders to survive, like you—like all of you." His hand moved toward his rifle.

Brandon released August's arm and leveled the M16 at the man's head. "Don't bother."

"Church, I'm on your side. Believe me. I wouldn't be here if I wasn't."

August shook her head. "You expect us to believe you?"

"It's true. Marx has gone too far. I hid the boy, his mother and the woman on the council. I didn't take them to the restricted area. That's what I came to tell you. That boy is the same age as my son. I would never harm a child."

She exchanged glances with Brandon. "Is that true?

"That's what he told me a few days ago. I believe him about his son."

"Where did you take them?" August asked again, determined to get an answer even if she had to hit him again.

Roman grunted and rubbed his throat. He swallowed hard, then said, "There's an empty utility room on the south side of the survivor entrance. I'm the only one who has access."

"Lydia and I'll go check," Rachel said.

August prayed Snow and Noah were safe.

"Take my keycard." Shipley lumbered to his feet, still clutching his throat, and looped the black cord with the card attached with one hand over his head. He tossed it to the floor.

Rachel snatched up the card and she and Lydia rushed out of the library.

"Can you stop pointing that thing at me?"

Brandon glanced at August for confirmation. After a few seconds, he lowered the rifle.

"If you're going to pull this off, there's more you need to know."

August gritted her teeth. "You know what we're going to do?"

"Have for a while. I'm a mind-reader, remember? It didn't take much to figure it out. That's why I left you in the armory alone to steal the weapons. And by the way, singing doesn't work."

She looked at Brandon, worried. "How do we know he hasn't already outed us to Marx?"

"Unfortunately, we don't."

"I haven't said a word to him. I promise you, on my son."

"What else do we need to know?" Brandon asked.

"The others with paranormal abilities. They can help us."

She stared at the man, anger rising two-fold, her muscles tensing. "Oh, now it's 'us.'"

"How?" Brandon asked.

"There are some survivors who can do some pretty amazing things, things no one would dream possible."

August wasn't convinced she could or should believe him. "What does Marx want with them?"

"Can I sit?"

Brandon pointed his rifle to a chair next to one of the tables.

The redhead sat, his eyes shifting from Brandon and then to August. "Marx believes he can heal his daughter."

"The man is insane." She folded her arms across her chest. "Haven't you figured that out yet? He's using you to do his dirty work."

He frowned. "Everyone who has the golden blood developed a special ability. He thinks if all the powers are used together at the same time along with the blood, he can cure Kenna."

August clapped her hands together and burst out laughing. "Now I've heard everything. Do you know how totally crazy you sound?"

"I'm not crazy. While you've been inputting data in the research lab, the scientists figured out the paranormal powers are amplified when telepathically banded together. You are the conduit to bring them all together. That's what they told Marx. August, you're the person who can fix her—because you died and came back to life. There's something different about you."

She was a conduit. Like a lightning rod. The thought made her laugh more. "This conversation is way too nutty for me." She narrowed her eyes at Roman. "Are you prepared to kill Marx, if necessary?"

"Yes. I agree things need to be different. It can't go on like this."

"They will be different," Brandon said. "I can promise you that."

Lydia and Rachel walked in, smiling.

"He was telling the truth—they're safe, thank God," Lydia said. "I told them we'd be back for them soon. There are too many guards everywhere right now."

August let out a sigh of relief and spotted John in the doorway, panting with a sullen look on his face. "John, what's wrong?"

"You need to come now. It's Luke. He's been hurt."

CHAPTER SIXTEEN

Please, God, no. Not my brother. August sprinted toward the medical unit with tears streaming down her cheeks.

Luke had been trying to fix something in the biofuel plant, the way Dad always liked fixing things. He'd fallen off a ladder after being electrocuted. That's all John had told her. With her heart lodged in her throat, she ran around the corner and slowed only to push past the two guards to get into the clinic.

One of the guards snatched her elbow and spun her around. "Where do you think you're going?"

She shook free and turned back around.

The nurse she'd met intercepted her.

"My brother, Luke Madison—where is he?"

The woman took a deep breath as if making a life or death choice. She pulled August toward her protectively. "Come with me."

Leading her deep into the medical facility, the nurse made a right turn into an expansive ward filled with hospital beds. Two-tone blue curtains segmented each area for imagined privacy.

"He's in the last one."

August followed her gaze, emotion welling in her chest at the thought of Luke being alone, like some lost or damaged animal, abandoned. She remembered his birth, his first steps, even how angry she'd been the day of her father's experiment.

Pulling the curtain aside, she sat on the bed beside his still and broken body. While she held his cold hand in hers, he blinked. Since he wore a neck brace and couldn't move his head, August carefully moved up on the bed, so he could see her.

She sniffled, tears filling her eyes. His face was pale, a light shade of gray. His skin felt slick and cold. "Hey, Luke. It's me. I'm here."

He inhaled short gasps and didn't answer.

She noticed the IV port in his arm and the clear bag hanging at the head of the bed. How much pain was he in?

His fingers crushed hers, and he made gurgling sounds.

"Shh. You don't have to talk."

"I can't...move...my...legs."

He was paralyzed. Any hope August had deflated, and her heart sank. Even if he somehow recovered, Marx would find him useless. She knew what he did with useless citizens. "It's okay. It's all going to be okay. We didn't make it this far to give up, did we?"

The words stuck in her throat when he tried to answer and couldn't.

He'd always talked, determined to have the last word since the day he started to form sentences. She looked for the nurse, standing silently a few feet away. "He's in pain. Is there something stronger you can give him?"

She shook her head, and August read the bad news in her eyes. They didn't have enough of those types of drugs, the drugs he needed, or he wasn't going to improve. She turned her attention back to her brother. "Do you remember when you were in the second grade and you got beaned at your first real baseball game?"

He tried to laugh, wetness leaking from the corners of his eyes. "First at-bat ever."

"It wasn't the last," she reminded him, rubbing the back of his hand. "You were runner-up for Mr. Baseball last year. You got back up and kept going. Nothing ever stopped you."

His eyes flickered open for a moment, and she swore he rolled them. "You hate baseball."

True, and she hadn't gone to nearly enough of his games. She wished she had. "Maybe not that much, but I love you."

He clenched his teeth against the pain and gasped. "I'm sorry I was late that day. We should have all been together. You, me, Chloe and Dad. I...disappointed everyone."

August tried in vain to halt her tears with no success. "I know, Luke. It's okay, I forgive you. You took such good care of Chloe out there. She loves you so much. When it really mattered, you took care of things."

"Tell Chloe I love her," he said, closing his eyes again. "Keep her safe."

"I will. I'm going to take down Graysen Marx. I'm going to do it for everyone he's stepped on, most of all for you. I'm going to win for you."

A small smile skittered across his face, and he suddenly relaxed, as if the pain had receded. He gave her hand a squeeze. "I believe you. Get him, August."

For the next hour, they sat in silence, holding hands until air rattled in Luke's lungs. He started to wheeze heavily.

Please don't take him—I just found him.

But August couldn't fight something she couldn't see.

As Luke's labored breaths slowed, he let out his last breath. She gave in to the pain this new world had dealt her. Bowing under the weight of more loss than any person should bear, August laid her head on his chest and cried.

• • •

No matter what August had said to Luke, she couldn't stop the machine that Liberty had become under Graysen Marx. Why Luke? He should have been thinking about cars, girls, and sports, not trying to scrape life out of the ice. Instead, he had been forced into hard labor, doing work he knew nothing about. No wonder he'd been hurt.

Now he was gone—like her father.

Fresh tears choked her, the loss too great. She cried until she couldn't breathe, knowing she'd have to tell Chloe.

After aimlessly roaming the tunnels, lost in pain, August couldn't remember how she had ended up back at the library.

Brandon came up beside her. "How is he?"

She shook her head and reached for his hand. He steadied her, and she inhaled a trembling breath. "He—didn't make it."

John stood and held his arms open. "I'm sorry, kid."

August darted into the shelter of his embrace like she had with her father when her mother died. John didn't say a word, just rocked her back and forth. She heard whispers and sniffles from the others. When she emerged, she felt grateful for their presence and their silence.

They scooted their seats around a rectangular table and made room for her to sit.

Lydia slid an arm around her shoulder. "I'm so sorry about your brother. We all are. It just adds fuel to the fire."

"There's no fire big enough."

"What do you mean?" Brandon asked, holding her hand. "Enough is enough. We have to go through with our plan. Don't tell me you've given up."

Did she tell him she didn't feel much of anything? Luke's death, her father's culpability and death in the experiment that changed everything, and what happened to survivors cast out of Liberty had stolen her resolve. None of them mattered. None of them made a big enough difference.

Across the table, Rachel shook her head. “We're right on the edge of turning this place around.”

“We are,” John said.

Lydia patted her shoulder and said, “Together, we have the ability to change this place. People need to know what Graysen Marx is doing and be free to make decisions about their lives, even if they want to live in the cold.”

“She's right,” John said. “I'd go back to the armory in a heartbeat.”

August hung her head, feeling only disappointment, exhaustion, and anger. She counted every strange new thing she'd learned, been forced to do, or witness. It would never end, this conveyor belt of trading work for food and security. One man ruled them all.

I “*Tell*Chloe She couldn't grow up in a place like this. Graysen Marx would steal her spirit. Chloe didn't deserve that, none of them did.

I promised Luke. August raised her head and looked up at Brandon, and then at each of her friends. “You're all right. I'd rather die trying to have a better world, a better life than live like this. I can't let Chloe grow up thinking this is all there is.”

“That's my girl.” Brandon kissed the side of her head. “Everything is still in place.”

A silent agreement pushed them all to their feet.

Lydia kept watch at the doorway while they dug their weapons and ammunition out of the garden dirt, hiding them in their coveralls. The women walked out first.

August perked up, feeling purposeful, prepared to put their plan in motion. The kind of purpose that, should they fail or lose their lives, their actions would carry meaning into the future for others.

CHAPTER SEVENTEEN

As August and Brandon headed toward Graysen Marx's living quarters, fear built in August's stomach. What they were about to do could easily go wrong. There were too many variables that could fail. Like getting caught. What if the others didn't make it to the armory and comm-center? She pushed the thoughts from her mind and tried not to worry.

Brandon peeked around the corner at the entrance to the living quarters. "It's going to be okay. Shipley was telling the truth. Four guards."

She inhaled a long deep breath, relieved the redhead hadn't lied to them. Not that she fully trusted him. Trust had to be earned, and Roman Shipley had a lot of work to do.

John checked his watch and lowered his voice. "We're a go. The others should be in position now."

"You take the two on the left. I'll take the other two," Brandon said to John and turned to August. "No matter what, if we get in a jam, kill if you have to."

"I can do that." Her gaze traveled to John, grateful he was in her life. "I had a good teacher."

John smiled. "Okay, kid. You're making me teary-eyed. Let's get this over with."

August reached into her pocket with trembling fingers and felt the security blanket of the gun.

"Ready?" Brandon asked.

She and John nodded.

As they rounded the corner, queasiness took over and she thought about Luke, her promise to him. She was doing this for him, for Chloe, for everyone at Liberty. Someone had to.

"You're not supposed to be in this corridor," one of the guards said.

"That's okay," John said. "We won't be here long."

The guard looked at him like he was crazy.

"Get out of here, old man," another guard said, taking two quick strides, approaching him.

She recognized the male's voice, and his face—the teenager who'd put the woman's face in her stew in the dining room.

Anger boiled inside her. August quick-drew her gun and pressed the barrel against the guard's temple before he had a chance to blink. Brandon pointed his rifle at the others then used the end of the weapon to direct them away from the door.

The teenager's brown eyes darted back and forth. "Hey, we're only doing our jobs."

"So are we." John gathered up their weapons and slid them on the floor down the corridor about twenty feet from the door.

August kicked the teenager in the groin, a reminder that he wasn't going to treat women like crap ever again.

He dropped to his knees, clutching himself, moaning.

She'd half expected him to get up and fight, but he didn't.

John smirked like a proud father. "Good shot. That should keep him down for a while."

August pulled out a handful of plastic zip ties from her coverall's pocket.

"Turn around and get your hands behind your backs," Brandon said.

The men did as instructed, except for the kid on the floor who was still incapacitated. August sucked in a breath and snatched the teenager's arms, jerking them behind his back. John hastily secured the cuffs in place and duct taped the guard's feet to each other so he couldn't move.

Brandon jabbed the M16 at the three other men. "Sit down next to your friend."

Once they scrambled to sit, John winked at her, his gaze traveling to the guards. "You're all going to be good little boys and stay put. If you move, I'll shoot your asses. Or she will."

Their eyes moved to her, studying her for a second, realizing John was serious.

August glanced at Brandon, her insides a nervous wreck, and he mouthed, "I love you."

At that moment, all the anxiousness drained from her body, his words giving her the extra push she needed to succeed—for Luke. She smiled and mouthed back, "I love you, too."

Extracting the keycard from his pocket, Brandon swiped it through the reader. The lock clicked. He pushed open the door and raised the M16 to chest level. August followed him in, and John brought up the rear.

They hadn't made it inside more than three feet when her throat closed. "Chloe!"

Graysen Marx had her sister positioned in front of him, shielding his body, his two large hands clamped on her shoulders so she couldn't move. A guard stood on either side of him, their weapons aimed directly on them.

• • •

Fear swept over August, and she gulped, terrified Graysen would harm her sister.

"August," Chloe said in a puny voice. "I'm scared."

"Please let her go," August begged. "She has nothing to do with this."

"She's a sweet child. Reminds me a lot of Kenna when she was the same age." Graysen smiled thinly. "Put the weapons down. All I have to do is give the order and my men will shoot. I'm sure you don't want to traumatize your sister any more than she already is, especially after—"

"Okay." August bent and put the gun on the floor, knowing he was going to mention Luke. She couldn't allow him to tell Chloe, not like this. She looked at Brandon and John. They both placed their weapons on the floor.

"We can talk about this," Brandon said.

One of the guards scooped up their weapons then returned to Graysen's side.

"I think we're way past talking, Church. Love certainly makes you do crazy things."

"Why are you doing this?" August asked. "Obviously, you knew we were coming."

"Don't ever be fooled, Miss Madison. I know everything that's going on inside the settlement. You're the one who gave the note to that Snow woman. Did you really believe the three of you could overtake Liberty?" He laughed. "I'm most surprised at you, John. How did they convince you to join their little rebellion after everything we've done for you? We didn't have to feed you and your friends."

"It didn't take much to convince me. When you see evil, you need to kill it. Let the little girl go, Marx, and we'll work this out, man-to-man."

The air hung heavy with tension.

Tears formed in Chloe's eyes, and August's heart broke in two for the second time in hours. She had to do something. "She's upset. Can I at least console her? Please."

Graysen patted Chloe's head. "You're a big girl. You're okay, aren't you?"

She shook her head and peered up at him. "No. You're a mean man. I want to see my sister."

Out of the corner of her eye, August watched Brandon pull a flash-bang out of his pocket. "Chloe, remember how I used to tell you to close your eyes and cover your ears when you thought there were monsters in your bedroom?"

The little girl nodded slowly.

"Do it now for me, and the monsters will disappear. Keep them closed no matter what until I tell you it's okay."

Chloe shut her eyes and put her hands over her ears.

Good girl.

Confused, Graysen glanced at his men. "Get them subdued and take them to the restricted area."

Brandon heaved the stun grenade down the long hallway toward the bedrooms.

"Flashbang!" one of the guards yelled.

A sharp, thunderous bang shook the living quarters.

She heard Graysen Marx shout, "Kenna!"

Chloe cried uncontrollably. "August...I'm...scared. My head hurts."

"It's okay, Chloe. Be brave. Keep your eyes closed." August gave her head a shake. She felt disoriented like she'd been hit in the chest and head with a sledgehammer. Her ears buzzed and rang loudly.

At the same time, the smoke alarm went off, sounding muffled deep under water.

Graysen staggered sideways and let go of Chloe.

A disoriented John charged at one of the guards like a linebacker wearing high-heels for the first time. He knocked the rifle out of his hand in one motion. They crashed onto the coffee table, shattering it into a pile of wood. While they wrestled, Brandon punched the other guard and got him in a headlock.

August tried to make her way to Chloe through the smoke, stumbling, pushing furniture out of her way as if her limbs were wading through thick soup, the vibration in her head overwhelming.

Two hands grabbed her by the back of the neck and dragged her backwards. August screamed, unable to do anything, her brain and limbs unable to communicate.

Chloe opened her eyes and yelled, "You're not going to hurt *my* sister again!"

Her blue eyes darkened, and she scrunched up her face. She stared at the couch, fierce anger flashing in her eyes.

Orange-red flames burst in small patches across the seat of the couch. Two candles on the shelf by the TV lit by themselves.

August's jaw dropped open. She couldn't believe her eyes. Chloe could start fires using her mind. How was that possible?

Graysen screamed at the guards, exchanging punches with Brandon and John. "Get her! She's one of the gifted."

The guard broke free from John and hopped to his feet. He raced toward Chloe, picking up a gun from the floor.

Gathering as much strength as she could, August lifted her foot and back-kicked Graysen in the leg. He grunted and his hands loosened on her neck then let go.

She took off running, her head thick and fuzzy, and hurdled over Brandon and the second guard, rolling on the floor, exchanging punches.

A gunshot popped.

August felt tight pressure, scorching hot and wet, in the center of her body. She wrapped her arms around her stomach and lowered her head. Sticky blood touched her fingertips, fanning across her overalls.

She looked up at Chloe. Her small face blurred in and out. Images of the life August once had roared double-time through her mind: her mother, father, Luke, Chloe, and Brandon.

Tears exploded, and washed away her vision, the salty wetness touching her lips.

Peaceful calm took over, and silence fell around her.

August was pulled down, her breathing and heartbeat slowing to a crawl.

Then everything went black.

And her heart stopped.

• • •

Brandon's voice faded in August's head. *Please be alive. You can't leave. I love you.*

August tried to move her limbs but couldn't feel them, not in the normal sense. They existed, yet no longer mattered. Was she dead? Alive? Somewhere in between?

She saw the living quarters like before, the couch, the flames, everyone moving in slow-motion. A guard fought with Brandon, stalled in hand-to-hand combat. John reached for the guard who'd shot her. Graysen raced through the smoke toward Chloe, near the fire.

He couldn't have her. Not now that she had demonstrated her power. He could never have her.

Her thoughts swam from one thing to the next, trying to understand where she was. Maybe this where she waited to find out if she had died or maybe a place before she came back to life. Radiant multicolored energy surrounded her, supporting her. Unintelligible voices floated softly, like living things, rising then ebbing in volume. She recognized some of the voices by their random and vague thoughts.

Could she speak to them?

Chloe kept calling her name, her tone soothing August. *August. August. August...*

Her baby sister had surprised them all with her volatile power.

Then panic jolted through August like a lightning strike. How could she help her? What was she *supposed* to do? *Help me!*

Hello? A different voice rose through the chatter. *Can you hear me?*

Roman answered first and read the mind of the guard he needed to evade. *I'm on my way.*

Harper didn't sound angry for the first time ever. *He's glowing blue now.*

You can trust him. He's with us.

We need to be let out!

August communicated the same way, through her mind, her consciousness. *What's happening?*

Whispered chants swirled and sounded like they were traveling on the tail end of a breeze. The scene in Graysen's living quarters ticked by, one slow frame at a time. He closed in on Chloe, baring his teeth, his face red. August glimpsed inside his mind at the raw anger, fueling his fear for the life of someone he loved, his daughter.

He ordered one of his guards to kill Brandon.

No! Her mind splintered. He wasn't like her. He couldn't come back. She needed him, loved him.

A casual voice edged into her terror. *Brandon will be fine. I can see everything.*

August remembered his friend, Morgan, who could see things before they happened. *Where are you? What's happening? I have to come back!*

Listen! he demanded.

She struggled to make sense of her new environment and quiet her mind enough to hear. *Listen to what?*

Every voice in turn joined and duelled for her attention.

Stronger, they repeated, until the word became a mantra.

Their energy merged and filled her, and she experienced their gifts separately, all stemming from the same source. She saw Graysen's vicious red aura and heard strange music playing under the surface. The skin on his face and hands were blistered, burnt in the fire Chloe had set using her own power.

The voices spoke as one. *We are all here. We are stronger together.*

She *was* the conduit Roman had said. August trusted the message and formed her thoughts back to them. *The time is now. He kills the weak. He must be stopped.*

Rustling voices agreed, including a small, weak voice she identified as Kenna's. August listened, and the scene in Marx's quarters sped up, her physical body energizing.

It's happening!

Her lungs fought for air. Her heart stammered against her ribs, and she opened her eyes where she'd fallen. Staring up at the ceiling through the haze of smoke, the fighting continued around her.

Gulping in a huge breath, she screamed, "No!"

Everyone stopped.

Brandon's jaw dropped. Chloe whimpered when Graysen released his hold on her.

August scanned the room, still fueled by the metaphysical connection to the ones with paranormal gifts. Her limbs woke, nerves sparked, blood surged through her body, and she stood.

John tackled the guard tussling with Chloe, prying the weapon from his hand and restrained him while Brandon whacked the other guard with the end of his rifle, knocking him to the ground with a thud. John hurried and secured him with a zip tie.

The collective force electrified through August like a live current, exhilarating and terrifying at the same time. Aware she could lose control of the vast reserve of power at any moment, she focused on Graysen Marx. He operated out of fear. Fear of those he didn't understand, the aggressive bands of renegades, and most of all, losing his daughter.

"I am the nightingale," a small, strained voice sang from the other side of the room.

He turned to the slight teenager in the doorway, wearing pale lilac two-piece pajamas with a unicorn printed on the top.

"There's a mouse in my father's house."

John went to intercept her.

"No. Let her stay." August raised her hand, and he stepped back. "She's one of us."

Kenna giggled. "One of you, two of you. More of you than rats in a tunnel."

Brandon stepped between Graysen and his daughter.

"Let me attend to her. She needs me."

When Brandon wouldn't move, Graysen dropped to his knees. "Please."

August walked to him and stretched out her hand.

Brandon shook his head. "August, no. What are you doing?"

She sidestepped his concern, would explain everything later, when they could be alone and at peace.

John had already put out the fire using a fire extinguisher from the kitchen. He placed a sooty hand on Brandon's shoulder. "Let her do what she needs to do, son."

Graysen gripped her hand without any prodding.

Energy sloughed off August the moment they connected. She held her breath, unsure how her power worked and followed her instincts.

"I—don't understand." Brandon stared at her with wide eyes as Chloe crept up beside her and took her other hand. "You were shot in the abdomen. What is happening?"

She pulled away from Graysen's touch and watched his skin heal before her, the blisters shrinking then disappearing. Her gaze shifted to his daughter. The young girl would die unless August did something about the tumor pressing into her brain. She could see the mass in her mind, like an x-ray, and felt hopeful she could help the poor girl.

But not yet.

August laid out her agenda, calm and forceful. "Your fraudulent Infinity Council will banish you from Liberty. You will not return or raise your hand against this settlement. Ever."

He cackled as if he had room to maneuver in the situation. "You're crazy. I made Liberty. You freaks owe me your lives."

Brandon picked up Chloe and held her tight. "This place is a hell-hole because of you, Marx. When people find out what you've been doing, they won't have any trouble turning you out. I promise you that."

The man sneered, not ready to give an inch.

Kneeling in front of him, she understood the depth of his fear and how to use it against him. She looked directly into his eyes and spoke gently. "I know you've been looking for me. You know I'm the one who can heal your daughter. I just showed you what I can do."

He looked at Kenna. She clapped her hands with glee.

Did she fully understand the conversation?

He turned back to August. "What do you want?"

"She's innocent, so I will heal her." She smiled at Kenna, then scowled at her father. "Your daughter will stay at Liberty with us and you will be banished to the ice. She's one of us now. She'll be safe, happy and healthy as long as you never come back."

"You are going to regret this."

"I won't heal her until you're gone. For good. You have my word." August swallowed hard, remembering her promise to Luke. "My promises aren't like yours. I keep mine."

She could tell he was digesting her ultimatum, forced to decide between his own safety and the health and wellbeing of his child.

Graysen finally hung his head in defeat and growled, "Fine. You win. Heal her."

• • •

Behind the stage curtain in the assembly hall, Brandon watched everyone filter in, exhaustion evident on the residents' faces. Hopefully, this would be the last early morning meeting they would have to attend for a long time.

He kissed August's hand, still shaken after last night. "You scared me. I really thought I'd lost you."

She leaned her head against his shoulder. "Me, too. I'm glad I'm still here—with you and Chloe."

"I can't believe you healed yourself and Marx, for that matter. I've never seen anything so incredible. And what Chloe did—wow."

"We couldn't have done it without her and the others. Roman really pulled through, too."

"I hate to admit it, I'm kind of beginning to like the guy. Don't tell him."

"As long as he stops reading our minds."

Brandon laughed. "Yeah, that." He paused for a second. "Are you sure you feel okay after what happened?"

"I'm fine. Couldn't be better. At least now we know for sure that I can die and come back to life."

"Please don't be doing that anymore, okay?"

August lifted her head and grinned. "Agreed. I'm not going anywhere."

"Are you going to tell me what it was like—being dead?" He shook his head. "I can't believe I asked that."

"That's okay. Later, I promise. We have something very important to do and honestly, I can't wait for Graysen Marx to leave. Everyone will sleep better knowing he's gone."

He peered at the crowd and then to the Infinity Council seated at the table to the left of them. "You're right. I know I'll sleep better tonight."

So far, they'd been able to keep last night's events under wraps. Shipley had put out the word there'd been a fire in Marx's living quarters, and everyone believed that was the extent of the problem.

While the last few people shuffled through the doors, Brandon smiled at Chloe in the front row, surrounded by Harper, Morgan and the others. There were some with abilities he hadn't met yet. He still couldn't believe what had happened. If they had helped August, he owed them big-time.

"She really likes you," August said.

"Who?"

"Chloe. She said you reminded her of Luke."

Brandon felt her take an uneven breath and heard the heartache in August's voice. It ripped him apart. He couldn't imagine how difficult it had been to tell Chloe her brother had died. He wished he could have helped, been there for both of them, but August wanted to break the news to her on her own terms.

August straightened and pointed to Eve Petty heading to the podium. "I think she's almost ready to start."

The woman had been brought up to speed around midnight after Shipley had taken her on a gruesome tour of the restricted area, convincing her immediate change was needed. His authority went unquestioned when they briefed the rest of the council. The man had been invaluable.

They'd also learned more about the council members. The oldest was Seth Wallen, a computer scientist. Katherine Meeks was part of the original Liberty team, a space engineer who oversaw the repairs and maintenance of the settlement. George Castellano was a computer scientist and Hawk Ritter had served in the air force before becoming a biomedical expert. Each of them brought something to the table, including the mayor which was why Marx had chosen them. Anticipation stirred in Brandon's gut.

From the back of the room, Shipley gave him a nod, and the doors closed one after another. His pulse accelerated, followed by a wave of nausea. The moment of truth had arrived.

Eve adjusted the microphone before beginning. "Ladies and gentlemen of Liberty, thank you for making the effort to join us this morning."

"We were dragged out of bed. Not willingly. That's for sure," a man in the back hollered.

Shipley hustled toward the man. Brandon shook his head to stop him.

"I understand your frustration completely. We spent the night listening to serious allegations against Graysen Marx. They were important enough to have to call this meeting."

An eerie hush fell over the room.

Brandon's skin prickled, and he clasped August's hand.

"I have asked August Madison and Brandon Church to share the details with you."

"Are you sure about this?" Brandon squeezed August's hand.

"I have to, if we're going to start fresh."

When they walked onto the stage together, a man stood and pointed, his voice full of rage. "Her father put us in this situation, and he's a guard member. Why the hell would we want to hear anything they have to say?"

"Please listen," Eve said. "It's important. It affects each and every one of us."

"Doubt it affects you or the rest of the council. You all have ignored what's been going on in the settlement, as it is," someone yelled.

"That is about to change." The councilwoman held out her hand, handing over the podium to August and Brandon.

Brandon stood behind August and would step up if she needed him.

A few beats of silence, then she said, "I'm sorry my father's experiment did this. I'm sorry to everyone who has lost someone. It never was his intention to hurt anyone. He wanted to make things better, the climate, life in general. He was a good man—"

"Right. A good man killed my family." A woman jumped to her feet in the second row. "How dare you. My children are dead."

Brandon put his hand on her shoulder and felt her anguish. Tears glistened at the corners of her eyes. She was the most courageous person he knew. He loved her even more. Not everyone would have to the strength to stand before thousands and admit her father's failure had killed so many.

"We have all lost someone we cared about."

"That doesn't make up for anything," the same woman said.

"I know it doesn't. There is nothing I can say or do that can. There is more you need to know." August grasped the edges of the podium. "Last night, a small group of armed opposition entered Graysen Marx's living quarters and took him into custody."

Gasps filled the air.

"We learned he had been using a restricted area off the west sick entrance for his own agenda. He has been mistreating the elderly, ill and individuals he had supposedly banished. Instead of sending people outside or helping the sick who required medical attention, he decided to have them processed into...food."

"Liar!"

Concerned, Brandon moved to the microphone. He didn't expect his knees to shake, but they did. "It's true, the stew and meatloaf we've all been eating."

He bowed his head as shouts and snipes continued. Eve had warned them it wouldn't be easy.

August pressed on. "The council has seen the area and can validate the truth. Graysen Marx has turned us all, unwittingly, into cannibals."

John stood, followed by Davis, Ian, Lydia, Rachel, and Snow. Most of Brandon's crew members stood to offer their support.

"Everything they are saying is true," John yelled above the noise.

A handful of men and women got up to leave. They were permitted to go and could leave Liberty if they chose. Things had already changed. Others yelled, "Stop lying."

One of the guards in the back strode down the aisle with his rifle. "Where is he?"

A line of citizens shadowed him, making their way toward the stage.

"Bring him out," the guard said.

Shipley shot off a short burst of blanks. He darted off with five of his men to take control. They circled the group and wrestled the weapon from their rogue member, then herded them, pushing and shoving, back to their seats.

"I beg you to continue in a peaceful manner," August said. "There has been more than enough death and destruction, enough loss."

"Kill him!" one woman screamed.

Another, "Send Marx outside!"

Brandon agreed and cringed. He looked at August, knowing a majority was needed.

They had to get it.

Eve motioned to the rest of the council. They formed a semi-circle behind August and Brandon in a show of support. When she nodded again, a pair of guards brought Graysen Marx out on the stage, front and center. His messy hair and pale skin told of a long, rough night. He didn't look like a million bucks anymore, his charisma dissolved under the weight of his deeds.

August looked at him. "Face the people of Liberty. They will tell you your fate."

Marx stared at the floor, unwilling or unable to look at any of them in the eye. Brandon hated the man. He could have done so much good, but chose not to.

"None of you have had to deal with my choices," Graysen said, shaking his head. "No one on this stage knows anything about running a city. You'll find that out when you get hungry."

"We're already hungry!"

"Bastard!"

August took a deep breath and addressed the crowd. "If you truly want change, a place to live where you matter, where your voice matters then raise your hand in favor of banishing Graysen Marx from Liberty. What he has done is despicable and will not go unpunished."

Brandon held his breath and waited. Hands shot up in the air and hope bloomed inside him.

"All opposed?" she asked.

Relief engulfed his body, and he noticed August's shoulders relax. No one wanted to be fooled anymore or terrorized in the name of safety. They wanted a chance at a better life, where they cared about each other, took care of the sick and elderly, and had a say in decisions affecting their lives.

Five minutes later, Eve Petty handed August the official results written on a piece of paper. "Go ahead, dear. You read them."

August's hands shook. "Graysen Marx. You will be escorted out of Liberty just before sunset. For everyone else, there will be no work until the afternoon shift. Get to know each other. Find your family and friends. Things will be changing. We promise you. It's time to look ahead to our future, to your children's future. Liberty will be what it should be—our home." She held a hand in the air. "United we stand."

Cheers erupted and the crowd chanted, "Liberty!"

"We did it." August threw herself into Brandon's arms, her embrace doing more to bolster him than anything else in the world ever could. "You were amazing."

Over her shoulder, Shipley and three other guards removed Marx from the stage. Members of the Infinity Council milled together, talking quietly, as the hall began to empty.

Only then did he release August, kissing her softly in quiet celebration. When he looked up, Eve walked over to them and smiled. "We can't thank you enough. Even though we don't understand everything, I know—we know—we're better off today than we were yesterday. We'd like to invite you both to join the council, if you're willing."

He nodded, and August answered for them. "We would be honored."

"Wonderful." The woman hugged August first, then Brandon. "I'll tell the others and we'll meet this evening."

They would have a lot of work to do and none of it would be easy. Sending Graysen Marx out in the cold took precedence, followed by healing his daughter. He hoped the teenager could supply them with more information about Liberty and the experiment.

"Let's go." He tugged on August's hand and pointed to their group of friends from the armory and the *Eagle*. "We have a lot to catch up on."

CHAPTER EIGHTEEN

The last glimmers of the maroon sun hovered above the horizon against the ghostly white ice. August stood next to Brandon inside the Liberty Guard entrance and watched Roman and three other guards escort Graysen Marx past her. He stopped beside her, wearing a heavy winter parka, hat, and gloves.

"I expect you to keep your promise and make my daughter better."

"And we expect you to keep yours—to never come back here."

"Good luck keeping everything running and feeding everyone. You *will* regret this."

She had expected a threat because that's who he was. Instead of focusing on Kenna, he had to take his last shot at her.

"If you do come back, I'll shoot you myself," Brandon said.

"Church, you surprise me. Love does wondrous things. You finally grew up and sprouted a set of balls." His eyes narrowed at August. "Remember what I said."

She was not going to allow him to upset her in any way. This was the start of their new life, a new beginning. "Get him out of here."

"Are you sure you want us to dump him at the armory in Icehaven?" Roman asked.

"It's the best place for him. He won't last long with the Sproggs and Bleeders. That way, his blood won't be on any of us."

Roman shook his head. "He's already thinking about how he can escape."

That didn't surprise her one bit. She looked down at the heavy rusted chains and padlock around both of the man's ankles outside his winter boots. The handmade shackles would hold him until the men arrived at the armory to set him free. Then Graysen Marx would be on his own. August got in his face, the toe of their boots touching. "If he gives you any problems, Roman, you know what to do."

The redhead gripped their prisoner's arm and yanked. Chains clanked and clinked as he chaperoned Graysen to one of the guard vehicles.

August let out a long breath, happy to be rid of the man. She felt Brandon slip his arm around her shoulders and heard John's voice behind them. "Why did you give him some food and supplies? He deserves nothing."

She turned, glad to see him, and understood his concern. Snow, Davis, Ian, Rachel, Morgan, Lydia, and Chloe followed him in. They circled around her and Brandon.

"I had to. If I didn't, I'd be no better than him. None of us would be. I wasn't going to do that. My father taught me to be kind, even under the toughest circumstances. Believe me, it was a difficult decision."

"Wise man," Ian said. "Wish we could have met him."

"You mean, you don't blame me for what happened?"

"God no. Why would we?"

Relief rippled through her, and August realized how lucky she was to have them in her life, that they'd taken her in, became her friends. Her new extended family.

"We have to let go of the past, all of us." Lydia smiled at her. "We know Marx somehow had a hand in the experiment going wrong. We just don't know all the details yet."

"We will one day," Brandon said, holding her a little tighter.

Kenna held the answers. As soon as August could heal her, she hoped the girl could help them. She was prophetic, could see the future. August wasn't sure she wanted to know what lay ahead. But going back in time could provide them with what they needed to know.

"I'm glad you didn't tell everyone at the meeting about us, about what we can do," Morgan said.

August had thought about it long and hard. The citizens had enough on their plate. Telling them served no purpose at the moment. All it would do is scare them. Eventually, they would tell them. Until then, their gifts would be kept secret as much as possible. She wondered how many others at Liberty had golden blood and special abilities that Graysen didn't know about. He certainly didn't know about Chloe, never tested her blood because she was a kid.

"You aren't seeing something that's going to happen, are you?" Brandon asked Morgan.

"Not a thing, I'm happy to report. I found a book in the library. Apparently, what I can do is called precognition. I call it a pain in the butt."

Everyone laughed.

"Is the mean man gone?" Chloe asked.

August picked her up and gave her a hug. She needed to talk to her about using her power. She needed to learn how to harness it, otherwise, the settlement could go up in flames. August pointed to Roman's truck pulling out of the building, red taillights glaring in the twilight. "See, he's leaving right now."

"I don't like him."

"None of us do." August kissed her cheek and thought about Luke. Guilt swamped her, and she fought back tears. *I could have saved him, healed his injuries.* If she had only known the power she had. She missed him so much. He'd be proud of her, the same way she was proud of him. He had saved Chloe.

"Can I go back to sleep now?" Harper said, stalking through the doorway.

August laughed. "She's never going to change, is she?"

"I doubt it. Pure diva." John shook his head. "Glad you could make it, Harper."

The woman gave him a hug, surprising everyone.

"Where do we go from here?" Snow asked.

"Brandon and I are meeting with the council tonight. They offered us a spot on the board. Obviously, our food problem is at the top of the list. Also, it's time for friends, families, and couples to be housed together. No more separation."

"We have about two-hundred children here," Snow added. "There are some who lost their parents and siblings. They don't have anyone."

"I would like to help with that," Lydia said through tear-filled eyes. "If Dax were here, he would want it that way. I know he's looking down on all of us with pride."

August's heart ached for the woman. Maybe having a child or two in her life would help her deal with her loss.

Rachel chimed in. "I could help, too. Maybe we can start a school?"

Davis, the man of few words, grinned from ear to ear. "That's a good idea. Need to keep the little buggers busy."

As more ideas were thrown on the table, August realized how much they were all in tune to make Liberty a real community, a city they could be proud of. There was still one nagging unanswered question.

"I'm going to talk with one of the scientists in the lab, Dr. Higgs. Maybe she can shed some light on why only some people's blood types changed and they developed paranormal abilities, but not everyone."

"There has to be an answer," Harper said.

August smiled. "If my father was here, he'd agree."

"Well, I don't know about the rest of you but I'm hungry," Ian said. "Why don't we leave these two lovebirds alone for awhile? I'm sure they could use some time together."

August put Chloe down and patted the top of her head. "How about you go with Snow and the others for dinner?"

"Can we have pancakes?"

"Probably not. I'm sure they can find you something you like. Not stew. I heard there might be chocolate for dessert."

Chloe's eyes widened, and she gave August a toothy grin. "Okay."

After everyone left, August and Brandon stood quietly and watched the sun lower and disappear.

"I'm worried."

"I know." He ran his finger along the side of her face. "You always get a little wrinkle above your left eye when something's bothering you."

Knowing Graysen Marx was out of their lives, reality had set in. They were taking on a huge responsibility, lives were in their hands. "If the leader of the Sproggs makes good on his promise, we need to be ready."

"I already talked to Shipley. We're going over a new security plan, first thing in the morning."

"Food. What are we going to do? We have to come up with a solution for the long-term."

"We will. Just not tonight."

She eyed the braided bracelet on his wrist that she'd given him. Her breath caught in her throat. "Does that mean I'm your girl?"

He glanced at the piece of leather and shot her a smile. "You are definitely my girl. You've always been, August. Does that mean we can spend every night together now?"

August kissed him, the warmth and safety of his lips on hers. When she pulled away, he said, "I guess that's a yes."

She'd tell him tomorrow about not being able to have children. She knew in her heart he'd be okay with it. "Definitely, a yes."

August had found strength when she didn't know she had it in her. She'd made new friendships and looked forward to having Brandon as part of their family, although she missed her father and Luke.

They would figure out the food production, maybe one day help supply food to other communities, expand the dome technology, and perhaps build new settlements if the ice ever disappeared. Most of all, they had survived her father's experiment for a reason. Because of it, they had become better humans, more caring, willing to help, and stand up for others. She planned on moving forward with no regrets because regrets only sucked the life out of you, her father always said. This was *their* new world. Liberty. Freedom. Justice for all.

Author Note

We hope you enjoyed the story and characters of *Icehaven* as much as we enjoyed creating this bold new world.

Please leave a review and visit www.sumofalltears.com to connect on social media and keep up with news, events and more.

Liberty, the next thrilling book in the Sum of all Tears series, is available now to pre-order at iBooks, Barnes & Noble and Kobo. Coming soon to Amazon.

About Kim Cresswell

Kim Cresswell resides in Ontario, Canada and is the bestselling and award-winning author of the action-packed WHITNEY STEEL series.

Her romantic thriller, *Reflection* (A Whitney Steel Novel - Book One), has won numerous awards including RomCon®'s 2014 Readers' Crown Finalist (Romantic Suspense), InD'tale Magazine 2014 Rone Award Finalist (Suspense/Thriller), UP Authors Fiction Challenge Winner, Silicon Valley's Romance Writers of America (RWA) "Gotcha" contest. Kim also signed a 3-book German translation deal with Luzifer-Verlag for the first three books in the series: *Reflection*, *Retribution* and *Resurrect*.

Lethal Journey won RomCon®'s 2014 Readers' Crown (Thriller).

The Assassin Chronicles TV series was in development with Council Tree Productions. The TV series is based on Kim's upcoming 4-book paranormal/supernatural thriller series: *Deadly Shadow* (May 2018), *Invisible Truth*, *Assassin's Prophecy*, and *Vision of Fire*.

To learn more, visit kimcresswell.ca

Books by Kim Cresswell

Whitney Steel Series

Reflection (A Whitney Steel Novel - Book One)
Retribution (A Whitney Steel Novel - Book Two)
Resurrect (A Whitney Steel Novel - Book Three)

The Assassin Chronicles

Deadly Shadow (The Assassin Chronicles – Book One)

Novellas

Lethal Journey
Dawn of the Storm
Dawn of the Enemy

True Crime Quickies (Short Stories)

Real Life Evil (Book One)
Murder on Sunset Strip (Book Two)
Garden of Bones (Book Three)
Edge of Madness (Book Four)

True Crime Anthologies Published by Grinning Man Press

Serial Killer Quarterly "21st Century Psychos"
Serial Killer Quarterly "Partners in Pain"
Serial Killer Quarterly "Unsolved in North America"
Serial Killer Quarterly "Cruel Britannia"
Serial Killer Quarterly "They Almost Got Away"
Serial Killer Quarterly "Lostmord: Murder in German"

About M.K. Chester

M.K. Chester is an RWA award-winning author of historical and contemporary romance. Her first novel, *Surrender to the Roman*, is currently published with Carina Press. Her three-book historical series, Bryeton Books, focuses on love, loss and redemption in small town America at the turn of the 20th century, while her latest release, *Crashed*, is the first book in the contemporary New South Series.

M.K. is a native Buckeye who lives in Tennessee. She's married to a veteran, recently became a MoM (Mother of Marine), and will soon become a grandmother. She adores her Scottish Terriers and is fighting MS.

To learn more, visit mkchester.com.

Books by M.K. Chester

Bryeton Books

All in Good Time (Bryeton Books – Book One)
The Bootlegger's Bride (Bryeton Books – Book Two)
Tied Together (Bryeton Books – Book Three)

New South Series

Crashed (New South Series – Book One)

Single Titles

Surrender to the Roman

CPSIA information can be obtained
at www.ICGtesting.com
Printed in the USA
LVHW042225031219
639337LV00018B/394/P

9 781999 558819